About the Author

Alan M Keef has a business building small railways for the industrial and leisure markets that he describes as a hobby that got out of hand, but for all that, it has taken him to some of the less glamorous countries around the world.

Writing *The Finding* was actually started in the Mkonge Hotel, when he had a day to kill, and little else to do.

His having lived in the Cotswolds for nearly twenty years and, having spent a small part of his education and rather more of his business life, in and around Carlisle, provides a background to this story.

Having written a number of non-fiction books, this is his first full-length novel.

He is widowed, remarried and lives and works in Herefordshire.

THE FINDING

Alan M Keef

THE FINDING

Vanguard Press

A CIP catalogue record for this title is
available from the British Library.

ISBN 9781784656 28 7

*Vanguard Press is an imprint of
Pegasus Elliot MacKenzie Publishers Ltd.*
www.pegasuspublishers.com

First Published in 2020
Vanguard Press
Sheraton House Castle Park
Cambridge England

Printed & Bound in Great Britain

Dedication

For Susan and Frances,
the two ladies in my life.

Prologue

"Come here, the Sissies."

"We hate that. Why do you have to keep on with it?"

"Easy. One of you is Sis and the plural of that is Sissies. As you're family, I honour you with being the Sissies!"

He bowed low in mock, very mock, servitude.

"But that suggests that we're sissies," said Dianne.

"And you know we're not. And it sounds bad," added her sister Daphne.

"I know you're not but does the rest of the world?" Gerry continued to needle them.

"Well, it will if you carry on the way you do."

"And who's going to stop me?"

"We are!"

And the two girls set about him in a friendly rough and tumble that should have hurt but Gerry seemed immune to their kicks and punches.

Once out of breath and the fracas settled to everyone's satisfaction it was Daphne who said, "You called, Gerry, what did you want?"

"I had an idea."

"Brain working today then," said Daphne.

He stuck his tongue out at her.

"Now I can drive…"

"You can't. You haven't passed your test."

"Yeah, well. But I can drive. I can work the pedals and do all the right things to get along the road."

"But that's not driving."

"Course it is. Anyway, as I was saying what do you say to us borrowing Dad's car, going off, taking the boat and have a blast round in it."

The twins exchanged a glance. Dianne raising a black eyebrow said, "Without the old fogeys in tow?"

Gerry nodded his head.

"Ooh, I don't know," said Daphne.

"Neither do I, but when?" said Dianne.

"Sometime when Dad's not here."

"You going to take the Jag?"

"No, the Mini."

"That old rust bucket!"

"It'll fall to pieces with three of us in it."

"But at least I know how to drive it, That's the one I've been learning on."

"What'll Mum say?"

"Or Muriel?"

"They needn't know."

Daphne and Dianne looked at each other.

"We'll think about it."

The idea appealed to their slightly warped view of life and at twelve going on thirteen and becoming teenagers they were game for anything – the worse the better. They had always scrapped and competed with their elder brother on the basis that whatever he could do they could do better. The fact that he was five years older than them meant nothing. In reality, of course, that was not the case and they tended to spend a lot of time being disappointed. They were identical twins with Dianne having an edge for being the more extreme. Their raven-black hair, coal black eyes and well-developed figures made them stand out in any gathering.

The next time their father was abroad on business they approached Gerry about his idea of a bit of boating. He was game to show off his prowess with both car and boat to the Sissies.

"So how do we get out without Mum or Muriel knowing?"

But Gerry had his answer ready.

"If she's out to see friends, which she always does when Dad's away, she'll take the Jag. Likes to show off a bit," he said. "Muriel is always busy in the factory so we can slip out in the Mini."

He was oblivious to the irony of what he was saying.

"Your driving's not too bad, I guess," smiled Dianne.

"Apart from a few kangaroo jumps," added Daphne.

They had peeled his L-plates off the car and set off in fine style. Gerry was indeed quite a good driver and most road users would not have been aware of his shortcomings.

They arrived at the club where the boat was kept and where they were well known. It was their good fortune, or perhaps not, that nobody queried that they were on their own. Gerry busied himself taking the cover off the boat, checking the petrol and all the other things needed. He was only slightly alarmed to discover that there were no life jackets in the usual locker but they were only going out for a quick spin, weren't they?

11

The boat itself was flashy and fast, much like their father thought Dianne and shared a smile with her sister; sometimes they almost knew what the other was thinking. The outboard would have appeared monstrous to an outsider but Gerry was competent with it and had watched his father going through the routines many times before. He had it running smoothly in no time at all.

"Come on, Sissies," he called.

"We've told you," they said in unison as they clambered in.

"I know," he said in mock acquiescence.

They set off down the creek and out into open water. The sea was a great deal rougher than Gerry had bargained for but he was not going to let on to that. And the spray was a great deal colder too, but again he was not to be put off. He gunned the engine and the boat came up on the plane and bounced from one wave to the next.

Daphne and Dianne sat back and enjoyed the ride with their black hair streaming out behind them.

"We ought to be going back!" yelled Daphne over the roar of engine, wind and water.

"You sure?" queried Gerry, although in truth he was glad that the first spoken thoughts of doing so had come from one of them. He also knew that Daphne was slightly more timid than Dianne.

"Yeah, we've had our fun. Let's get back and no one is any the wiser." They both nodded their heads this time.

He swung the boat to port at just the wrong moment. He put on too much helm without reducing speed and it dipped into the trough of a wave which neatly rolled the boat over. Fortunately Gerry was a strong swimmer and he managed to drag Dianne to the upturned hull before it drifted away and then push and shove her up onto it.

"Can you see Daphne?" he shouted at her.

Dianne looked around perfunctorily. She was cold, wet, frightened and really only concerned about herself.

"No."

Gerry swam around the upturned boat to no avail and with considerable difficulty climbed onto it himself. He had hoped to stand up on it to get a better view of the surrounding water but it was much too unstable to do that. He had to content himself with swivelling round on his bottom. There was no Daphne to be seen.

"Now what?" asked Dianne. She did not seem to be aware that her twin sister was not there.

"We wait for someone to come by and pick us up."

"Who?"

"Another boat, fisherman or something. I don't know." Gerry felt a darkness pass through him. It gripped at his throat, then slowly its icy fingers sank into his chest. "It will be OK," he finally managed, although he knew it wouldn't be OK. Would never be OK again.

"Can't you attract attention?"

"No. Flares are underneath us and I'm not going back in the water. Dad keeps the radio at home."

Dianne's piercing wail cut the air. Gerry's gut twisted at the sound.

"Get help," she sobbed, but it was a whisper, a begging little girl's voice. "Get help for Daphne."

"It'll be OK," Gerry repeated. He was oblivious to tears streaming down his own face and he felt sick and dizzy. "It's going to be OK."

It was nearly an hour before they were spotted by a passing yacht. The crew managed to get them on board and in turn called the lifeboat. By this time they were so cold that they were only just able to help themselves and were beyond caring what happened to them. With consummate skill the lifeboat crew righted the speedboat and were astounded to discover the body of another person underneath. Daphne. She had received a devastating blow to the head in the capsize that had rendered her unconscious. Hypothermia had done the rest.

Chapter 1

For God's sake, she had only made this considerable diversion because somebody had said that she should not pass through Tanzania without staying at the Mkonge Hotel in Tanga. 'Not much of a hotel but glorious position,' was the recommendation. Maybe. At least from what she could see so far. She turned the registration form round and shoved it, violently, back across the counter. The tall elegant African receptionist looked at it in a studiously bored manner before suddenly jerking her head up and saying:

"You? Miss Jennifer Suffram?"

"Yes, why?"

It was with difficulty that Jennifer refrained from biting back to the effect that: 'Would I have written all that if I weren't?'

Not answering immediately, the girl started rummaging around in a drawer under the counter. With a triumphant flourish she produced a dog-eared brown envelope with *Miss Jennifer Suffram* written and underlined across it, with, in the top left hand corner *To be called for*. Never having been in the place before, to say that she was surprised was the understatement of the her trip. She later considered that she opened it with remarkable care, bearing in mind her mood at the time.

There was no address, nor even date at the top of the half sheet of A4 pad paper and it finished with just *Love, David*. She let out a long "Oooooh" and allowed herself to be shown to her room in a hazy dream.

She flopped her rucksack onto the floor and waited for the air conditioning to bring the room temperature down to a comfortable level before opening the envelope again and reading more fully what was written in the letter. It was scrawled, there was no other word for it, and she had to read bits several times before being sure of what was being said. The gist of it was something like this:

Dear Jennifer,

If you get this it will be something of a miracle. I diverted from my planned schedule just in case our paths might cross again – it was the only place I knew you might go – and then only might. I wish we could have had the whole flight to chat rather than just the last half hour, just as I wish we could have met instead of my writing this. Did you get to the Ngorogoro Crater and the Serengeti as you said you would or did the tourist touts put you off? They do me so I have never done these things. Did you camp or did you live like a lady? My trip was briefer than expected and not much good business-wise either, that's how I had time to get to the Mkonge and dear old Tanga. Maybe we can meet back in the UK sometime, I would wish that we could. Let's try.

Love, David.

"You wish, you wish. What about my having a wish? I've been wishing for you all the time I've been here." She nearly screamed it out loud. "And now you just re-appear out of the ether like some sort of mirage."

For the umpteenth time she relived the flight out to Nairobi. She had been to some trouble to get a window seat but regretted it almost as soon as she sat down. Whilst not normally claustrophobic she had felt penned in by the tall slightly older man sitting next to her. He at least could stretch his legs into the aisle whilst she, almost as tall, could not. As always on long haul flights, and she had to admit to this being her first, one lives in a little world of one's own, merely accepting as one's due the food and goodies handed out by the cabin staff. She imagined it must be a bit like being in prison – take what you're given and be grateful. She had no interest in whoever might be sitting next to her and she doubted if he had any interest in her other than the that taken by all men in women. But the problem arose that she must go to the toilet. Nature would not let her wait until they landed – and anyway goodness knows what African toilets might be like. She would leave that bit of exploration until she had to face up to it. She just had to disturb Him sitting next to her. As she returned immigration cards were being handed out and it was at this juncture that he spoke for the first time.

"And what brings you to Nairobi? Holiday? And first time in Africa I think?" All questions, all at once.

"Yes, yes and yes," she mumbled in reply. "Or at least yes and yes to the second two," she added with more confidence as she realised what he had said.

"Gap year and backpacking?" Another question.

"No and sort of." That should put him in his place.

"Now that requires some explanation," he said. She was afraid it would. "Yes, at risk of being rude and you never speaking to me again I think you are a bit older than gap year but you had a great big rucksack with you at the check in desk."

Hey! Had he noticed her there as well? It would appear he had.

"You're right," she replied resignedly, "I am older than the gap year bit, by rather more than I intend to give away, but I can't settle to a career as everybody seems to think I should. It sounds hippie and 1960s but in a funny sort of way I'm hoping to find myself. Whether I shall like myself if I find me is another matter, but we shall see," she finished apologetically. Gosh, why had she said all that in the first few minutes to a total stranger? But he appeared not to notice anything unusual, merely saying:

"And the sort of?"

"Ah, well, I don't have to do this on a shoestring, indeed my parents wish I wasn't doing it at all. I can afford to stay in decent accommodation or hotels if I want to. I plan to mix and match if possible."

"Sensible girl." He sounded patronising, which raised her hackles a bit, so she decided to carry her war, so to speak, into the enemy's camp.

"And anyway, that's all about me, what are you doing? Business, I imagine. All expenses paid, I expect. By some poor soul who can't afford it, I don't doubt." She ran out of breath.

"To follow your format; yes, sort of and no. Anyway what's your name?" he replied.

"Jennifer," she replied without even thinking. Good thing she hadn't handed out her surname but this was getting silly, she had to calm down. "And now it's your turn to explain."

"The *yes* is that I am indeed travelling on business. The *sort of* is that we are a family firm. I'm the son, David, incidentally, and as a consequence I don't have carte blanche or even a fixed budget to spend. I just have to keep it within sensible levels for the business I am doing, which I fear won't be much."

This was quite a speech.

"And what are you trying to sell anyway?"

"We make specialist pumps and claim to able to pump anything that is in liquid form, in this case molasses. This is also where the *no* should really be a *yes*, my customer can afford what I hope to sell him without any difficulty, but I suspect he's not going to buy."

"Sorry," she said, "for being a bit scratchy. I guess I'm a bit paranoid now I'm actually here, well, nearly anyway. I've now got to do the things I've said I'm going to do. You know what you're doing, I don't."

"Understandable," David replied and was obviously considering something. After a moment or two he continued, "By accident or intention, at least you've come at the best time of year, November, after the big rains and before it gets too hot. Advice is always dangerous but the best I can give you is this. East Africa is full of almost every race, colour and creed under the sun but pretty well all of the expatriate community and most of the Africans too, for that matter, are only too pleased to see a new face.

19

As everywhere they are not all trustworthy but, if need be and you seek help, it is usually forthcoming for very little cost, if any."

Another speech but she was grateful for it. It calmed her nerves and that was needed as they came in to land. But he was carrying on and saying more. His advice might just be worth listening to.

"I know you're headed for the tourist trail to see all the things you should see but if you can manage the time, go to Tanga and spend a couple of nights at the Mkonge Hotel. Tanga is very definitely not a tourist destination, although it was once a very important place. The Mkonge is similar, not a brilliant hotel but with a situation second to none. Give it a try, just for me."

What else he said she really could not remember but she was eternally grateful to him for staying with her to collect her bags, as her rucksack was the very last item to appear on the carousel by which time most of the other passengers had gone. The customs formalities spat them out into the bright African sunshine and he was gone, to catch an internal flight, and, horror of horrors, she was alone and on her own.

Jennifer lay back on the bed and mused. She had enjoyed herself, or least she thought she had. Many people, African, Indian, Greek, English, Dutch, you name it, had helped her on her way with only thanks being asked; and she liked to think she had helped a few others in return. It was just as David had said it would be. She sat bolt upright. She took the envelope and looked at it. Yes, her name was written across the front and spelt correctly too. How had he known? She was sure she hadn't told him anything more than just Jennifer. She relaxed and went through their conversation again word for word. No, she had definitely not told him.

These musings led her on to her own trip now she was nearly at the end of it. What had it achieved? She had spent quite a lot of money, well, not that much really, it certainly could have been worse. The big question was, did she have to continue trying to convince herself that she had enjoyed it? Was it only something to have done rather than to do? Had she found herself as she had promised David, and everyone back home, that she hoped to do? Again, she sat bolt upright. He, he was the key to it. She needed him, to have made it all worthwhile. She had sat next to him for six and a half hours, yes, shout it out loud, six and a half hours without realising that he was the key to her life.

She lay back and wept. She did not even know his name. Loneliness threatened to overwhelm her.

The next morning, she was more in control. She sat at breakfast and took in the splendid situation of the hotel. David was right, it was a beautiful place. It was worth the detour, and why did he suddenly feel so familiar? Making sure it was the same girl on duty who had given her the letter, she enquired as to his surname and address in England, if indeed he was even English. He had had no recognisable accent so she had automatically presumed he was.

"Ah, yes," said the girl. "That is Mista Ware. Yes, he from England. He comes here quite often, two, maybe three, times a year. I will look his address for you. Ask later when I have time."

There was hope there at least. The hotel register should know all about him, but then, as she had learned already, this was Africa.

When she went to the desk later in the day to collect her key, a hotel registration form was produced with the name Ware, David on it and under the address section just Carlisle.

"Is near where you live?" asked the receptionist with a broad, kind, but knowing smile.

"No. It's at least 400 kilometres away," Jennifer replied. Having spent a month in Africa she was now thinking in kilometres rather than miles.

"The manager say that he know him well and he never give full address. He must have done one time and we must have had once but cannot find. Also he say that Ware may not be his proper name. Maybe we have somewhere, but…" she shrugged and waved her hand dismissively.

Jennifer spent a couple of days enjoying the somewhat restricted delights of Tanga. She walked to the derelict German clock tower. She took a taxi – at least it purported to be a taxi, anywhere else it would have been considered just so much scrap metal – to the Amboni Caves which she saw by the light of a flaming brand of palm leaves. She saw the dhow harbour and the War graves, drank coffee in the two half reasonable eateries, wondered whether she had the nerve to gatecrash the yacht club and finally wound up on the point staring vacantly out across the Indian Ocean thinking of David. She was having trouble remembering him. Tall, well not excessively, perhaps a bit over six foot, say six foot one or two. Hair, dark, brown or black? Not black anyway, so let's say brown. Eyes, must be brown. Fat, no. Thin, no. Just right then? She giggled. Dress? Casual when she saw him but then he was arriving in a tropical country. Open-necked shirt, casual trousers and brown shoes. Luggage? Well-worn and not much of it. Obviously travelling light and used to it.

Jennifer sat on the scarred and half-broken bench and yet again started reviewing her life to date. She had been doing this on a continuous basis since she left school and a fat lot of good it had done her. The whole idea behind her month in Africa had been to sort herself out but if she was brutally honest with herself it had not done so. It was back to familiar story.

"Let's itemise it this time and see if that helps, as though I was writing a CV," she said out loud and suddenly looked round to see if anyone was there to be listening. Fortunately, there wasn't, or at least not within earshot, and then only a few children kicking a Coke can around.

"Family," she said, much more sotto voce. "Mother, father, elder brother. Yes, we are a family. Mum and Dad don't fight, Paul and I don't fight. OK, we bicker, but we don't fight. Dad runs the farm, not that well if truth be told, and Mum runs him, us and everything else that moves but she does it so nicely that you would never notice. Paul knows what he's doing, he's going to take over the farm – and then it will hum." She smiled at the thought, Paul always knew exactly where he was heading and what he was going to do next. Not like her who only ever knew what she was not going to do. The smile disappeared.

"Home, that's next on the agenda," she mused. Home was fairly palatial by most people's standards. Valley Court and Valley Farm, the names were interchangeable, was a largish establishment. It consisted of a good -sized family house built of the local creamy coloured stone near Cirencester in the Cotswolds, together with a farm of several hundred acres, she could never remember just how many (much to her father's disgust). It stood, as its name suggested, up a steep-sided valley at the end of a half-mile drive or farm road, the terminology depending on who one wanted to impress, and was in most ways an idyllic spot in which to grow up. She was amused to remember that this had been especially so when the valley had been snowed in and she couldn't get to school. It had been in the family for a number of generations and her father had taken on additional adjoining acreage on the higher Cotswolds on which he grew corn at a fair profit. The Prairies he called this land as opposed to the more gentle meadows in the valley.

Her childhood and girlhood had been typical of her situation. All very 'county'. She shuddered slightly at just how different her upbringing had been, compared to that of most other children. What would the children kicking the Coke can have made of it? So self-contained. Ponies and horses of her own until she had rebelled against that one. A good private education, yes it was good, she did at least appreciate that. She hadn't been to boarding school and, in truth, the family almost certainly couldn't afford it.

Thinking about it she realised that until this trip that she had organised and paid for herself she had never been abroad, even to the continent. It was only now that it really dawned upon her that in all probability they quite simply couldn't afford that and her education. She hadn't missed it though and she was grateful they had made that choice for her. She had enjoyed school, maybe simply because it got her away from the stultifying influence of the valley where nothing changed. Year on year it was always the same, lambing, ploughing, seed time, harvest, hedging, fencing and then the same routine started all over again. There had to be more to life than that. Her father didn't think so and neither did Paul.

"I did well at school," she continued. "Lots of GCSEs and two and a half A levels. I could have gone to university. Why didn't I?" She blushed to remember the uproar when she refused point blank to do what everybody else was doing and indeed what was expected of her. She really didn't like to remember the row about that. They were not a family that had rows but this had really been one and had gone on for a long time. More like a war than a skirmish which was what most of their disagreements turned out to be. As usual they had been sitting around in the large drawing room with its everlasting wood fire that was only out for a short period in summer. It was her father who started it, probably with an eye to the likely cost.

"Time to think about which university you want to go to," he had said quite casually.

"I'm not going to university," she had said equally casually.

"But of course you are, darling. Everybody does." Her mother speaking.

"Everybody may do, but I'm not."

"But why on earth not?" exploded her father. "Here we are, given you a good education so that you can have the world at your feet and you just casually say that you're not going to do it! Why, for goodness sake?"

"I simply don't want to."

"But you can't just not, because you happen not to want to."

"Why not?"

To her surprise her parents did not seem have an answer to that. It was just the fact that she was not being conventional that seemed to upset them.

"Well, it'll help decide what you want to do with your life."

"But surely I need to know that first," she had countered.

"Jennifer. You're acting like a three-year-old, having a tantrum because you don't want to go to bed."

"Mum. I'm not. I've had enough of being educated and told what to do all the time."

"But university isn't like that. You should ask Paul."

"Paul?"

"Well he went to university."

"He didn't. He went to the Royal Agricultural College just down the road."

"Same thing."

"It's not the same. Not like a university anyway."

"But all broadens your mind."

26

This put a shadow of doubt into her head but she was having none of it.

"Maybe, maybe not, but I want to get out into the real world."

"But university will give you more experience for when you get out into your so-called real world."

"I'd avoid the real world for as long as possible, if I were you," her father had commented with real feeling in his voice.

"That's not helpful."

This from her mother, to which her father had simply grunted.

In retrospect she realised that it was her sheer reasonableness and absolute determination about what she was or was not going to do that had upset everyone. The persuasion was subtly carried on at school and a proxy war developed with her teachers acting as foot soldiers on behalf of her parents. They, at least, had much more cogent reasons as to why she was being silly. Not the least of which, she suspected, was that one less person going on to university might affect their position in the school league tables published in various newspapers.

"No, really, why didn't you?" she asked herself. "It would have got you away from the valley and all that that stood for. Instead you're stuck with it.

"I really and truthfully don't know," she answered herself, "I suppose I just didn't want to," she added rather lamely.

"Selfish bitch," answered her conscience.

"Well, I didn't. So there," she retorted.

And after that debacle, what had she done then? Her father had stood on his dignity and found her a job with a local firm of auctioneers and surveyors where he hoped she might see sense and the error of her ways. He hoped that she might conceivably take an interest, even gain herself some qualifications or something. In fact, it had been the 'or something'. She had, in his eyes, degenerated into being a mere telephonist. In practice she was front office and the public face of Halliwill & Stoddard and enjoyed it thoroughly. That was even if she had to admit there was no future there and that in six months she had risen as high in the firm as she was ever going to unless she did something more professional, and that she was determined not to do.

"On the other hand," said her conscience, "You could go to university now. They have mature students, you know. That would be good for you and the family and everyone else would approve. You would have seen the error of your ways!"

She considered this for a while but finally came back to her old mantra. "I've had enough of education to last me a life time – and it will have to!"

Her conscience pricked again, "What about…"

"Don't even think about it."

"It's what you're here for."

"Things have changed."

And they certainly had, primarily in the form of a certain David. David who, for goodness sake? Why did he have to appear, totally derange her equilibrium, and then disappear.

And finally, the here and now? Well, she was supposed to be sorting herself out, finding herself, as she had said to David. David? Why had he come along to complicate life? She hadn't forgotten him after she left Nairobi but logic had said she couldn't do anything about it. At least that was until she had arrived here and been given his note. But why no address? Why no contact number? What was he playing at? Playing with her? Why? Why? Why? Had she been younger, much younger, she would have thrown a tantrum.

But then common sense prevailed for an instant and she realised that after all that deliberation she was back at the beginning again. She had to come to a conclusion.

"Spoilt little rich girl!" she shouted to the trees overhead. Even one of the Coke can kicking kids looked up this time. She ticked words off on her fingers.

"Spoilt? Yes. Yes, for sure."

"Little? No, definitely not, I'm nearly five feet eleven inches and twelve stone." She was quite offended at the thought.

"Rich? Not really, but many people might think so."

"Girl? Yes." She sat up straight, pressed out her bosom and looked down. "Yes, definitely girl!"

And with that had she now found herself? No. It was not herself she had to find, it was David. She continued to stare at the sea and then, quite suddenly, her mind was made up. It was time to go home. She must shake the dust of Africa off her feet and get back to England and civilisation. No more messing about or pretending she was a student doing her gap year. Decent accommodation and back as soon as reasonably possible. Next morning she would call at the travel agents to confirm her booking, then book a seat on the bus to Mombasa and thus to Nairobi and the big bird home. Only one diversion would she allow herself and that only because it was in part how she had come to be in Tanga in the first place. She wanted to do the tourist bit and take the train from Mombasa to Nairobi.

And the following morning she set about doing all these things. First was into the travel agents to confirm her flight. The train she found she could not book at long range but she was assured that there was only very rarely a problem with lack of accommodation. Then to book onto the bus for Mombasa. Tanzanian bus stations were always a nightmare with touts yelling at her from all directions offering services that she did not want. However, she had become immune to them and usually found a hut containing a reasonably honest individual who sold her the ticket she wanted. This occasion was no exception.

The day after that saw her seeing her trusty rucksack into the bowels of the bus along with a lot of lengths of iron bar, plastic bags of maybe flour and the worldly possessions of those making the journey. She took her seat, an aisle one, and hoped the bus would fill up and soon depart from all the racket outside. Eventually it did after a final altercation between the driver and the man in the hut. As soon as she was out of Tanga she realised that this was going to be journey like no other she had done. The road was close to being non-existent. Most of the other roads she had travelled had been at least in part surfaced but this one never had been and was simply a dirt track through the trees; indeed it was down to the underlying rock in places. The only real evidence that a road was intended to pass this way were concrete bridges over minor rivers and streams but most of these were single track and had lost their railings. Villages were few and far between and then just a string of huts along the road with a so-called store liberally advertised in garish paint.

The border post with Kenya came at Linga Lunga and was heralded by a ribbon of shacks along the road offering every service a traveller might want from money changing downwards. Having been turfed off the bus all passengers' passports were stamped by bored customs officials. After all, these people were leaving the country and their problems would begin on the Kenyan side. There was some argument about something in the underbelly of the coach but probably a few shillings or even dollars passed and all was well and the coach was on its way again. A mile or so of no man's land and the smartly appointed Kenyan customs buildings appeared. Jennifer was pleased to see the clean paint and aura of order that they presented but she was to be disappointed. She and others were shuffled from one office to another, apparently randomly. They went through her documents with a fine-tooth comb. They made her turn out her rucksack which, with the amount of dirty washing in it, was more embarrassing than anything else. By the time she was back on the bus she felt humiliated and more like a common criminal. A very tall African in the seat behind did his best to console her.

"They've got a big boss man here today," he said. "All the way from Nairobi. So they're making a big show of doing their job properly. Not many Europeans on this bus so they have to make an example of you. If I'd known I would have come another day. It wastes too much time."

At that moment the bus driver leant on his horn, long and loud.

"You see," her friend continued, "some will be left behind."

And sure enough the bus moved off leaving a percentage of its passengers attempting to run after it.

"But what will happen to them?" queried Jennifer, envisaging herself being abandoned in this place.

"Oh, they will have to get on the next one in place of those left behind on that one. See, we have some new faces with us now."

Jennifer looked and indeed there were new passengers aboard. Not a good introduction to Kenya, she thought.

"Bad job but now we shall get a film to pass the time," was her companion's only interest in the matter.

On the plus side the road was now surfaced and the vehicle rattled along it at a good speed. The jungle or woodland or whatever it was disappeared and the countryside opened out into ranching fields with the odd derelict sugar mill thrown in for good measure. Where there was woodland it was coconut plantations with the tree tops so high it hardly classed as such. Suddenly she found herself being poked from behind.

"Look. Look!" cried the African pointing at the television screen at the front of the bus.

Jennifer had been more interested in the land she was passing through than the film and it seemed that it was reaching a climax of a particularly gory killing and he was delighted by this and thought she should be too. She made appropriate noises and returned her attention to the passing countryside. She realised they must be getting close to Mombasa as the bus started to stop at apparently random road junctions but these had signs for beach hotels and the like. There were even a few white people trying to catch this or any bus that came along. Soon the inevitable shacks and shanties started to appear as they neared their destination when they quite suddenly found themselves on the ramp to the Mikindini ferry and Mombasa was in front of them. After all day spent travelling it seemed to be only minutes before Jennifer found herself standing in the street wondering where on earth she went next. As so often it was her co-traveller who came to her rescue.

"Do you have somewhere to stay?" She heard his voice behind her.

"No. Not yet."

Before she had a chance to explain that she had been given a hotel name and that all she needed was a taxi, he had taken her in hand.

"Now my name is John, after Bible man who have his head chopped off!" He seemed to have a somewhat macabre sense of humour to say the least. "What sort of place do you want, eh? Hotel? Hostel? B & B if they have such things? A piece of sidewalk to call your own?" He laughed again at his own joke. She was getting tired of this man but he might still have his uses.

"Oh, a medium-priced hotel will be fine. I have been recommended to one." She pulled a piece of paper from her pocket and showed him.

"Ah, that is very handy as that is where I plan to stay. We will share a taxi."

Before she could demur he was off along the line of buses to where she presumed there were taxis. Right first time.

"But wait," she called, "I have to go to railway station first to book onto the train to Nairobi."

He looked at her as though she were some specimen from outer space.

"You are going by train to Nairobi?" He was incredulous. "The bus is quicker, and cheaper."

"I dare say but I want to go by train." She was adamant and fortunately he took the hint.

So they shared a taxi to the station and he sat rather closer to her than she would have wished. Once there she left him in the taxi and went to book her ticket. In itself this was no problem except that despite what she had been assured in Tanga, tomorrow, when she wanted to travel was fully booked so tonight it would have to be. Oh, well, she would have to miss out on whatever delights Mombasa might have for her. She explained this to John. To her astonishment he was incandescent.

"Why you do this!" he shouted. "We were to go to hotel. Have night together then I show you Mombasa."

"We most certainly were not," she retorted, equally annoyed that he should presume thus.

"Oh, yes, yes. Now you owe me money." He stood over her menacingly. The taxi driver was studiously watching the traffic in the adjoining road.

"What on earth for?"

"I help you at border. I bring you here. I arrange hotel. I pay for taxi. I…" He petered out.

"You're joking!"

"No. I not joke. You owe me." At least he wasn't shouting now, just being sullen about it.

It always came down to money. She knew that, but this was sheer blackmail, creating a scene in the front of the railway station. He had obviously planned all this and his plans had now gone awry. However, she wanted to get away from him and if it cost, well it cost. She was on her way home and only wanted to get on with it.

"OK. How much?" she asked resignedly.

"Sixty dollars," he replied, quick as a flash.

"Now you are joking!" She was appalled. She didn't think she had that much left on her and she was feeling very much alone as this confrontation continued its public way.

"OK. Fifty."

"No way."

She reached into her money belt, took out a twenty-dollar bill, handed it to him and, to her own surprise, turned on her heel and walked away. Astonishment was added to her surprise when she heard the taxi start up and drive away. She had expected another shouted tirade. When the noise had died away, and she could differentiate it from all the other noises, she dared to look back to find that it had indeed departed. And so, it appeared had the unlamented John. He would get a much better exchange rate into local shillings than she could ever hope for.

"Gee. You did well there. You OK?" A genial but overweight American tourist in a loud batik shirt and shorts commented to her.

"Sure," she replied. It was kind of him but she had had enough of interfering strangers. She felt a bit wobbly but endeavoured to walk on as though nothing had happened. However she did not move away from the station and kept other Europeans in sight so far as possible. She had come to another conclusion. She did not like Kenya or the Kenyans and wanted to get out of the place as soon as possible.

Evening and departure time came soon enough. One day she would get used to the tropical habit of the light turning itself off just as you thought evening was coming. She was grateful for having a sleeping compartment to herself even if she found she was herded in with all the other tourists for the evening meal. Small talk she could manage but holiday small talk consisting largely of people grumbling about what was not worth grumbling about or comparing how they had got a better deal here or there, she found depressing. She slept well enough although at one moment there was so much banging about, she wondered if the train was still on the rails. She was in some trepidation as to whether the dreaded John might have reached Nairobi before her but the coast seemed to be clear.

Therefore, it was with some relief that she was able to alter her flight yet again for that self-same night and finally shake the dust of Africa off her shoes.

***

Another hotel room. Another continent. Another person. A youngish man lay on his bed mentally flagellating himself. What a fool he had been. He had deliberately gone out of his way to leave a note for an unknown girl at a hotel that she would more than likely never visit. To cap it all he had not even had the courage to sign his full name. Despite her protestations about not having to travel on the cheap she probably couldn't afford it and wouldn't go there anyway. Why should she? Just because he'd recommended it? Don't be silly. Thus, he could rationalise his own stupidity to himself and tell himself that he should forget all about her. He was well aware how tempting some of the accoutrements of foreign places could seem until you got them back into the harsh light of an English winter.

He only knew her full name because he had surreptitiously looked over her shoulder as she had filled up the immigration card. He should have also been able to read where she came from and was reasonably certain that he had, but to save his life he could not remember it. At least it was England, or somewhere in the UK, he was pretty certain of that. Yes, definitely. She had had a British passport. He had furtively – why the hell had he done it furtively? Was he not quite entitled to look in a phone book? Well anyway he had looked up Suffram in all the phone books in the office without success. So she wasn't local to northern England or southern Scotland. That didn't help much. He would have to find a full set of telephone directories somewhere, library he supposed. Unusual name, Suffram, there might be something on the Web. He'd perhaps try that when he got home. His mind wandered on to private detectives and other nonsense before coming back to kicking himself again. Here he was, well liked emissary of the family firm, confident in any sort of business situation, capable of dealing with governments if necessary, completely thrown off balance by an unknown girl he had only met for about an hour in total. He hoped he had been helpful in befriending her and smoothing her way through the airport. But why, oh why did she continue to haunt him so?

He tried to visualise her. Just a bit shorter than himself, he guessed. Hair? Mousy. That wasn't very complimentary, was it? But probably the best description, even so. And cut longish, not short anyway. Eyes? He didn't remember seeing them but a light hazel brown seemed appropriate. He hoped that one day he might be able to check up on that. He doubted they were blue and hoped not. He had had some bad experiences with blue-eyed girls. Figure? Definitely not glamorous, but very much all there. Homely might be a better description, and he guessed that that too would be worth checking out if he ever had the chance. Face? He remembered that her face had struck him. She was slightly fresh faced and ruddy cheeked. She also had a very mobile face. She seemed to smile or laugh at the slightest thing. Very attractive.

Maybe a country girl. Perhaps that's why they had clicked? Clothes? Jeans, blouse and sensible shoes but, unless he was mistaken, cut slightly better than usual. Yes. This he definitely had to pursue. His mind wandered back to private detectives and how much they might cost.

***

"Hi, Mum, I'm back." Thus Jennifer announced her arrival back in England to her mother.

"Hello, darling. Super to hear you again. Where are you now and when are you going to be where?" came her mother's clear and well-enunciated voice back down the line. It was music to her ears after a month of having to translate broken English or for others to understand her mangled Swahili.

"I'm due at Kemble just after twelve thirty. Can you meet me?" Jennifer replied.

"Yes. Of course I can," and then a note of concern crept into her mother's voice. "Of course I will, but would you prefer Richard to? I know he's free." Obviously, her mother dearly wanted to come but was being gallant by offering Richard instead.

Her mother's diffidence was as nothing to the pause in Jennifer's head. Richard! She really hadn't thought about him after receiving David's note and not much before that. And he was her boyfriend, almost her *fiancée*. She paused. Jennifer wasn't aware of the fact but her mother noticed the pause and interpreted it correctly.

"No, I, er, don't think so. I just want to get home and have a long bath and be a bit more civilised before meeting anyone."

"OK." Her mother sounded relieved. "I'll see you at half past twelve then. Byeee." And she was gone. Her mother never wasted time on pleasantries when finishing telephone conversations.

Jennifer sat in the train looking out of the window but she wasn't seeing the scenery. Although she knew the journey well enough; if asked she would have had no idea where she was. Richard. Dear dependable Richard. Shamefacedly she had to admit that she hadn't given him a thought since she received the letter at the Mkonge Hotel.

Her mind went back to their first meeting. Her brother Paul had corralled her into going to a Young Farmers Club dance with him because he was, for some inexplicable reason, short of a partner. He was quite honest about it; he didn't want to be dancing with his elder sister but equally he didn't want to be alone. However, he did dance with her and in one of his more extravagant whirls she lost her footing and cannoned into a very solid young man standing at the bar. She sort of slid down him onto the floor covered in most of his glass of beer.

"Hey, steady on, old girl," boomed a voice from somewhere up in the ether. Paul was remarkably contrite as they both helped her up from the floor. He even went so far as to replenish the man's beer and then to make introductions as it seemed that they knew each other by name at least. It was only by this stage that he realised just how wet with beer she was.

"Oops. Sorry, Jen. Do you want me to take you home?" he asked but Richard, that was his name, weighed in.

"No, Paul, old chap," Despite his obvious youth his English smacked of another age. "I'll sort your sister out. Try and dry her off so that she can continue to enjoy the evening or take her home if she really wants. You find yourself another partner."

It was a not very subtle way of telling Paul to get lost. He, Richard, would partner Jennifer from here on. What Jennifer herself thought about it all was of no issue. She felt like a parcel being handed on from one man to another. But Richard was all solicitude.

"Now come on, old thing, let's see if we can get you dried out somehow." And with that he took her by the hand, like a small child she thought, and led her to the building's toilets, grabbing a scarf from the rack of coats as they passed. He almost pushed her into the Ladies.

"Now take this and see if you can dry off sufficient to be presentable. If the Gents is anything to go by the roller towel is somewhere near the floor and you can use that as well."

"I do hope that this is yours," she said. "I wouldn't want to ruin someone else's."

"It is actually. It'll wash or clean or something. I'll wait out here for you."

It turned out that she did know him herself but only as a voice on the telephone to put through to another member of staff. It was a point of contact if nothing else and he did indeed take her home that night. To her brother's total chagrin she was home later than he was.

"Thank you for introducing me to Richard," she said the following morning, "But, please, next time I'd rather not get pneumonia with it."

"Sorry," he said even if he did not sound very sorry. "I'll try and be more careful. Not a bad bloke though, is he? Bit pompous, but that's what being an auctioneer does for you, but mind you he's a bloody good auctioneer."

"Hence the voice?"

"Yeah. You can hear him from one side of the cattle market to the other, even if he's not actually selling! You seeing him again?"

"This afternoon, actually, after work."

"Hey, you're not letting the grass grow under your feet are you, sis."

"Taking a leaf out of your book, little brother."

And so began a beautiful relationship.

As the train slowed for Swindon, she mused about their relationship. It remained stiff and formal. Yes, it had had its excitements, its pleasures, its ups and downs but did she love him? He loved her; that was for sure. They had made love, but did that mean anything other than that they both enjoyed a bit of sex? Although she had produced all sorts of other reasons, she now had to admit that Richard was the real reason for her trip to East Africa. She had needed time and freedom to think. And had she thought? Well, yes, and no, had to be the answer to that. She had thought, yes, indeed she had, but not necessarily about Richard. It was David who had taken over her thinking time, to the exclusion of everyone else, including Richard.

The trouble was that she was sure Richard was about to ask her to marry him and the world seemed to have great expectations in this respect. Jennifer was well aware (she had, after all, been told enough times) that if she had a failing it was that she always knew exactly what she did not want to do but never what she did want to do. That had been a problem all her life, school, university or not, job, everything. Including Richard. If she hadn't been sure about him a month or so ago then she was even less sure about him now. She had hoped that being away from him might make the heart grow fonder, as the old saying had it. Well it hadn't. And if he had been about to propose marriage then he was even more likely to want to do it now. But how to tell him? Well actually that was easy, she would just have to be brutal and at this moment she knew she could be but she did not kid herself. She knew only too well from past experience that it was fine to be firm and determined sitting here on the train but much more difficult in real life when she got home. It was also going to be much more difficult to deal with everybody else, especially her family and particularly her slightly domineering but, for all that, much-loved mother.

The trouble with the trouble about Richard wanting to marry her was that he really was the right person to be her husband. Even she could see that. Undoubtedly, he loved her, even doted upon her. He was tall and with his fair hair and blue eyes he was handsome by anyone's standards. He dressed well, even meticulously. He had the right connections. He was due to pass all his final exams and become a fully-fledged auctioneer any time now. He earned a good salary and he moved in the same circles as she did. Although their parents didn't know each other in the full sense of that term, they did know of each other and they both approved. She imagined them all walking about with their fingers permanently crossed on her or his behalf. She giggled to herself at the thought. She was about to blow all these cosy little plans apart. Or was she? That was the nub of it. As the train drew into her station, she knew that she had finally made her decision. Like the addicted gambler and as though she hadn't known all along, she was going to stake her all on the unknown.

"Good flight?" her mother enquired after the usual huggings and joy of returning were over.

"Yes, on time all the way and the trains to here too."

Jennifer shivered with the December cold. She was still mostly dressed for the heat of Africa and had so far managed to simply pass from one form of transport to another without having to get seriously out into the English weather. Her mother noticed.

"Come on, get in the car quickly before you catch your death of cold. Why haven't you got a coat on for heaven's sake?"

"Because I haven't got one with me. It's hot in Tanzania. Remember?"

Her mother grunted and changed the subject.

"I haven't told Richard that you're back yet."

"Thankyou." Was her mother fishing for information or was she just being tactful? By some telepathy had she realised that Jennifer was not much further forward than when she left? It would have to wait.

It was when they were sitting over a drink in front of good fire in the drawing room later that evening that it all came out. It was her father who put both feet in it, either inadvertently or deliberately. He had a habit of making outrageous remarks that the rest of the family then found they either had to face up to or think rapidly of alternatives and excuses. Both her parents were very perceptive but the difference was that her mother was generally more tactful with it.

"So what about old Richard now?" her father asked in a lull in the conversation.

"Simon, darling," her mother cautioned.

"Well, she's had a month to think about it. Should have an answer by now," he ploughed on. "Made up her mind what she's doing and all that," he continued.

There was a long pause. Jennifer reddened and even her father began to think he had said too much. He was about to apologise when she took her courage in both hands and said:

"I'm not marrying Richard if that's what you are talking about. Not now, at least."

There; she had spoken her innermost thoughts, but why had she had to leave that proviso at the end? She knew in her heart of hearts that it was final. But what if she couldn't find David? She would cross that bridge when she had to.

There was another pause, shocked silence this time. It was her mother who spoke first.

"Have you met someone else?"

"Yes, and no." This reminded her of another conversation.

"Is it anyone we know," asked her father.

"That's a stupid question," cut in her mother. "How could she possibly meet anyone we know in Africa of all places."

"Yes, I suppose that's true." And he subsided only adding, "But I suppose it's possible."

Playing for time Jennifer said, "That's not as daft as it sounds. I did meet somebody I just about knew at school and several people I met had unexpectedly come across friends of theirs also out there."

"Well, there you are then," responded her father, but largely for her mother's benefit.

Another long pause.

"Well, darling, you can't keep us in suspense indefinitely," encouraged her mother.

"Well, you see, I sat next to somebody on the plane out," she began.

"One usually does."

"Simon," cautioned her mother again but in a very controlled voice.

Jennifer was actually quite glad of this interruption: it gave her a few more seconds in which to marshal her thoughts and decide just how much to say.

"We only chatted for the last twenty minutes or so before we landed in Nairobi. He very kindly waited for my bags to come through. Do you know they were the very last ones on the carousel? Nerve-wracking. Anyway, in

46

that time he recommended that I should stay in a certain hotel in Tanga if I could make it there, although he realised it was well off my itinerary. And I did go there, God only knows why. But it is very beautiful, just as he said. But when I got there they gave me a dog-eared envelope with a letter in it for me. Well, half a piece of A4 pad that I suppose you could just about call a letter. He had obviously been there whilst I was humping round the rest of the country but the strange thing is, how did he know my name? I never told him and he never told me his. And I still don't know it." She began to feel desperate.

Her mother came to the rescue.

"But if he wrote to you, he must have signed the letter."

"Yes. He did. Just David."

"No more?"

"No, nothing."

"Oh," her mother brightened. "But where does he come from?"

The pig-headed streak in Jennifer was coming to the fore.

"No idea. No, that's not strictly true, but there was no address on the letter."

Even her mother was getting exasperated.

"This is crazy. Are you saying you are throwing up Richard for someone whose name you don't know or even know where he comes from? I presume at least he's English."

Her mother was working herself up. There was no telling what politically incorrect comment she might make next.

"Yes, yes," said Jennifer hurriedly. "I had enough sense to enquire of the hotel who he was and where he came from and the girl at reception was very helpful – seemed to read my thoughts even. It seems they know him well and that he stays there quite a lot and as a consequence he doesn't complete the register and all they have for him is Carlisle, UK."

"Carlisle." Her father came out of his reverie. "That's a long way off."

Her mother was, as ever, practical and to the point.

"Oh, well, that's easy then. You can look him up in the phone book." Then a sudden thought struck her. "You do know his surname I suppose?" she enquired guardedly.

"Er, well, er, no, not really."

"Oh, Jen, for heaven's sake. What are you messing about at?"

"Well, his name's Ware, David Ware," she said, "Although I'm not convinced about the Ware bit. Even the hotel was dubious about it. But I do know his firm make pumps in Carlisle."

"Pumps?" interjected her father. He didn't say it but he might just as well have. Both mother and daughter heard the unspoken, "Trade then, not gentry or professional."

"Yes, pumps," Jennifer hurried on. "So he ought to be possible to find from Yellow Pages or if necessary I shall have to go to Carlisle and look for him. It shouldn't be impossible," she added a bit lamely.

Her mother was seeing the rarely seen steely side of her daughter. The one that had decided she was not going to university. The one that had gone off to Africa to find herself and now appeared to have done so even if it was not what she and everyone else was expecting upon her return. Being ever practical she asked, "What about Richard then?"

Jennifer drew a deep breath. "I shall have to be brutal. I hope I've steeled myself for it."

As if on cue the telephone rang.

"Talk of the Devil," muttered her father.

Her mother answered it. "Valley Court."

An auctioneer's voice boomed down the line. "I hear the wanderer's returned then. Is she there?"

Her mother handed the phone over to Jennifer as if it was red hot and mouthed, "I'm not making excuses, it's your problem."

She departed out of earshot. It was not going to be easy but she knew what she had to say and she was quite determined to say it.

Meanwhile back in the drawing room:

"What do you make of all that then, Simon?"

"Well, you know what she is. She's plenty old enough to know her own mind. I guess we've just got to accept it. You know, I've had the feeling for a while that she's just been marking time, waiting for something to happen, maybe this is it."

"If she can find him."

49

"Oh, she'll do that, you mark my words. If she really wants to do something, she'll do it. Feel sorry for Richard though. Nice chap. Good sort and all that."

"So we just let her get on with it."

"First, we can't actually stop her and second she'll do it anyway whatever we say."

At that moment Jennifer returned looking very flushed and plonked herself back into her chair.

"Dad, can I have a strong whisky, please? A lot has happened in the last few hours."

"Of course. I'll get it. In fact, I think we all need one." And he went off to get drinks all round, but whether for celebration or drowning sorrows he knew not.

Whilst he was gone mother and daughter did not speak.

When he returned with tray, glasses, whisky and water it was Jennifer who broke the almost morbid silence. As though a weight had been lifted from her, quite cheerfully she said, "My trip was worthwhile after all. At one stage I quite thought I was wasting my time and money. It feels hateful to say it but now I feel free. For maybe the first time in my life I know, really know, what I am going to do next."

"Then we'll drink to that," said her mother in a relieved voice.

So we celebrate after all, thought her father to himself.

Chapter 2

Henry Thomas Wear was finding having a small child about the place a serious constraint to his *bon viveur* lifestyle. It was true that he loved both his son, Gerry, and his wife Millie very dearly but the child really got in the way. When he was a baby it seemed to be easier to park him somewhere and mostly the child was pretty obliging about being left. His mother and Millie's parents vied with each other to have him but they all seemed to have suddenly aged and were much less keen to have an obstreperous three-year-old left on their hands. This was not least because Henry and Millie's evenings out tended to overrun into the small hours of the next day.

So it was with some relief that he came back from the golf club fractionally earlier than usual and shouted up the stairs to his long-suffering wife, "I think I've found someone to look after that brat of yours!"

"Ssh, you'll wake him," came the tart response.

"Sorry, didn't think. It's not that late."

"I can do without having him awake unnecessarily at eleven o'clock at night, thank you very much."

"Sorry."

"You could be lucky. Anyway, who is it?"

"Somebody Freddie knows."

His wife was not impressed but without noticing he carried on regardless.

"Girl called Muriel. God, why are we blessed with all these old-fashioned names, Henry, Millicent and now Muriel!"

"As I've said before, none of it's our fault. You think of something better and we'll change them all!"

"This Muriel is some sort of relation to Freddie. There's another old-fashioned name when you think about it. His ward or something. Don't think she's his bastard child but it's always possible."

Henry was renowned for calling a spade a spade but it still shocked Millie occasionally.

"How old is she and what does she know about looking after children, especially one like Gerry?"

"How do I know?"

"Didn't you ask him?

"You expect Freddie to know that sort of thing? You can ask her, she's coming round tomorrow afternoon, about four o'clock!"

"Sounds as though it's all arranged then."

"Sort of is. Subject to you approving her."

Even Henry realised that he might have been pushing his luck a bit so he changed the subject.

"Come on, old girl, time we were in bed."

"I've also told you before that you don't 'old girl' me until we're both turned the ripe old age of thirty. And you've got longer to go than I have!"

"I'll thirty you, you, cheeky young lady," he said and lunged towards her, but she was too quick for him.

"Oh, goody!" she said and scampered for the stairs.

***

Names were something of a sore point with Henry Thomas. His father had started the family firm in Carlisle making pumps under the name of T. H. Wear & Co Ltd. He was Thomas Henry Wear and Henry thought it lacked a singular lack of imagination simply to reverse his own names for his son. This had rankled with him since he was small boy but then his father had certain other blind spots as well. He had almost literally smoked himself to death at the early age of fifty-one despite continuous warnings from family and friends alike.

Henry had only just about acquired himself a glamorous wife, who he found to be quite remarkable in bed, when he also found himself in charge of the family business about which he knew very little.

"My God," he had said to whoever would listen, "now the old man's popped his clogs I've actually got to run this outfit."

"Perhaps you shouldn't have spent so much time chasing women, wine and golf in that order!"

Words to that effect was all the sympathy he got from most of his friends.

Freddie Lambart was alone in being a bit more helpful than some and had given him some assistance in how the company system worked and had been remarkably impressed with what Henry's father had set up. This was possibly because his own family ran a haulage business and he did know some of the pitfalls of family businesses.

53

"Any fool can run that show," he had said. "Even you!"

Henry was not impressed by this comment but had indeed taken to the company as though it had come with his mother's milk, which perhaps it had. More to the point he found that T. H. Wear & Co Ltd made good profits that in turn allowed him to enjoy life to the full. In this, Millie, despite her old-fashioned name, joined him to the full. So it should have been no surprise to him when he found he had a child on the way.

But it was!

"Now what are we going to do?" he complained.

"Carry on regardless," Millie said. "I reckon it was that day we went up on the moors, love in the raw behind a gorse bush. Lovely."

And she hunched her shoulders up with the memory.

"Yes, well, there'll have to be less of that now."

"Why?"

"What about your condition?"

"Ooh, no need to worry about that for a while yet!"

Henry wasn't convinced and awaited the arrival of his son with some trepidation and quite a lot of whisky.

***

"You'll like her," Millie greeted him when he got back from the office the next day. "Oh, yes. You'll like her."

"Who?" he replied casually.

"Your friend Freddie's ward or whatever she is."

"Oh, her, Muriel was it?"

"Yes, her. Don't play the innocent. She says you've met and she winked at me!"

"Well maybe, if she says so. I meet a lot of people you know. Describe her to me."

"Jet-black hair. Quite tall but then she'd got stilettos on. Figure to die for. Cleavage you could lose yourself in. We could have a lot of fun with her."

Henry was attempting to remain on the planet.

"And does she know anything about children? Especially cantankerous boys."

"Don't know. Didn't ask!"

"So what did you talk about then?"

"Oh, this and that. By the way she's starting at the end of the month. Has to give a week's notice where she is."

Henry spluttered:

"But we never said anything about her being full time. Just the odd evening when we want to go out and come back late."

"Think how handy it will be when we want to do something, even as simple as going shopping." Henry winced. "Or lunch at the Golf Club." Henry didn't really want Millie too close there either. "Or up to the moors!"

"I guess you win, as always," he said with resignation. "But I'm looking forward to seeing this protégé of yours."

"Not mine, yours!"

He hadn't the will to try and argue that black was white any longer and so it was that Muriel Bouche came to the household of Henry and Millie Wear.

***

In fact Muriel proved her worth in double quick time. She seemed to have an affinity with Gerry and be able to control him where others couldn't. This may have been because, although only rising three, he was very like his father. He was very happy to be in the company of others provided he was the centre of attention. Muriel was happy to let him be that and young enough to empathise with him. For a start she came in on a daily or as required basis but, quite frequently, stayed the night when the Wears were particularly late back.

"Henry," said Millie one breakfast time after Muriel had been with them for about a month. "We need a larger house."

"Can't afford it," said Henry without giving the matter the least thought.

"You don't have to. I've got a bit of my own and there's a nice large Victorian house at the bottom of the town that would do us well."

"Still can't afford it."

"Now we've got Muriel, we could have her full time if we had accommodation for her. Just think how that would help. And having her in the house could have other advantages as well."

"Such as?"

"Don't go all pi on me, you know what I mean."

"And Gerry can have his Auntie Muriel with him on a full-time basis. You've got a point."

"See? It's all very tidy. I'll go and have a look at that house tomorrow. I think Mrs Jones used to live in one of those. Said they were huge inside. Be ideal if we have any more family, which is likely knowing the way you go on."

Henry was completely unfazed by these comments.

"And if Muriel's now part of the family, as you're suggesting, we can share her between us."

"If that's what you would like!" he added, just in case he had misread the signs.

"Yup," she said.

He hadn't.

***

A few days later and a little less than a month before Christmas Jennifer returned to the offices of Halliwell & Stoddard. She felt very much a stranger as she walked through the door. Having seen East Africa at least to some extent in the raw she felt that this was a very artificial world to which she was returning. However, the staff had not changed in her absence and she was welcomed back with a good selection of ribald comments.

"How was Bongo-Bongo Land?"

"Don't be foolish."

"Had she seen any lions and tigers?"

"Yes, but tigers don't live in Africa."

"What was the food like?"

"Plain but OK."

"Have the black boys got nice smooth skin?"

"No comment."

"Well, did she meet anyone worth meeting?"

"Yes, but I'm not telling."

And so on and so on. Even Mr Halliwell made some pleasant comments and Julie was ecstatic to see her back. "I can't think how you can stand being on reception and being nice to every Tom, Dick and Harry who comes through the door or bothers to ring up. I've been counting the days until your return."

It was nice to feel wanted.

A day or two later she found an excuse to escape from the office and descended on the telephone directories in Cirencester's library. There was only one D. Ware in Carlisle and the address didn't look right for her David. What did she mean 'her' David and what was his address likely to be anyway? It just didn't look right but she noted down the number and promised herself to give it a try. In the business section there were four, one Ware in Carlisle itself and that was a butcher's. There was one in Maryport described as 'Engineer' but that didn't seem right either and the other two were a soft furnisher and a gifte shoppe. Move on to Yellow Pages. This was equally discouraging. There was no direct mention of a pump manufacturer. There were a couple of local hire firms and one national company specialising in pump hire. She tried various other types of engineering that she thought might apply but nothing leapt out of the page at her. Again, she would try the local firms and see if they knew anything.

In some trepidation she tried the D. Ware that evening. A man's voice answered:

"'Allo." Loudly. That was a bad start but she had to carry on.

"Is that Mr Ware?"

"Yea." It was getting worse.

"Would you by any chance be the Mr David Ware that I met in Tanzania?"

There was a roar of raucous laughter.

"Nao, luv, never been out t'country. In fact, barely been out Carlisle, so tain't me."

"Oh. I'm very sorry to have troubled you," she finished, grateful that this Mr Ware couldn't see her blushes.

"No trouble, luv, hope you find 'im. Bye."

She put the phone down with his voice ringing through her head. What a strange accent the man had, half Scottish, half Geordie, half Lancashire. Well it couldn't be half, could it? A third of each then. Her David (there she was, at it again, being possessive) hadn't a trace of an accent.

Of the hire companies the national one came with a central office in Birmingham, at least she recognised that accent, and was singularly unhelpful unless you wanted to hire a pump. Of the two in Carlisle one was equally unhelpful but the other thought that somebody did make pumps in the area but they didn't know who, what or where. Thought the firm was very specialised, which sounded hopeful, and something like Pedro Pumps rang a bell with them. She went back to the directories but with no luck. Neither the farm nor the office had yet got as far as the World Wide Web, and no one she knew had either.

Jennifer's brother Paul was one of those elusive people, everybody knew where he had just been or where they had last seen him but as to where he was just now when you wanted him was another matter entirely. This was a trait he had had since childhood, and Jennifer along with other members of the family had many and varied memories of looking for him. This was usually accompanied by increasing panic as the possibilities of what might have happened to him began to gnaw at the brain. It was always that he was last seen in the stone barn, the hay barn, the milking parlour, or was it actually the slurry pit that he had found?

Their father was stoic about it.

'If he comes to grief, so be it. If not, he'll learn what's safe and what isn't.'

In truth, and like most children, he had an innate sense of what was practicable to do and what wasn't, but the attitude did not go down well with their mother.

Paul was in fact five years older than Jennifer. Neither was aware that there had been an intervening miscarriage to create that gap between them. There had been the usual competition, fights and slights, actual and perceived, as in any other family. Paul tended to use his sister when convenient, as on the occasion when she had first met Richard, and then drop her again when he didn't want her around. She didn't mind too much because it meant that she could go along with the crowd of Paul and his friends or she could stay at home instead – whichever suited her.

Their education had been different too, as Paul had gone to boarding school, at least from aged thirteen onwards. In Jennifer's view those must have been some good farming years with which to provide the wherewithal to pay for it! This had only increased his swagger to his younger sister when remarks got presaged with, "When I was at school…" She had become equally adept at fending this attitude off by referring to him as, "Grandad, here says…" Nevertheless there were times when she wanted his advice and this was one of them.

Unlike his father, and certainly unlike Jennifer herself, he was something of a workaholic, always rushing hither and thither and with a good purpose in his rushing about. And it showed. Since he had started to have a more active role in the running of the farm and estate things were noticeably better. All the gates now shut properly, some age-old junk they had played on as children had disappeared, most of the fences were now stock proof and, joy of all joys, the endless paperwork was up to date, or almost so anyway.

The latter chore Paul usually did on a Saturday morning so Jennifer was reasonably sure of catching him in the farm office then. The snag was that she had to work at least alternate Saturdays and often more than that. He had moved out of the family home a year or so previously and lived in one of the estate cottages. She could have seen him there but again he was difficult to pin down and as a matter of principle did not welcome visitors, even his sister, except by prior arrangement. Despite his efforts with the farm this was partly because he lived in a mess, and knew it. If his house was tidy and presentable it was usually because he was expecting one of the girls from the Young Farmers Club and everyone knew what that was about. Visitors were then even less welcome.

So she barged into the farm office and sat down across the desk from him.

"Paul, I need to talk to you," she announced.

"Mmm, yes, what about?" came the mumble from behind the computer.

"I want your advice about David."

"About what?" came the dreamy response.

She brought her hand down hard on the desk so that every loose object jumped in unison and some of them fell on the floor.

"Eh, what…? Steady on, Jen." Paul came out of his reverie. "David, did you say?"

"Yes. I need your advice. About David. Are you with us at the moment or still in computer land?"

"Yes, yes. I'm with you. But why my advice? Surely you should have a heart-to-heart chat with Julie or whoever in the office. All girls together and all that. I'm only yer average bloke."

"Many a true word spoken in jest," grinned Jennifer, and just avoided the notebook thrown at her. "No, truly you know you have much more experience of these things than me even if I am your sister. What I want to know is, should I go chasing after him?"

"You don't even know where he lives," said Paul perfectly reasonably. Jennifer looked sheepish.

"I know, and that's the worst part. I know it's Carlisle but I don't know just where and all the usual sources just don't produce the name. I suppose I could be spelling it wrong but I don't think so. No. The point is, should I go to Carlisle to try and find him? Answers, please."

"It's a hell of a long way to go," answered Paul judiciously, "And for what may be a complete non-starter."

"Maybe 300 miles but that's not that far by African standards anyway. Not unless you're a country bumpkin stuck in a rut down here." Another book flew in her direction but again she avoided it. "You want to be careful of doing that, you may lose vital information you know. Seriously, the question is: should I go?"

"It's a bit pushy. Especially for a girl."

"I know. But we do live in the equal opportunities era, you know."

"Yeah, but that's not quite the point."

"Suppose I came looking for you, Paul. What would your reaction be?"

"Depends on whether I wanted to see you or not."

"And would you? I mean if you were David, would you?"

"How would I know?"

"You're making it difficult; do you know that? But if a girl you'd met somewhere came looking for you, what would you think?"

"Like I say, it depends on whether I wanted to see her again."

"That's not helpful. What would you think of her?"

"I suppose I'd be flattered and I'd know she'd got guts, especially if she had come 300 miles."

Jennifer nodded as thoughts raced through her head.

Paul looked at her and tried to be solemn. "But you won't be happy until you have, will you?" he said.

"No, I suppose I won't."

"By the way, what do the parents think?"

"One, I'm crazy. Two, how am I going to find him? Three, he won't be one of us, you know." Paul made a face. "Four, how do you know if he wants to see you? Truth be told three should probably be one."

"Yea, I get the picture. So get on with it then. What's keeping you?" And he looked back to his computer.

"Thanks, bro, so I go with your blessing?"

"Of course. Get it out of your system if nothing else." Jennifer said thank you again and ruffled his hair as she used to do when she was small and wanted to upset him. Then she ran for it before any further missiles could be launched in her direction.

***

So the first full weekend of the New Year saw her heading up the M6 on a Thursday afternoon of a long weekend she had talked Mr Halliwell into letting her have. Having just taken two years' holiday in one go he took a little persuading but she reminded him that she had worked all the days over the Christmas break. The latter she didn't actually mind as she found Christmas at Valley Court a bit hollow and hypocritical. As the office had to be open anyway even if only with a skeleton staff with not a great deal for them to do either, she found she was appreciated more there. She promised to work some extra Saturdays as well.

She had to stop for fuel and something to eat (she had forgotten how bad, not to mention ruinously expensive, motorway food could be) but more to the point she bought an A to Z street map of Carlisle. For the moment it was pretty useless as she had no idea where she was going or what she was looking for, but it gave her confidence. And it was confidence she needed the nearer she got. It was easy to plan from several hundred miles away. She would find his office, or she would bump into him in the street, or she would just happen to pass his house as he arrived home from work. In all these scenarios he would be delighted to see her. She might find his office but would he be delighted to see her? Probably not. By the time she reached Penrith she was ready to turn tail and run for home. But it was too late for that. She wasn't going to stay anywhere grand and she found a modest hotel passably close to the city centre that was normally, no doubt, full of men working away from base but was nearly empty on a Friday evening.

She slept badly but to the evident surprise of the establishment polished off a full breakfast complete with baked beans and black pudding in the morning. She felt ready for anything after that. She then retraced her steps to a large lay-by just off the motorway where she had seen an 'Information for Lorry Drivers' sign in the half dark the previous night. Plan A was to drive round all the industrial estates and see if she could see the name written up or perhaps a firm that made pumps. This was where her street map might come into its own. She was surprised at the number of places there were for her to look, but she set off purposefully enough. Engineers of all sorts, printers, sign makers, car repairs, a dairy, haulage contractors (several), joinery manufacturers, an engine re-manufacturer (whatever that was), a non-ferrous foundry, she found them all but no pump maker. A cup of coffee from a sandwich van nourished her but enquiries for a pump maker, name of Ware or something, anything like it brought only blank looks. By lunchtime she was totally depressed. It was time to sit back and take stock. Time was running out as they, whoever or wherever they were, would doubtless close for the weekend today and probably early at that.

So what had she achieved so far? Precisely nothing. Well that wasn't quite true, a bit like herself, what she did know was all negative. She knew where he wasn't. He wasn't in any of the obvious new industrial estates but what else was there? She was more used to looking for remote farms than factories. If they were an old firm might they be nearer the city than out at its limits? That one she hadn't even considered. She supposed they could be in the surrounding area, not in Carlisle at all, Carlisle simply being the nearest place that anyone would have heard of. That would be much more difficult. She would try the inner areas and see what happened.

Bingo. She struck lucky almost immediately but, she had to admit, it was sheer chance. She was at a set of traffic lights waiting and wondering which way to turn when a couple of vehicles up in the next lane she spotted a van with written across the back, 'PEDRO PUMPS' and below it 'Pump Makers to the World'. When the lights changed, she ignored every rule of driving and cut across the traffic to 'follow that van', as the movies would have it. She didn't have far to go but it was an area she would have overlooked, grimy brick buildings behind the station and the street still with cobbles for a surface. The van turned through a gateway and into a yard at the end of a long building right up to the road, and the only concession to the latter part of the twentieth century was a tyre and exhaust centre nearly opposite. She went past and came back to investigate further. Here she found what did indeed appear to be an office at the opposite end of the building to that at which the van had turned in with its own smaller yard that had a few cars parked in it. This would appear to be the executive end of the establishment.

This was it. Now she had to gather up all her courage and see if David did indeed exist here. It was her only chance. She had to brazen it out. She hoped she wasn't too conspicuous. The only person around seemed to be a tall, gangly, overalled lad outside the tyre centre. She parked in the road; there was no need to make her presence more obvious than was necessary. She walked up to the office door and went in. She found herself in a small lobby with a frosted sliding glass window with 'Reception' written over it and one hard chair in a corner. She tapped on the window. Half of it slid back and an older than middle-aged woman with tinted hair looked back at her. She didn't speak.

"Do you by any chance have a David Ware here?" Jennifer enquired. Her voice sounded slightly odd, almost as though it came from somebody else.

67

"Don't think so. And you are?"

"Oh, it's personal. I think we met on holiday," she replied.

The lady appeared to think this over and then came to brisk decision. "No. Sorry I can't help you at all. Nobody here of that name and nobody has been on holiday recently. Sorry again. Good day." And the glass slid shut.

Jennifer found herself standing looking foolishly at the glass as someone started typing again on the other side. So that was that, or was it? She turned and went back out of the door where on the wall she saw two small brass plates that she had missed as she came in. One said 'T.H. WEAR & SON LTD, REGISTERED OFFICE' and the other 'PEDRO PUMPS LTD, REGISTERED OFFICE'. Her heart leapt for joy. She was right after all; so what was the silly woman in there saying? She felt like going back in and confronting the woman but her courage had had enough for the time being and she limply returned to the car.

What now? She was pretty sure she had found the right place, also that David did indeed exist but he was obviously being 'protected' by Mrs Tinted Hair who was supposed to be reception. Her first choice would be to sit it out and see if David appeared in order to go home. After all the day was creeping on and they probably finished early on a Friday anyway. As though her perceptions had been answered there came a flurry of cars out of the other end of the works followed by a few stragglers. She looked at her watch. Four o'clock. Yes, they did go home early on a Friday. She guessed the office staff would not be too far behind. At half past four a man came out of the far gate, closed and locked it behind him, walked up the street to the executive end, opened the door to the offices and shouted, "Good night, Muriel, see you Monday!"

Then he went and got into a battered blue van and drove off. All went quiet again until five o'clock when a man, a woman a little older than Jennifer, a girl much younger and finally the tinted hair woman came out, carefully locking the door behind her. *She must be Muriel,* Jennifer thought to herself. The man and the one Jennifer's age got into cars and drove off but the others all walked. Fortunately it was dark with only streetlights for illumination and Muriel, if that was her name, went the opposite way. Jennifer was all set to start looking for something under the dashboard if she had come her way.

So, very obviously, no David. She sat staring up the road straight through the gangly youth who was idly kicking a flat football round the tyre centre forecourt. She started the car and drove slowly away wondering what her next move should be. Before she reached the turning at the end it struck her like the proverbial bolt of lightning. The name on the brass plate was T.H. Wear not T.H. Ware and it was the name of Ware for which she had been looking all this time. She braked hard and stopped when another thought struck her. Back at the Mkonge Hotel there had been some confusion over whether his name was Ware as in the place, Wear as in wearing clothes or Weir as in something water goes over. The manager had been absolutely adamant that it was the first of these and would brook no argument to the contrary. She wondered why but, more to the point, she had another avenue of approach.

Back at her hotel she borrowed a local telephone directory from the desk and took it up to her room. Never mind people called Ware it was Wear she wanted. And sure enough there were some. Only one in Carlisle but it was a T. Wear and, joy of joys, a D. Wear at Brampton wherever that was. There were several more but all much further away, Maryport and Silloth. She reached for her A to Z and decided to at least find where the one in Carlisle was. It was getting too late and too dark to first find her way to Brampton and then find an address when she got there or, for that matter, to go looking for somewhere in Carlisle itself. She would have to contain herself until tomorrow.

On Saturday morning, with the aid of her street map, she found a bungalow in a select, sedate and retiring area which was further reinforced by an elderly lady putting out the milk bottles. It didn't seem right but there might be a connection. In due time she would be proved correct on this one too.

Her next port of call was going to be the works again. If it was the right place he might be there on a Saturday even if nobody else was. She drove past and then back again and parked where she had yesterday. There were a few cars in the works car park but none at the office end. The door was open so somebody must be there. Before she could react the youth from the tyre bay was approaching.

"You looking for somebody?" he enquired as he arrived next to her. "See you here yesterday. Don't like people just hanging around," he added, by way of explanation.

Jennifer gulped. If it was that obvious, she would never make a detective. The face she put on was braver than she felt.

"I'm looking for a David Ware. They tell me in there that he doesn't exist but I'm almost sure this is the right place."

The youth looked blank.

"Or is it David Weir?" she tried as an afterthought.

She watched realisation dawn.

"Yeah, yeah, got yer problem," he proclaimed. "They spells it W-E-A-R but pronounces it We Are, right? Sounds a bit like Weir but it ain't. And it ain't Ware neither."

She could have hugged him, oily overalls and all. This solved the problem that had bugged her all along.

"So is there a David We Are over there then?"

"No. Not today. 'Ee's never in on a Saturday, even if 'ee's in the country. Dunno what 'ee does on a Saturday but 'ee's never in."

She must have looked crestfallen, because he went on:

"'Ee's usually in on a Sunday morning though. That's if 'ee's 'ere. Again dunno why."

She perked up.

"Are you sure about that? I could be here tomorrow."

"He's pretty much always been in when I work Sundays, but that's not every Sunday," he backtracked slightly but carried on with quite a speech. "You'll know if 'ee's 'ere cos 'ee drives a VW Golf same as your'n but

71

red and more modern. Last year's model. Dunno why 'ee don't drive something a bit posher, 'ee could afford it. And, yeah, if you come back tomorrow don't come too early, 'ee's never 'ere before eleven. Did the old bat throw you out?"

"And some." Jennifer was still smarting from the way she had been treated.

"Like that she is. Dunno what gets into 'er."

"I wouldn't give her house room." She didn't know why she was confiding her thoughts to this youth.

"Nor me. Looks after 'im like she's 'is mum, she do. Not to say as 'ee don't need it though."

Jennifer was stunned. All this information all of a sudden. In her excitement the last part of this speech passed her by but she would remember it later, much later. Now she needed just one more piece to complete her jigsaw.

"Do you happen to know where he lives?" she asked.

"Ah. No. There you 'ave me. I don't think 'ee lives in t'city but where I dunno. 'Is dad lives in t'city and I do know as 'ee don't live at 'ome. Not any more, 'ee don't."

Again there was an undercurrent in what he said but once more it went over her head.

"Thank you. Thank you very much indeed. You see, I met him on holiday and I've been trying to catch up with him ever since."

"Ah. Yes. I see." He tapped the side of his nose conspiratorially. "Good luck tomorrow," and shambled off.

"Thanks again," she called after his retreating back. This produced a wave of an oily arm.

She sat back into her car and drew a deep breath. Most of what she had wanted to know and had been endeavouring to find out since returning to England had fallen into place in five minutes' conversation with a droopy youth in a tyre depot. So what now? She had effectively a day to kill. Be a tourist? If she had to be. No. The obvious thing was to find this place Brampton and then find the address she had from the telephone book.

Brampton itself was easy: straight along the main road towards Newcastle, turn off that road where signposted. She found herself in an attractive small market town with a triangular 'square' with its own town hall or butter cross or something. The address she had turned out to be even easier as it was a flat overlooking the square probably with a good view of all that went on. She didn't see a red VW Golf parked anywhere, but then part of the square was taken up with market stalls.

"Courage again, Jennifer," she said to herself as she marched up to the door and rang the bell. It was an anti-climax. There was no reply.

***

Sunday morning saw her back outside the factory feeling very conspicuous. The gangly youth was nowhere to be seen today although she half expected him to show up out of sheer curiosity. More to the point there was a red Golf in the office car park. Her heart missed a beat, indeed several, as she repeated her previous manoeuvre of driving past, turning round and then, taking the bull by the horns, driving into the car park and parking beside it.

"It's now or never, girl," she said, probably very loudly, as she got out of the car. As she approached it she wondered if the door would be locked but, no, it opened as before and she was in the lobby again. Silence. She wasn't sure quite what she had been expecting but empty, eerie silence was not it. She opened the sliding glass from her side. No one, obviously. If he was here he'd be in his office wherever that was. She tried the door and this too opened as though she was expected. The door the other side of the general office was ajar and she went through that to find herself in a passage that had a general smell of oil and was littered with odd lumps of steel lying about on the floor. Of the three doors the first was probably Accounts, the second possibly David's (it wasn't very tidy) and the third very obviously the drawing office. The door at the end, open and leading her on, led down a couple of steps into the works proper. As the rest of the place was deserted and as there had to be somebody here, even if it wasn't David, she pushed on and was hit immediately by the smell of machine tools, oil and metalworking. It was a smell she had not come across before but was not unpleasant and she knew she could cope. There was sound of movement and someone called, "Hello?"

"Hello," she called. "Anyone about?"

"Yes, in the assembly bay," replied the voice. How the dickens was she to know where the assembly bay was?

"Coming," she answered and went in the general direction of the sound.

There she could see a man in a white coat and, yes, it was indeed David, even though he had his back to her. She knew that in all the books and films she should rush to embrace him but her willpower nearly failed her at the last moment and, like a cat, she was ready to cut and run. Perhaps fortuitously at that moment he turned round.

"David?" she said with a slight question in a voice that she hardly recognised as her own. "It's me, Jennifer. Remember? At Nairobi airport? I got your message."

The shock of seeing her was plain for all to see but there was joy with it as well. She had her mother's intuition and that did not desert her at this critical moment.

"Jennifer! What the hell are you doing here, of all places?" he exploded.

"Just looking for you," she said simply.

"But here? On a Sunday morning? In the factory? How did you know…?" His voice trailed off.

"It's a long story," she said and tears came unexpectedly to her eyes. "I'm sorry," she stammered.

His face was picture of happiness and embarrassment but her sight was too blurred to see it. He recovered first and quickest.

"Come on," he said. "Come and sit down while I make a cup of coffee for us both and we catch up where we left off." He led the way back up the two steps and into his office (she had guessed that bit right) and made her sit one of the chairs. He then departed through one of the doors opposite into what she glimpsed as being a remarkably smart little kitchen. There she could hear him busying himself with kettle and cups and coffee and things.

Had she been able to see him she might have heard him whisper to himself, "Wow, this I like, but how did she find me?" She would have seen him draw deep breaths, rub his eyes just to check he was really awake and in truth wipe away tears of his own. She would almost have seen his brain asking itself just how he should play this one and then decide not to move too fast. She was too important to him to chance putting her off by rushing in where angels would fear to tread. Then all business he called out, "How do you like your coffee?"

"Black, one sugar," she called back. She was mentally more composed but felt a wreck.

"That's just as well because I'm not too sure about the milk. It's remarkable there's any at all over the weekend."

He came back into with two mugs of coffee and sat in the other visitor's chair beside her.

"Sorry, we don't run to cups and saucers and these are the best of the mugs." She looked at hers, which advertised a firm of packaging suppliers in Gateshead.

She laughed and the tension eased.

"I got your letter," she said.

"Good heavens. You mean at the Mkonge? You mean they actually remembered to give it to you? Well, they must have, I suppose or you wouldn't be here." He looked suddenly puzzled. "But I didn't put an address on it as I remember," he added.

"No, nor your name either," Jennifer chided.

"Er, no," he said. "Silly wasn't it?"

"Why not?" She just had to ask but he ducked the question, replying conventionally and lamely to the effect that it was lovely to see her again. She felt frustrated.

"More to the point, how did you know my name so precisely, Miss Jennifer Suffram, and yet hid your own?"

"Oh, that was easy," he said, brightening. "We sat next to each other, remember, and I just looked over your shoulder as you filled up the immigration card. Tick the box for 'Miss', name 'Suffram', forenames, 'Jennifer Mary', address; I have a pretty good memory for things I want to remember but that one escaped me for quite a while until Cirencester materialised out of thin air some time later. More to the point, however did you find me?"

"That," she said, "is a much longer and more tortuous story but at its most basic the Mkonge gave me your name, wrongly, but they did get Carlisle right. Ultimately I followed one of your vans to here and the lad over the road told me to come round today."

"John? Yeah, he's a few bricks short of a load but he's OK," David mused.

Conversation flagged. There was so much that each wanted to ask the other but both were nonplussed as to where to begin. Again, it was David who reacted first. He looked at his watch and said, "It's a bit early but let's go for some lunch. I think I know just the place." Then he added, "Oh and do you mind if I just tidy up what I was doing in the works before you appeared out of the blue?"

The tension eased but Jennifer needed to know something else first before she moved on to whatever might come.

"That sounds nice but just hang on a minute, there's something I need to know before we go anywhere." David was surprised by her forthrightness and, truth be told, so was Jennifer. This was a new Jennifer from the slightly lost young woman he had helped in Nairobi. He raised an eyebrow to her.

"Go on," he said.

"Why wouldn't that woman in there," she pointed in the general direction of the reception office with her empty coffee mug, "even acknowledge your existence? For want of a better description, I'm a professional receptionist and if I treated anyone, but anyone, like she treated me, I should be out on my ear in double quick time and quite right too. OK, I had the pronunciation of your name wrong. And incidentally why do you pronounce it in that funny way? But that's no excuse for literally slamming the hatch in my face."

She paused for breath and could feel that she was flushed about the face. In the pause that followed she was afraid that David might slam the figurative door in her face as well. In reality he was equally worried by the outburst and needed those few seconds to collect his thoughts.

"Ah, Muriel," he began apologetically. "She's a bit too fond of trying to mother me these days."

"That's just what John over the road said," Jennifer interrupted him.

"Did he now?" muttered David thoughtfully. "Anyway let's deal with the pronunciation first and then you may understand. I only say may. I truthfully don't know why we pronounce it the way we do. Whether the word is corruption of Weir or Ware, whether it's a joke lost in the mists of time, or possibly to create confusion with one of our competitors I have no idea but that's the way it is. It is kind of distinctive, if a bit confusing for outsiders."

"I'll say." It was Jennifer's turn to mutter but David ploughed on.

"It has the useful effect of us knowing immediately if someone comes looking for me who we don't know and perhaps don't want to know."

"Are there many of those?"

"Yes, quite a lot actually, reps and so on. And others too, but that's all another story. You being an attractive young lady –" he looked sideways at her but she did not react, "– would not have helped where Muriel is concerned. She's something of a thwarted spinster. Did you also happen to say how or where we met?"

"I said we met on holiday. What's wrong with that?"

"Again, quite a lot. OK you were on holiday but I wasn't and haven't been away for over a year. All her alarm bells would start to ring. The mothering instinct would begin to take over and her common sense would go out of the window. She would have visions of some gold digger come to pinch the family fortune, if there was such a thing. She would make a snap decision that here was somebody who was not good enough for the 'We Are' name and block you out – literally."

"But why, for goodness sake?"

"Please believe me," he was almost pleading, "these are long stories that are certainly not for now. Muriel is not

79

really the battle-axe she appears to be; she can be very sweet even if a bit overbearing. Please forgive her, eh?"

"I'll think about it," Jennifer pouted, not at all satisfied with the answers she had received even if it was obvious she was not going to learn anything further at the moment and would have to be content. David became all action.

"I must go and just clear up what I was looking at or I shall have people grumbling that I've been interfering with their work tomorrow morning," he said. "Stay here or want to come?"

"Just you try and stop me," replied Jennifer with a genuine show of enthusiasm.

They went together down the passage and through the door into the works. She became aware of that smell again and was surprised that she had ceased to notice it when seated in the office but she was sure it was there in the background somewhere. David busied himself moving some parts into boxes and looking very closely at others before replacing them on shelves. She wandered around looking at machines that did she knew not what. It all looked impressive and it seemed to stir something inside her. She was sure it shouldn't appeal to her but somehow it did; it looked interesting. But after all she was a girl, and a country girl at that, and girls, especially country girls, didn't work in a grubby factory and get their hands all oily. Equally certainly, ever so nice schools for girls didn't mention this sort of thing as a career.

But David was soon finished and whisked her out of her reverie and through the office front door, locking it behind him. He was as good as his word and they descended on The Millrace pub overlooking the river a few miles out of the city. Being early they were there before the Sunday lunch crowd and so could collar a quiet table. David went for some drinks and came back with a pint of the local beer, which he declared to be good having persuaded Jennifer to have a half of shandy made with the same beer. She had to admit to his good taste and it relaxed her a little. They were both a bit tongue-tied now that the initial pain and pleasure of meeting again was over and as a consequence made a great issue of deciding from the menu although the choice was not that great or exciting.

"It looks like," David offered, "chicken and chips, chicken and salad or maybe chicken and chips with salad. Must be special menu for wet Sundays."

"But it's not wet and you've missed the Cumberland sausage and chips or salad," Jennifer countered. "And anyway what's special about a Cumberland sausage?"

"Nothing really except its long and coiled up like a rope. Try one?"

"OK. Decision made." David went off and ordered. Whilst waiting they wandered onto the outside patio and Jennifer felt calmer in the weak January sunshine as the water idled by and some ducks came over to have a look at them. These in turn attracted an unusually superior-looking swan.

"I've nothing for any of you," she said in mock distaste before they returned to their table. Conversation was in short supply but their meal came quickly and it was David's turn to create surprises.

"So how's life at Valley Farm or Court or whichever it is today?"

Jennifer was stunned.

"How do you know…? You said you couldn't read the address on the immigration card. And anyway, that doesn't have both in it. Why are you grinning like that?"

It was his turn to blush.

"Well, you see, I've been and had a look." Before he could continue Jennifer rounded on him.

"Then, why in heaven's name didn't you call and come and say hello? Men are supposed to do that, you know, not me come traipsing all the way up here."

David put his hands up in surrender.

"Hang on a mo, before you eat me instead of the sausage. If you had kept to what you told me was to be your schedule you would still have been in the Serengeti or the Ngorongoro Crater or somewhere. We have a competitor down your way but occasionally we combine forces on a job and for that reason I had to be only a few miles from Cirencester, so I thought I'd just have a look see."

"Quennington," she said.

"Spot on," he said admiringly.

"Godsells," she said. "Mr Halliwell knows them. I don't."

"Well, as I say, I had to go and see them and borrowed the local telephone directory from the receptionist just see if there were any Sufframs in the area and, well, there were. I found, at some difficulty I might add, the entrance drive but knew there was no point in calling for the reasons

82

herein given," he finished with mock pomposity knowing full well that he doubted that he would have had the guts to do so if she had been there. The excuse was true, but he was glad of it all the same.

"She must have been more obliging than a certain Muriel," commented Jennifer.

"It was a he actually."

"Ah, male chauvinist conspiracy," she retaliated, but there was a large smile on her face all the same.

"And what was to be your next move?" Jennifer enquired guardedly.

"Well, I've been expecting to have to go that way again for a while but so far it hasn't happened. Then I might have come and enquired."

"Only might?"

David coloured. "Yes, only might," he said and looked away.

Jennifer found an emptiness in her stomach as she dropped her hand onto his. "Oh, David," was all she could say. He did not move his hand and she did not move hers even if she did think she had been a bit impetuous. Brightly she got back onto safer ground.

"So where do you live? In Carlisle, in a village, out in the country, what?"

"Brampton," he said.

"Ah," she said.

"Ah?" he queried.

"Yes," she said. "Amongst my researches, once I'd had the name sorted, it was also the local telephone directory. One in a smart area of the city, but elderly, Mrs was putting the milk bottles out, possibly your parents?"

She looked at David. He nodded.

"Second one in Brampton. I rang the doorbell but there was no reply.

"My, I'm glad you didn't find me, my flat's a tip at the moment. Got to give you ten out of ten though for deduction, Miss Sherlock Holmes." He smiled.

"Elementary, my dear David," she responded and flushed at what he had said. "A good thing I caught up with you today then or I might have caught you out, or rather in."

"And what about you then? Your name isn't the commonest; I've never come across a Suffram before. Parents? Brothers? Sisters, whatever?"

"Yes, I suppose the name is unusual, but having lived with it all my life I've sort of got used to it," Jennifer laughed.

"One does." He spoke feelingly.

"For what it's worth the story goes like this. You know the Cotswolds are renowned for their sheep and wool, or were years ago, and the prosperity of places like Cirencester was built on all that? Well, an ancestor introduced a Suffolk ram into his flock and it had a good and noticeable effect on wool production. You have to imagine all the old boys talking about 'him wi' Suffolk ram' and somehow the name stuck, or at least a corruption of it. We still keep sheep and have Suffolk rams so that's how it is."

"I wouldn't have guessed it, that's for sure," David commented. "And the rest of the family?"

"Parents. Yes. Getting older but still active. Brothers? One. Paul, now running the farm. Sisters? None. So there's just me. How about you?"

There was a pause as though David wished he hadn't got into these questions even if they were inevitable.

"Parents. Yes. Suddenly very elderly although not that old. Otherwise also just me. Running the family shop as you saw."

"Another drink?" he added, as though wanting to change the subject.

"No, thanks," she replied. "Remember, I've got a lot of driving to do." And looking at her watch, added, "And I soon have to get going if I'm going to be home at anything like a sensible hour and I don't want the family staying up to find out if my mission has been successful or not."

"They wouldn't?" he queried.

"They might. Indeed, almost certainly will. They all think I'm totally crazy coming up here like this. Plenty of comments about chasing wild geese, pigs flying by, etc, etc."

"Well, I'm glad you did anyway. I should probably have got to you in the end but there's no telling when that might have been or whether I would have had the courage to have actually come and asked for you." Intuitively she realised that it was probably quite an effort admitting his weakness and she did not pursue it.

"I'll run you back to your car," he continued in order to cover for himself.

"I'm glad you're not abandoning me here," she joked, "but seriously, I must have your phone number. Home and work."

"Ditto," he said. "Although I've actually got yours."

Jennifer looked surprised.

"I got it when I got your address. Remember?"

"Ah."

Back in the office car park neither knew quite what to do next or how to part company. Finally, David put an arm round her shoulders, drew her to him and gave her a long kiss. Confused, delighted and in a slight panic she jumped into her car, started the engine and prepared to drive off.

"Bye," she called through the open window, "Oh, and by the way, put a flea in Muriel's ear for me, OK?"

He laughed, but he stood and watched until she turned to corner out of the end of the road. He didn't see John at the tyre dealers quietly watching them nor did he hear him say a satisfied "Ah" to himself.

***

David let himself back into the factory offices in something of a daze. He found his way to his desk and collapsed into the chair. He saw nothing of what was on that desk, the bits of paper with messages and reminders on them, his diary with appointments for the coming week, nothing of the whiteboard on the opposite wall with its more urgent messages and squiggly multicoloured diagrams of how jobs should be done. He lent forward with his elbows on the desk and his head in his hands, then threw himself back with his legs stretched out on the floor in front of him as though in paroxysm of pain.

"Wow!" he said finally and out loud to the empty room, adding, "Who is this girl who has the guts to come all this way looking for me?"

He relaxed and reviewed his day. It had started quite ordinarily. He had got up at about his usual time and had breakfast. He had picked up the Sunday paper on his way into Carlisle for the morning eucharist at the Cathedral. Nothing unusual in that, for him anyway; but what would she think? He had come on to the works as he always did so that he could check out the odds and sods of business life without having anyone breathing down his neck and without the telephone ringing. And then Jennifer had walked through the door. And she had found him grovelling around in the assembly bay! He would have had lunch out anyway but he had had it at a slightly better establishment than normal because she had been with him. And it had made him very happy. He had to admit that. At his age he was no longer a teenager but he knew he was all of a flutter inside where it mattered.

And the rest of the day? He normally went on to high tea with his parents and spent the evening with them. Funny, now he came to think about it, how she had found them and he was sure would have gone in asking questions. That might have been awkward if she had not seen his mother on the front doorstep. Well, he guessed he would still go and see them but did he tell them about her or did he keep quiet? He thought he would have to keep quiet even if the conversation got a little dry, after all nothing might come of it although he was sure and hoped that it would.

Which thought provoked more turmoil in his mind. What next? The ball was very obviously in his court. He didn't consider himself shy but knew only too well that he was exceptionally so in these sorts of circumstances. He knew her address and telephone number. It was now too late to post anything with the idea it might get there the next day. He would have to think about that, but in the meantime, it had to be business as usual and off to a dull evening with his parents.

***

Jennifer was over halfway home before she came even remotely down to earth. It was really only the necessity of a loo and something to eat that stopped her at Keele Services. Here the adrenaline kicked out and she wondered how on earth she had managed to drive the last 200 miles as she had no memories of it whatsoever. She just hoped that she had not caused too much mayhem on her way south, cut in front of too many lorries or grossly exceeded the speed limit. She really must go sensibly from now on but it was only another couple of hours to home, anyway.

Refreshed she started off again and fell to thinking about what she must have been thinking about in the previous few hours. Obviously, it could only be one thing, or rather one person: David. First and foremost, had she remembered him correctly. Yes, her memory had been pretty good. He had been dressed for the tropics before so had maybe appeared a bit taller than he actually was. Now he was quite smartly dressed, even wearing a tie and on a Sunday morning in his own factory? Bit odd that. Hair was nearly black, just a trace of brown. Eyes, deep set in a craggy face and brown, slightly bushy eyebrows. He was perhaps thinner than she remembered and more reserved. She had quite obviously caught him off guard and he was more than a little surprised to see her. He seemed somehow diffident, even shy – had the regular traveller style he affected in Nairobi been a ploy or a put-on? He seemed almost like two people. And then what about her and him? He was obviously pleased to see her and had made some sort of moves to find her. Good point that. Had she been too pushy in going to find him? She hoped not and felt that they would ultimately have met up again somehow if he could have forced himself to make the move. No, that was unkind, and she was not in an unkind mood, but it was probably true even so. And so on, and so on, it all whirled round in her head until she found herself driving up the drive to Valley Court more or less as she had intended. And as expected her parents were waiting for her return. Really! She was no longer a fourteen-year-old out on her first date but she was too tired and too happy to make an issue of it.

"Did you find him?" was the immediate question.

"Yes, I did," was the equally immediate answer followed by her father once again requiring drinks all round in order to celebrate.

Thus, ensconced in their familiar chairs the inquest into her pilgrimage to places north was just beginning when the telephone rang. Her mother went to answer it. She came back with a twinkle in her eye,

"Someone called David on the phone, wonders if you're back safely."

Jennifer blushed all over her face and into her hair as she hurried out of the room. Her parents exchanged knowing and amused looks as the door closed behind her.

"David?" she said. "How sweet of you to ring. And how did you know I'd be back by now, I've really only just walked in the door... Yes, I guess you do know how long it takes to get down here. You sound horribly official. Are you still in the office...? No, I thought you must be at home by now... Yes, the journey was good but I don't remember much of, it's really a wonder that I did get back here safe and sound... That would be your fault... Yes, we will make something more sensible of it next time... I'll allow a bit more time..."

After some more conversation she rang off and put the receiver down allowing her whole being to do a double jump as she punched the air with both hands Yes, this was definitely what she wanted. She straightened herself up, brushed herself off and returned to go through all the gory details of how she had found him. She thought she had been quite clever and quite enjoyed relating the tale. She thought, too, that they were genuinely interested in her story.

Later she wondered just how much courage it had taken David to make that call. Quite a lot, she suspected.

Chapter 3

Whether Muriel knew what was happening to her was something she often wondered about in later years but at the time life was new and exciting. In particular it got her away from her mother and talk of a father that she had no recollection of ever having met. Despite that he seemed to cast a long shadow over her family such as it was. A much, much younger brother, too obviously an error of pills on her mother's part, gave her what experience she had of looking after children. She knew she could be a hard nut but she blamed that on her upbringing or lack of it. She did her best to contain it as she had soon found that being nice to people was generally the easiest way of getting what she wanted.

And getting into this Wear household was what she wanted at this moment in her life. They appeared to have plenty of money, judging by the way he splashed it about. She had been in on the viewing of the possible new house with Mrs W and she liked what she saw even if she thought it odd that Mr Henry didn't even bother to go and see what his wife might be buying. Yeah, she definitely liked this idea. Even if it was a bit of an old-fashioned sort of place, it was large with a decent-sized garden that would be a novelty to her at least. It also had big rooms, one of which she had been promised if she moved in with them on a full-time basis. Knowing what a sexy bastard Mr W was, she was pretty sure what that would lead to but, hey ho, you only live once!

***

"They've taken my offer," Millie announced at supper a few days later.

"Good."

"We shall need a bit of a mortgage and you will have to fill up all the forms as you will be paying even if the house is going to be mine."

"Joint, surely?" Even Henry seemed taken aback by this revelation.

"No, it's going to be mine. You know you spend too much money enjoying yourself, not that I don't enjoy it too but I want some security in my life and this is going to be it."

"But Millie, this is going to look very odd, isn't it?"

"Who's to know? You can be the martyr paying the mortgage and all the world will think it's your house! I can be the little lady back home doing all the right things for her hubby."

"You can do that all right," he said casting a lecherous glance at her.

She just sat demurely at the table.

"That's all right then."

"What about Muriel?" he said, only partly changing the subject. "And Gerry," he added in an effort to be family orientated.

"She came to see the house with me because I wanted a second opinion."

Henry seemed completely unfazed that his was not that opinion.

"She seems hell bent on moving in with us and has even picked a room that she would like! I haven't finally agreed to that yet. The room, I mean, not her coming with us. I think she sees it as a step up in life which I'm guessing has been pretty hard for her up to now."

"It has, I think. From what Freddie said, and if you're furnishing it for her and the room's large enough, you better get her a double bed."

"I was planning on it as I guessed that was what you would want, or should I make it king size for all of us?"

"One thing at a time, old girl, or you'll frighten the living daylights out of her before we've even started."

Millie didn't actually comment about that but changed the subject.

"And there's a nice room for Gerry just along from hers."

"That's good. So when do we move in?"

"Be a while. We've actually got to buy it first, sign on the line and all that and then it's easier to do what we have to do to the house before we move in. Decorating and such, you know." She wasn't letting on just how much needed doing; that could wait.

"So do we keep Muriel on a daily basis for the time being or do we try and fit her in here?"

"Daily for the time being, I think."

93

"Unless she threatens to take off and then we pin her down."

Neither of them knew that there was no chance of this happening. By some primeval instinct Muriel knew that her future lay with sticking to them, come what may.

***

From being an obstreperous two-year-old, Gerry became an obstreperous three-year-old at about the time they all moved into the new house. It was inappropriately named 'Fellside', being many miles from any fells and not beside them either; obviously a choice made to help the developer's sales or one made by the first owner. Red brick, Victorian and distinctly out of fashion it may have been but it was a wonderful place for a small child with all sorts of nooks and crannies from which he could jump out to frighten his parents and his auntie. There was an overgrown garden too with thus further possibilities for making his family jump. It was, however, a bit sad that he never managed to create the paroxysm of fright in Muriel as he managed with his parents. In fact, more often than not it was the other way round; she was able to creep up on him with the desired effect.

Maybe the two of them were too much of a kind for one to be even remotely alarmed by what the other did. Either way she became a very good nanny to him, which suited everyone just fine. In fact it soon reached a point where when Gerry had a problem it was Muriel he wanted rather than his mother.

"Want Mu," he would say and could be devastated if she wasn't around.

"That boy doesn't know who his mother is!" Henry would grumble.

"The way we both mother him, it's hardly surprising," was Millie's answer to that comment but he seemed contented enough with it anyway.

"He'll be playing one of you off against the other when he gets older."

"He already is!"

"That's my boy." In his own way Henry was proud of his son, who appeared to be very much a chip off his own block.

It was not long before Henry was spending some of his nights in Muriel's bed. She finally had to ask him what determined with whom he was going to sleep, especially as very often it was just that; no sex involved.

"I flip a mental coin," he said. "No offence to either of you. At least none intended."

"As simple as that? I don't believe you!"

"Sometimes when you've changed the colour of your hair it turns me on and I have to be here with you. Millie always refused to do that, says it's too much trouble and I don't blame her."

"Is that all I have to do!"

But Henry was not really thinking about it.

"Occasionally, if I'm late back I do wonder who might have had the hardest day and sleep with the other one! But that's about the limit of it."

"Very practical. And what decides when we all have a good time together and then all sleep together?"

"Not having to get up in a rush in the morning!"

"Yeah. I'd guessed that one except that a certain someone has to get Gerry his breakfast!"

"But gets paid for it!"

"In more ways than one! You're harder than I am but it's a great life until we all weaken!"

"No chance of that just yet a while."

"I know."

And they made love again.

***

In due course Gerry went to playschool and then on to school proper. He was a precocious infant as his father must have been before him. He wasn't in trouble any more than any other child and certainly didn't go looking for it. In any case both his mother and Muriel kept a tight rein on him at home. His father's maxim that life could be a lot of fun without actually being in trouble or breaking the law seemed to come naturally to him. As a consequence, Muriel found herself with not enough to do all day and bored as a consequence.

As she did not want to leave the family there seemed to be only one answer, and she raised this with Millie over coffee one day.

"Isn't it time you had another baby?" she said. "Gerry's getting on and there'll be a big gap if you leave it too long. And I shall be out of a job," she added for good measure. "And I like it here."

Mrs Wear took a long draught of her coffee. She had been expecting this for a while.

"I know," she said. "I've been getting at Henry for a while about it but he says one's enough for the time being but he's been saying that for at least three years. He doesn't seem to realise how time passes."

"In a world of his own."

"Not all the time, but quite a lot of it. I don't want to upset him but, as you say, it's time there was another one around. Be good for Gerry too. To have to learn how to cope with a brother or sister."

Being the scheming young woman that she was, Muriel had a plan but was unsure whether to suggest it or not.

"We could…" she began. "But no, forget I spoke."

"No. Go on. If you've got a good idea."

"No. It's not very sensible."

This was playing right into Muriel's hands. She spoke all of a rush.

"Suppose we both came off the pill and see who gets a bun in the oven first? There now. I've said it."

Millie was not at all outraged, as Muriel would have expected. In fact, she had had a not dissimilar plan in mind herself but she did foresee the practical problems.

"So if it were you, say, how would you talk your way through without it being too obvious that it's yours? How do you fancy being classed as a single mother? And who's going to be the father? Even if you and I know exactly who it will be!"

"Hmm. I hadn't quite seen all those snags," said Muriel, although in fact she had and had answers to most of them. Time to play it a little cool. "I'll have to think about it a bit more."

"We both shall," said Millie, but she too had a good many of the answers. Their conversation moved on to more conventional matters.

About three weeks later it was Millie's turn to revisit the subject. Without much preamble she said, "I think you should come off the pill and see what happens. If that doesn't work then I will, and we go from there."

"I already have," said Muriel bluntly.

"That'll give him something to think about!"

"Nothing's happened yet."

"It will. Give it time."

"I am."

And it did take a considerable time before anything happened and Muriel's plans could swing into action. Her first move was to make something special of her hair. She went a golden blonde with it piled up high and, sure enough, it had the desired effect and Henry was in her bed in double quick time. When he was satiated, she dropped her bombshell.

"I've missed two," she said.

"Two what?"

"Two periods, silly. I'm expecting your baby!"

"You're doing what?" Henry yelled at her.

"Your baby. In here." She patted her belly which was not showing anything yet.

"You can't be."

"Well I am. Please don't shout, you'll wake Gerry."

It wasn't Gerry she had woken but Millie who guessed what the commotion was about and smiled to herself. Whatever next?

"But you can't be, you're on the pill."

"Correction. I was on the pill. I came off it a while ago. I thought we needed some more children about the place and you and your *wife*," she emphasised the wife, "didn't seem to be doing much about it so I thought I would."

"Oh. You did, did you?"

"Yeah." She looked smugly at him from under her eyelashes.

"I ought to chuck you out of the house in the clothes you stand up in and nothing else!"

"I haven't got any clothes on!"

"Exactly my point."

"And it would be very unwise, you know. Just think of the fun the papers would have with 'Girl thrown out of house naked!' 'Expecting employer's child!' Etc, etc."

"I had thought of that. The alternative is that I turn you over and spank you for being a naughty girl."

"Now that's more like it." And she turned herself over to receive her punishment.

She was not actually expecting it but Henry smacked her one very resounding blow on her upturned bottom with the flat of his hand. Millie heard it and laughed to herself.

99

"Hey. That hurt," said Muriel in an aggrieved voice.

"It was meant to. Now let's think about how we get over this problem."

"I'm not having an abortion, if that's what you mean."

"Fortunately for you, I don't."

"That's good, so what's your problem?"

Henry discovered that every snag he thought up about his new-found fatherhood Muriel had an answer for. She had too obviously been working on this for a long time.

"I could do with a problem solver like you at work," he muttered.

"Now there's an idea," she replied.

But Henry had moved on.

"And finally," he said, "what will my wife, of whom you spoke so considerately just now, think about this?"

"She knows."

"She knows!"

"Yeah, well she doesn't actually know it's happened. I thought you should be the first to know, but she knows that it was going to."

Henry really was flabbergasted this time. Both women in his life ganging up against him like this!

"I really should spank the both of you, I think," he said.

"Yeah, OK. But not so hard this time. Right?"

But Muriel did not offer herself to be spanked again.

***

Unlike many people, Jennifer actually enjoyed going to work. Monday mornings held no qualms for her. But this Monday morning she knew exactly what it was going to be like. Everyone from Mr Halliwell downwards was going to want to know her business. Worse still, it had even started before she left home. Paul, who never normally showed up in the house before she left for work, had made a point of doing so this morning. Unusually jolly, he had asked the inevitable:

"Well, did you find him then?"

Jennifer sighed.

"Yes, I did. And I can't cope with any snide remarks at this time in the morning. I shall have enough to come when I get into the office."

"As though I would."

"You would."

"Yes, I probably would, but come on tell us all about it then. I've got work to do, and for that matter so have you."

"Got a couple of hours then."

"Ninny, the potted version will have to do for now." Childhood exasperation with his sister was beginning to surface again.

"OK. Yes, I found him, Grandad." And she ducked to avoid his hand coming to clip her over the head. "I found his factory on Friday by sheer luck but got turfed out by a dragon of a receptionist. Found him there on Sunday morning but then I had been tipped off that he might be. We went out to lunch and I came home. What else would you like? Oh, and he rang to check that I had got home safely."

"Good, I'm glad for you. By the way how did he know the number?"

"He knows that sort of thing," replied Jennifer rushing to David's rescue even if she had asked the very same question of herself. "Hey, and I've got to get to work," she added in order to prevent herself having to give away any more details.

The office was just as she had feared. The comments were even more juvenile than when she came back from Africa. Once the initial rumpus had died down and the day's work had started Julie found the time to come and talk in between Jennifer returning to her telephone duties.

"Well done, Jen, I really thought we'd have the hankies out and be consoling you this morning, you know."

"More than once I thought you might too," admitted Jennifer.

"And how did you find him in the end?" Julie asked, all too obviously fishing for details.

The phone rang and Jennifer had time to think out her answer as she put the caller through. She decided there was nothing really to hide and happily recounted how she had found the factory and been thrown out of it. Muriel still rankled with her.

"Then I found him there on Sunday morning of all things."

"Whatever was he doing there then, doesn't he have a home?"

"I don't know. You know, I hadn't really thought about that. Odd," mused Jennifer. "As to what he was doing there; well, he was sorting through a lot of bits of metal that I suppose were important bits of something. Messy, but I rather liked it. Something was actually being made there. Not all pompous and how much is my house/farm/prize bull worth today, like it is here."

Julie shivered. "I think I'd prefer what we do here to a lot of bits of oily metal," she ventured.

Jennifer appeared not to hear and continued her reverie.

"It's his name that threw me, it's spelt Wear, as in wearing clothes but pronounced We Are but at the same time very like Weir. There's a funny accent up there, sort of half Geordie and half Scottish. Can be confusing till you get used to it. Yes, he does have a home but I haven't been there yet."

"Yet? What do you mean yet?" exploded Julie. "You haven't known him more than a couple of hours and you're already talking about going back to wherever he lives!"

Jennifer made a face at her and carried on.

"As I was saying when so rudely interrupted."

It was Julie's turn to stick out her tongue.

"He has a flat in a place called Brampton but as I say I haven't been there properly, yet." She emphasised the *yet*. "Although I have rung the doorbell. There was no answer. His parents live in Carlisle and I found them but fortunately didn't call because he wouldn't have been there. He said it was a good thing I didn't find his flat because it was in a mess."

"Typical man," commented Julie.

"No, not a typical man. Not to me anyway," retorted Jennifer. "But hadn't you better be getting on with whatever it is you're supposed to be doing or Mr H will be on your tail?"

"I guess so," sighed Julie. "But your adventures are much more interesting." But she did take the hint and go, much to Jennifer's relief. She liked Julie but she had an awful habit of adding two and two together and making it four just when you didn't want your innermost secrets revealed. And she couldn't be relied on to keep it to herself, either.

To Jennifer's further relief her adventures 'Up North' seemed to be a five-minute wonder and by the end of the day most people had lost interest. Julie, needless to say, wanted to know if she had heard more from him as the days went by. Telephone calls, a letter, a card perhaps? Jennifer had come to the conclusion that David was actually very shy despite apparently being in command of a useful-sized business. In truth on this occasion she too had made two and two add up to four but it would be a little while before she was sure of it. She was also having to admit that she was becoming a bit, no, quite a lot more than a bit, worried herself at the silence from 'Up North'. After all, she reasoned, it was up to David to make the next move, wasn't it? She had gone all that way on what could well have been a complete wild goose chase and on what most people fully expected to be just that.

It became a very long week. And the weekend seemed even longer than the week despite the fact that she was working on the Saturday. Paul became even more enquiring than Julie and, being family, quite unpleasant with it. In the end her mother put her foot down as though he was still a small boy and again it all subsided, but that didn't stop her worrying. Relief, when it came, was dramatic indeed.

The end of the working day, around five thirty, always tended to be chaotic at Halliwell & Stoddard. There always seemed to be a panic to get things done to catch the post for which the last collection in Cirencester was at six o'clock. On the Tuesday a week after her return she didn't leave the office until well after six and it was going uphill to seven o'clock before she got home. Her mother was unusually jumpy when she arrived. This was most unusual for her as she was normally in complete control of any situation.

"David rang," she announced. "Something's wrong. I can feel it. Anyway he left a number and asked if you could call him back. I said you would. But something's not right," she added again, quite unnecessarily.

Jennifer was puzzled.

"What sort of thing?" she said.

"No idea. But something is. He sounded…" Almost uniquely, her mother was lost for a word. "Weak," she said finally.

Jennifer didn't waste any more time. She went straight to the phone and settled down with it out of earshot of anyone else who might be around. She dialled the number he had given her and it rang a few times before being answered.

105

"David?" she queried. She wasn't entirely sure it was David who answered.

"Jennifer. Thank God you rang."

"David, whatever's the matter? You sound, well, awful."

Jennifer, too, was lost for a word.

"Jen, it's a lot to ask, but could you possibly come up here?"

"Well, yes. But I'm supposed to be at work this week you know. But what's wrong?"

He sounded relieved.

"In a nutshell I've broken my arm, and badly."

"Oh, David," she gasped. "However did you do that for goodness sake?"

"It's not a long story. I fell down the stairs and landed in a nasty heap at the bottom. And before you ask, I hadn't been drinking."

"I wasn't going to," she said with a touch of frost in her voice. "Yes, I can come. Now? Like immediately? And anyway, why me? You hardly know me."

His voice sounded more cheerful.

"Yes. No, tomorrow will be fine. I can't cope with those trying to look after me and I think I know you better than them, even if we have only met twice."

"I'm honoured, to be sure, but what about your parents or neighbours or anyone else you might know? Let's be practical, I'll come, I'd love to. But they won't thank you for dragging an unknown girl from the other end of the country."

"I know, I'll chance it but my mother's in a world of her own and nearly driving me crazy. And Muriel, well, I think I'm beginning to see your problem with her. She seems to have got the jumps and become irrational with it. And as for anybody else…" His voice trailed off. "There just isn't anybody. Please come." His pleading had a pathetic tone to it.

"OK. I know where to come even if I have only ever been there when you were out."

"Park behind the Moot Hall if you can and come in the door and straight up the stairs. Have you got a mobile phone? No? Oh, well if you get lost, get in a phone box and ring this number and I'll direct you. I'm not going anywhere."

She rang off and sat looking at the receiver wondering what on earth she had committed herself to and, more particularly, why? She had never broken any bones herself but she knew plenty who had fallen off horses and ended up in hospital. She didn't remember any of them being like this. Anyway, it was nice to be wanted and it would be nice to be seeing him again even if rather sooner than she had expected. Then it dawned on her as to just exactly what she agreed to do. She was supposed to be at work. She was not due any more holiday for a while; she had used it all up going to Africa. This was hardly compassionate leave even if caring for the sick was what she was doing. Mr Halliwell would not be pleased. She felt herself pale at the enormity of her situation but she had to face her mother, first.

107

Her mother was fiddling with some flowers in the hall all too obviously waiting to find out what all this was about. Jennifer didn't beat about the bush.

"He's broken his arm. Badly, he says, and wants me to go up there to look after him. He appears to have no one else. I'm going tomorrow morning."

Her mother did not seem surprised; had she been listening in?

"And work?" she questioned, knowing full well what the answer would be. She hadn't brought Jennifer up without knowing how determined her daughter could be on those rare occasions when the spirit really moved her.

"I'm going to ring Julie at home, I think I've got her number, and she will have to cover for me. Call it compassionate leave or something. I'll speak to Mr H when I know better what I'm doing and for how long."

She departed with the phone again and after some rummaging found Julie's number. She was surprised to hear from Jennifer and not a little aghast at her precipitate action.

"But how am I going to cope and what will Mr H say?" she wailed down the line.

"You'll manage and Mr H will have to get over it," Jennifer replied brutally but truthfully. Just at this moment she was an Amazon on campaign and nothing, but nothing, was going to deflect her.

"But what if he threatens you with your job? You know you're not due any more holiday," Julie continued to worry at her.

"Sod it," answered Jennifer, "I don't doubt I can find another job somewhere. My position isn't exactly indispensable. Even you can do it."

With that last barbed remark Jennifer could almost feel her colleague standing up straight upon her dignity as the reply came, "Yes and that's just what I'm afraid of. You waltz off playing at being Florence Nightingale, he gives you the sack and I wouldn't blame him, then Muggins here gets lumbered with being receptionist. You know I can't stand that."

She had to pause for breath.

"I know, I know," said Jennifer changing into a conciliatory mode, "but I shall only be gone a few days at most and then I shall be back. I'll phone Mr H tomorrow as soon as I know what I'm doing. You're a saint, Julie, you know that?"

Whilst not actually cutting Julie off she finished the call and went to pack some clothes. This presented more of a problem than she expected. How long was she really going to be away? Two nights? Three? A week? What was she going to be doing? Skivvying for David? Mostly cooking and cleaning she guessed. Was she likely to get involved in his business affairs, even with that Muriel? One thing was sure, in the state he sounded to be in it wasn't going to be a dirty weekend type affair. Pity, she thought. In the end she settled on casual workaday-type clothes, jeans and sweaters and at the last minute decided to put in her office clothes, just in case. She didn't know it then, but she was going to be glad of that decision.

Supper was quiet that evening. Her father thought her madder than usual and actually voiced his long-held wonderment as to where his daughter got her impetuousness from. Her mother was quiet but helpful and afterwards departed into the kitchen to make a huge shepherd's pie for her to take with her.

"But we'll never eat all that," expostulated Jennifer.

"I'll bet you will. Not all at once of course but you can cook it and then eat it as required when all other cooking fails."

Jennifer was doubtful but accepted it with good grace.

The evening dragged and finally, and in some trepidation, she rang David ostensibly to find out how he was, but actually to be sure that the expedition was all still on. She would have been heartbroken if it had been off but she half expected it to be some sort of bad dream. It was not. David still sounded depressed and fed up but was obviously expecting and looking forward to seeing her tomorrow. She had a long drive in front of her but an early night did not give any extra sleep and she felt distinctly jaded when she set off the next day. The motorway was clogged with traffic in a manner that she was soon going to find out about all too well, but she had not intended to arrive until after lunch in any case. She could not have arrived any sooner. She parked as instructed. He had said the door would be open but even so it was with some trepidation that she apparently marched into someone else's home. She was surprised to see that the bottom panel of the door had a piece of plywood roughly screwed over it but thought nothing of it, just then.

"It's me," she called up the stairs in the tone of voice that assumes the hearer will instantly know who it is speaking.

"I'm in here," responded a voice, again assuming that she would know where to go but it added helpfully, "Turn right at the top of the stairs."

She did as bidden and then stopped dead with a gasp and her hand to her mouth. "But you said you had broken your arm," she stammered.

"I have but that's not all of it," he replied.

"I should think not…" she trailed off.

"I just fell down the stairs." He was trying to be jocular. "And through the door at the bottom and nearly out into the street."

He grinned but she noticed the wince of pain. In an instant her brain took in the scene. A pleasant airy room with, surprisingly, a fireplace and an alcove with dining table and chairs. A large three-seater settee and an armchair, bookcase with books, pictures on the wall. All very cosy and comfortable and not at all like a bachelor pad. Her gaze returned to his injuries. One eye had the most enormous bruise round it and she guessed it had been closed. Cuts on his face were obviously only superficial and had scabbed over or been hidden by a few days' growth of beard that he did not have before. The hand of his good arm was bandaged at the wrist whilst thumb and forefinger were encased in elastic bandages. The fingers of his right arm protruded from the whiteness of a plaster that seemed to include his elbow as well. He had been sitting propped in the corner of the settee with his left leg resting along it. By the way the lower part of the trouser leg was split open it appeared this was bandaged as well. He struggled from where he had been sitting, but did not actually stand up.

"Why ever didn't you tell me about all the rest of your… your injuries?" she finished.

"You might not have come if I had," he said.

"Well I have to admit that I was a bit surprised. I've known people break their arms and legs but I don't remember them calling to the other end of the country for help. Especially to somebody they hardly knew."

"Silly, isn't it? And I hardly dared hope you would come."

Jennifer enjoyed the pleasure of that remark but David appeared not to notice. She scrabbled back to firmer ground.

"Well, now I am here, what's to do first?" she asked.

"Sit down and have a cup of tea while we sort ourselves out."

"OK, point me at the kitchen. I'm passable in a kitchen but nursing an invalid, that may be something else again."

"Through that door there. I hope it's not in too much of a mess."

It wasn't. She had expected to find a mountain of washing up and a goodly mess of half-eaten food.

"How did you manage to have it so tidy for me?" she called through the door.

"Mother came over this morning and did the washing-up. She's a bit miffed about you coming though. Thought she was going to have the chance to mother me all over again but once is enough of that." He sounded a little bitter.

She rattled around in his kitchen finding mugs, teapot, tea bags, milk, sugar and even a tray. She was impressed. Compared to her brother Paul's cottage David was very well house-trained. She wondered if it was him naturally or whether his mother was putting on a good show on his behalf. She rather thought the former as she felt it would take days for someone to sort out Paul's mess, not just half a morning. Perhaps as proof of this she even found some biscuits in an airtight tin. She carried the tray though to the living room and they sat down for afternoon tea. It was patently obvious that neither of them were used to this ritual and neither knew quite where to begin. Jennifer decided it was up to her.

"So, tell me, what exactly did you do?" she asked rather formally, more after the style of a doctor than a friend.

"I told you, I fell down the stairs."

She looked at him and frowned.

"Most people don't wind up like you from falling down a few stairs. Were you drunk and incapable? Was it these stairs or a fire escape as you evaded an irate father or what?" Why did he always seem to talk in nearly monosyllabic riddles? She remembered this from Nairobi and also the note he had left her.

"You want all the gory details then?"

"Please," she almost begged him.

"Yes, I did fall down stairs and it was those stairs just out there. No, I wasn't drunk, it was eight o'clock in the

113

morning and I was on my way to work. I suppose I may have been trying to avoid a second journey and was carrying too many things. I must have stumbled on the top step. With my hands full I wasn't able to grab at anything and thus fell from the top to the bottom, out through the bottom of the door half out into the street. You may have noticed it's been patched up."

"I did, but didn't take much notice," answered Jennifer. "By the way was it glass?"

"Yes, and I've got eight stitches in my leg to prove it."

"Oh, no!" exclaimed Jennifer in horror.

"Oh, yes," he carried on. "Anyway it nearly frightened the life out of poor Mrs Colmer who just happened to be passing, which was just as well as there was blood everywhere and she was able to call an ambulance. I think I must have blacked out for bit because I haven't any memory of what happened next; the first I knew was coming to with the sound of sirens in my ears as the ambulance took me into Carlisle."

"Golly," was all Jennifer could manage. "And when was this?"

"Wednesday morning after we met. Actually, I blame it on you!" he said with a bit of a twinkle in his eye.

"Me?"

"Yes, because I had been preoccupied with how best to make contact with you again without appearing too pushy or too formal and my mind was somewhere in Gloucestershire, rather than concentrating on what I was doing, when I was trying to carry too many things down the stairs."

"I'm flattered but it's a bit of an extreme way of going about it, you have to admit. A phone call would have sufficed. So what happened next?"

"True. Well they kept me in for two nights, which in itself is quite an achievement these days. I think it was to satisfy themselves that my blacking out was a result of the fall not the cause of it. They were also concerned as to how I was going to look after myself if they did let me out. Mother wanted me to go and live with them and Muriel said she could come out to keep an eye on me here. The long and the short of it was that between them they must have convinced whoever that I wouldn't be back in hospital immediately at least. It was arranged for a nurse to come here to change my bandages for as long as necessary. In the short term that was all OK by me because it got me back on my own patch and out of hospital."

"So how are you coping?" she asked. It was a leading question she knew but she had to see where all this was leading.

"Let me see. That was Friday. Mother brought me home and she and Muriel got me up the stairs. That nearly killed all of us. The weekend was all right as people had time and I was the latest wonder, but by Monday it was obvious it wasn't going to work long term. Then I thought of you and then quite deliberately, before I had time to prevaricate with myself, I rang and you weren't there. I was devastated. But you rang back and now you're here and all's well with the world, my world anyway."

"Which reminds me," said Jennifer, once more trying to get back onto firmer ground, "I need to phone the boss and try and explain what I'm doing."

"The phone's just there," David said pointing to the table next to him. "I'm afraid it's a fixed line and I can only move with difficulty so I shall be listening in. Sorry." And he handed the instrument across.

"No problem," she said, but it was really. She wished it was a hands-free like the one at home where she could retreat out of his earshot. However, whatever had to be, had to be.

She dialled the number and Julie answered.

"Hi Julie, it's Jen here, is himself around...? Maybe that's a good thing, is he very upset...? Oh dear. Really? He's threatened me with my job? Well maybe he'll have to do it himself then... OK, I'll phone him tomorrow. First thing? Well maybe... Yea, pretty knocked about. Fell down the stairs and through the glass door at the bottom and out into the street. Stupid thing to do, wasn't it?" She grinned sideways at David. "No idea how long I shall be here... Well he'll have to whistle for it... Talk to you tomorrow. Byee."

"Do I gather you are about to be out of a job?" asked David as she handed the phone back across him.

"Almost certainly," she answered.

"Hey, but you can't risk that on my behalf."

"Just try me."

"But you hardly know me," he said. "You might not want to stay."

This time she wasn't to be panicked.

116

"Well, there's only one way to find out and that's by staying here with you." And she grinned back at him.

"Great," he said, and it was not said sarcastically. He meant it.

"Actually, hand me the phone again, I ought to phone Mum and tell her that at least I have arrived, that you're more or less in one piece and that I don't know when I'm coming back. That'll make her fret!" She grinned wickedly again.

This conversation was a bit longer than that to Julie but followed much the same pattern. She explained in a bit more detail about David, touched on the possible sudden lack of a job, said she would be back due course and would phone in a day or two. She passed the phone back and then jumped as the doorbell rang and without warning, someone was suddenly coming up the stairs.

"Who's that?" she said. But before she could get an answer a woman slightly older than herself was in the room with them. David made the introductions.

"This is Melissa who comes to change my bandages and generally check-up that I'm being sensible."

"Aye, an' I'm needing to be doing that too," said Melissa. The Scottish accent was very pronounced. "He's a good boy really but he'll be doing more than's good for him if I'm no stopping him."

"I've heard the gory details but I'm not sure I'm ready to be seeing them yet," decided Jennifer. "I'll get my things from the car."

David started to say something and then thought better of it. She started off by bringing up the shepherd's pie and

117

passed through the living room studiously avoiding looking at what was going on there. She put it in the fridge and had a look to see how much other food there was. Not much. What were David's plans for eating later on? She was surprised his mother had not left anything. Perhaps cleaning and clearing up was all she liked doing. What was she, Jennifer, going to do about it? Was that why she was here? So many thoughts flew through her mind. She felt as though she had suddenly got married without anyone telling her and it was equally suddenly her problem to be keeping house. She would find out after Melissa had gone.

She went back down to the car and brought up her overnight case but then stopped at the top of the stairs, wondering where she should take it. Turning left at the top presented three doors. One she knew to be the bathroom, but the other two? One turned out to be an airing cupboard so the other must be a bedroom. Gingerly she opened the door to find a room, indeed a bedroom, nearly as big as the living room with a large double bed in it, a couple of chairs, an elegant chest of drawers and a built-in wardrobe. She left her bag just inside the door and was wondering what to do next when she heard Melissa winding up her visit, so she hovered on the landing until she re-appeared.

"He's doing OK," she said cheerily. "Horribly healthy really. Do me out of a job, he will that." And with that she was gone.

David was looking a bit pale when she returned to the room.

"It's all very well her being so cheerful," he grumbled. "I guess she's right but doing what she does leaves me completely knackered. If you'll pardon the expression."

"No problem," she said. "What about food? There doesn't seem to be too much in the fridge. I've brought a huge shepherd's pie that Mum made but we want more than just that. Had you anything in mind especially as you are in no state to be going anywhere?"

"No, I guessed I might have eaten my reserves by now," said David. "I had been worrying about this. Didn't my mother leave anything?"

"Doesn't look like it."

"Oh dear, she really has got the hump about your being here. Sorry, but it looks like you will have to go to the shop and see what you fancy. But I'm sure the pie will be fine," he added hurriedly.

"Where do I go, then?"

"Co-op is about the only choice. A bit basic but they've got most things just as long as you're not too fussy. About 100 yards down the street, you can't miss it."

"Good, I'll try them." And with that she was off down the stairs into some fresh air that she felt she sorely needed. She really was finding herself in at the deep end and it was becoming very deep indeed. Good heavens, she had only met this man twice before and the sense of *déjà vu* loomed before her again as if she had instantly become his wife, or partner at least. She was beginning to feel physically breathless at the speed things seemed to be moving. But she didn't really have much choice, did she? It was she who took off up the M6 like a lunatic when he called so

119

she had better jolly well get on and do what she had come to do. Worry about the consequences later. In fact, she reflected, lunatic wasn't a bad word at all for her at this present moment. Never in her life had she been so emphatic about what she was doing. These thoughts took her to the shop where she purchased enough to see them through until tomorrow and then, well, tomorrow could look after itself.

Again, she rattled around in a strange kitchen and produced a meal of which she was reasonably satisfied even if she did have to admit she had not done much more than put it together. Despite his injuries, David seemed to have a good appetite or, maybe, his eating had been erratic over the last few days. Once completed David became suddenly diffident and nervous.

"I have to raise one question," he said.

"Go on," she replied.

"Question of sleeping arrangements," he continued rather rapidly. "You have some choices to make. The Star has, or at least at lunchtime, had a room if you want it. Only a pub but quite civilised, I'm told. Equally I'm told this sofa is quite comfortable. Or," and here he faltered a bit, "my bed is a double and large with it, but you may not want that."

He was flushed and embarrassed as he finished.

"This problem had crossed my mind," Jennifer teased, because she had already made up her mind about this one if the opportunity arose. She pretended to ponder.

"I'll take your word for the sofa but I don't intend to find out." She noticed the shadow of a downcast expression cross his face as she continued, "The pub has probably got itself booked up by now so it looks like it will have to be your bed. I can risk it because you are in no state to do anything you shouldn't but I might have to make other arrangements when you can."

He didn't miss the glint in her eye despite the school-mistressy-type lecture and the wagging finger.

"I hope it's comfortable," she added.

"It is," he said, "or at least I think so. That's settled then. I'm glad." He seemed business-like again. She giggled.

"Penny for them?" he asked, suddenly alarmed.

"I've never shared a bed with anyone in cold blood before," she laughed, "not even with school friends. It'll be a new experience."

"Nor me neither," he answered, using the American *neether*. "That should be a comfort to both of us. If we need comforting."

They both laughed, but both realised all too clearly what they were getting themselves into and where it was all likely to lead. Neither said anything but both rejoiced at the possibilities.

When the time came, David was insistent that he did not need help to get himself to bed, he had after all been managing for himself since he came back from hospital. Yet he looked ashen and washed out when she finally saw him there. It obviously took it out of him, like the visit from the nurse. She was glad she had brought pyjamas rather than a fancy nightie; there would, she hoped, be time enough for that in due course.

***

Unsurprisingly their night was not without its disturbances but both were reasonably refreshed by the morning. David put himself through the same exhausting process in reverse to get up but did seem to be a bit less done in by it. He tucked into breakfast with enthusiasm. Once he was back on the settee and she had washed up, he became business-like again.

"Do you think you can find your way into the office for me?" he enquired.

She smiled.

"Well, I found it before without instructions and you can tell me where to go this time," she said. "Yes, you tell me what you want and I'll go fetch." Like a dog, she thought to herself, but also like a dog, she knew she would enjoy it.

"Good," he said. "I'll ring Muriel and tell her what's needed and she can have it all ready for you."

"Er. No," said Jennifer.

He looked up surprised.

"No. You tell me what you want, write a list or whatever and I'll go and see whether Muriel will let me in or throw me out." She really was very surprised by her own audacity but she had been stung by the woman's ineptitude and she needed to start as she meant to go on. If Muriel didn't like it: well, tough. If David didn't like it; well, she might have to modify her line but she would cross that one when necessary.

David was taken aback but was beginning to be able to put words and reason as to why this young lady who, as she rightly said, he hardly knew was such an attraction to him. She was no infatuation but a real live, thinking, working, down-to-earth girl. If he dared think about it they could go far together.

"Please don't upset her too much," he pleaded. "She virtually has to run the show when I'm away. I know that no one's indispensable but she comes close to it.

"At the moment, anyway," he added and managed to wink with his good eye.

Again she enjoyed the flattery but again she had to run for safer ground. She was glad of the afterthought that had made her put her smart office clothes in her bag.

"OK, I'll go and change then," was all she said.

"Wow," said David when she returned dressed in dark jacket and skirt with high heels to match. "Engineers' offices are not glamorous places like estate agents you know. They tend to be full of bits of metal and oily clothes."

"I know. I saw, remember? And I'm fascinated and this is where I begin to find out how it all ticks. But Mrs Muriel has to realise that she's not the only one who can put on an act and play the part. If she and I are going to co-operate at all then it has to be on an equal footing. Now, what was it that you wanted?"

It was her turn to be business-like and it was his turn to look worried.

"I've made you a list but it's basically any letters and faxes that require attention. There will probably be a string of phone messages, some of which I can perhaps deal with from here if they're urgent. You haven't met any of the staff yet, except Muriel through the window, but I think Christine will be in today. She's the accountant and does the books etc. and she may have some cheques for signing and details of anyone clamouring for money or will tell you if anyone perchance has paid us. I'm sorry I shan't be there to make the introductions but I'm sure you'll cope." He grinned. "Oh, and here's some cash, go and do some shopping if we are to eat any more. You'll pass a couple of supermarkets on your way in, take your pick."

So, once again wondering what on earth she was doing and why, she set off for Carlisle. She spent the journey rehearsing all the things she would say to Muriel if she got the chance but knew full well that when one starts thinking like that, the situation one encounters is always very different from what one had imagined. She deliberately pulled into the office car park as though she owned the place, but the building remained dead as though nobody had been there for weeks. The only place where she was noticed was across the road where John let out a loud "Ahh" when he saw her drive in, but would only tap the side of his nose when his mates asked him what that was all about. She got out of her car and walked across to the main door, which at least was not locked, as she had half expected it to be. She was not going to be humiliated by knocking on the frosted glass hatch windows so went straight for the office door. This was locked. By some sort of intuitive instinct, she recoiled from it, wheeled round, walked out of the door and back to her car. She didn't hear the hatch open or voices enquire who was there. She was gone by then.

She drove out of the office car park, along the road and back into the works yard. She had not been here before but fortunately the main door was open and she could see where she was in relation to where she had been previously.

She got out and marched into the works. She was taken aback by the noise, machines running, grinding going on, somebody somewhere hitting something with a very large hammer and above it all a cacophony of radios that sounded as though they were all tuned to different channels. She was halfway to what she knew to be the works entrance to the offices when a man in a white coat caught up with her to ask if he could help. She kept moving but explained that the front office door was locked and that this was the only other way that she knew of into the offices. He seemed to accept this and led the way, even opening the door and letting her pass through. She was touched by the wolf whistle that followed her in from somewhere in the background. The man in the white coat looked slightly embarrassed but let her go on without following, for which she was grateful.

She walked on down the passage which was dark and cold. Not cold in the physical sense but in the sense of being lifeless. She vaguely wondered why the lights were not on. Saving electricity perhaps, but she doubted it. There was a coat over the back of the chair and a handbag on the desk in what she had decided was the accounts office but, otherwise, the place seemed dead. She opened the door into what she knew to be the reception office. To say that the effect was electric would have been an understatement of a considerable order.

Jennifer, in that instant, discovered an attribute that she didn't know she had: total and instant comprehension. She presumed it came from her mother. Just, as she now realised, she had taken in David's situation, injuries and home in the split second as she rounded the corner into his living room, she now took in the situation before her and didn't like what she saw. The most immediate effect was total silence with only the background hum of the factory for noise. This was accompanied by total immobility of the three people in the room. Muriel – she was the only one for whom Jennifer could be sure of a name – had come to a standstill with a cream bun halfway to her mouth. A smartly dressed young woman sitting on the edge of a desk, probably Christine in here for coffee and a chat, had been hugging her coffee mug to her in both hands and swinging one leg as she did so, but the leg was now stationary in mid-air. Jennifer wondered for just how long she would manage to hold it there. Sitting at a desk in front of a keyboard was a young girl with mousy hair who just sat gaping as though she was watching some sort of horror movie.

It was Muriel who recovered first, not least because she had an inkling as to who Jennifer was and why she was there. That knowledge made her spiteful and attack is generally acknowledged as the best form of defence.

"And who the hell are you to come marching in that way without so much as a by your leave? And how did you know there was an entrance that way? Visitors come to the front door and I choose whether to let them in or not" she stormed, pointing the cream bun at the hatch and presumably the door beyond it, spilling a trail of icing sugar across the desk which she looked at with distaste. The other two women in the room stared at her in disbelief. They knew Muriel could be a law unto herself but this was going too far. Jennifer, even to her own surprise, remained icily calm.

"The door was locked so I came in the only other way I knew how," she answered.

"There is a hatch, you knock," continued Muriel continuing to gesticulate with the bun and scattering more sugar across her desk as she did so.

"And then you slam the hatch in my face, like last time," replied Jennifer, still very calm. Her ears picked up a restrained giggle from the mouse. Muriel heard it too.

"And don't you laugh like that, young lady, if you know what's good for you!" she almost shrieked and, turning back to Jennifer, she said in voice loaded with irony, "So I suppose you're the young flibbertigibbet that he's called in to look after him?"

"Yes," said Jennifer ignoring the jibe.

"So what are you doing here then? Why aren't you shacked up with him in Brampton, 'looking after' him?"

Jennifer could almost see the inverted commas around the last words.

"He doesn't need full-time attention, as I'm sure you know."

This elicited a grunt.

127

"And he's concerned," she continued, "about what's going on here."

"Doesn't he think I can manage the place in his absence?"

Jennifer noticed the 'I'.

"I've no idea."

Another grunt.

"So why are you here then?"

"David asked me to call in and collect any mail, faxes or messages for him."

"Sounds as though he must be getting better then," answered Muriel, but she didn't sound as though she was pleased.

"His brain works fine but it's the rest of him that's the trouble," said Jennifer hoping that a little light relief might ease the tension. Christine smiled, which was encouraging.

"Huh, doesn't he think we can do anything on our own? Anyway, how do I know who you are? You could be anybody."

"Oh, Muriel," said the woman sitting on the desk with reproach in her voice.

"Well she could be anybody sent to spy on us!"

"Oh, come off it. Who would want to spy on us? It's not exactly as though we've got government secrets in a place like this." She waved her coffee mug around the room and laughed at the thought.

"Well you never know."

Jennifer shrugged but didn't say anything. She wasn't going to get involved in this one even if the conversation was nearer the truth than most of those in the room would have supposed. She just looked enquiringly at Muriel.

"And anyway, what's your name? Do you have one?" she spat.

"Yes, it is high time we were introduced. I'm Jennifer Suffram. And you are…?" She knew full well of course but she was not going to be browbeaten into giving anything away.

"Muriel. Muriel Dawe." Nothing further was forthcoming.

"And…?" Jennifer indicated the other two women in the room.

"Christine, Christine Bouche. She keeps the books for us. And Miranda."

"And does Miranda not have a surname?" Jennifer was all sweetness and light.

"Spate," snapped Muriel.

Christine got up from the desk she was sitting on and moved towards the door saying as she went, "Well, I've got work to do. I have one or two things for David so if I could have a word before you go Jennifer, I should be grateful."

"No problem," said Jennifer and turned back to Muriel who was glaring at Miranda.

"And you've got work to do as well, Mir, so you just get on with it," she scolded, but it was the last of the storm and she turned her attention to Jennifer. Miranda's keyboard started to click.

"Sorry," she mumbled, "you caught me off balance."

Round one to me, thought Jennifer, *but it's not going to be the end of it, I'll wager.* She said nothing.

Muriel put the uneaten remains of her cream bun down on a piece of paper, dusted the crumbs from her considerable bosom onto the floor and waddled across to a long table beside the door. On this there were a series of columns of sheets of paper neatly layered out. Muriel started sorting through the first column. Jennifer stood and looked around her more carefully; she had been relying entirely on intuition and her previous brief visit to know where she was. The large room was surprisingly light and airy considering its forbidding exterior. There were two desks complete with computer terminals, one under the reception hatch that was obviously Muriel's domain although the whole room was equally obviously her personal fiefdom. Miranda occupied a desk with the second computer. There was a further spare desk, the one upon which Christine had been sitting, and there was the long table at which Muriel was now working. A photocopier and fax machine completed the inventory.

Muriel looked up from her sorting and seemed to be at least in mollified mood.

"Here's a collection of telephone messages that need his attention. A couple of letters that I can't deal with and ditto three faxes. I'll give you his Dictaphone and a tape so that he can reply if he wants. He can use the telephone I suppose?"

"Well, he managed to phone me," answered Jennifer.

"So I can see." The edge was back in her voice.

Jennifer ignored this and said brightly and with feigned ignorance, "OK, thanks for those. Christine said she had something for him as well. Whereabouts is her office or where does she work?"

"I'll show you." Again, the bare minimum that had to be said. Muriel opened the door into the passage and pointed to the next door along which was open.

"Thanks."

No response.

Jennifer knocked politely on the open door before going in and Christine rose to greet her, came round her desk and carefully shut the door behind her. Again, an instant first impression of a woman about her own age, perhaps marginally older, well dressed in a mauve skirt and green jumper that was better than Marks and Spencer. Her rich brown hair was well cut in a straightforward manner. Jennifer instinctively felt that here was someone to whom she could relate and also whom she could trust. This was borne out by Christine's first quiet comment as she returned to her chair.

"I've no idea about your relationship with David and I'm not fishing, but you could have made yourself a bad enemy there." She inclined her head towards the outer office.

"I'll have to chance that but she slammed the hatch in my face last time I was here. She knows jolly well that she made a mistake and she's trying to blame it on everyone but herself. I was determined to stand my ground this time so I came psyched up for the purpose. And by the way I don't know much more than you about my relationship

131

with David, I had only met him twice before but he rang, so I came. Odd what one does, isn't it?"

"Mmm," Christine pursed her lips. "I heard about that incident and wondered if it might have been you." She put her elbows on the table with the tips of her fingers together and sucked them gently for a moment or two, but never taking her eyes off Jennifer. Then she obviously made up her mind about something.

"There are maybe a few things you need to know. I think you and I may be two of a kind so I instinctively feel you're straight and I can trust you. You will understand that I have to be careful what I say because it is up to David to tell you what and when he thinks fit, but this is in confidence and just to steer you gently in the right direction."

Jennifer nodded her acquiescence to this apparent signing of some Official Secrets Act and wondered what on earth was coming next. She thought it best not to say anything. Christine continued quietly and with some hesitation as though she was afraid that the walls might have ears.

"You have to understand that Muriel has built herself quite a little empire here and great reliance has had to be placed on her since…" And here she paused looking for the right word or phrase. "David's father withdrew from the business. This has helped her ego no end, as she has often been the continuity between the past and the present. You can imagine it. Can anyone remember when we did such a job? What's the name of the managing director of such and such a company? If she doesn't know the answer off the top of her head and, in fairness she often does, then she knows where or how to find the information quickly. She has made herself little short of indispensable to the company and a tyrant to poor Miranda. I don't know why the girl sticks it. However, she and David have never really got on, but then he couldn't have coped without her and they both know it. Maybe David's bump on the head..."

"It's rather more than that," protested Jennifer.

"Yes, I know, but you know what I mean. Just maybe it's made him see through her and he now feels he has to stand on his own two feet. And once again they both know that too. It hasn't gone unnoticed here that he won't be nursed by her and that he's fetched in somebody else – you. I'm only part time here, three half days per week, but I somehow feel I have to be around just to see fair play, if you see what I mean. Anyway, I shall deny I ever said any of this but David's a nice chap and I wish you well with him. Look after him, for all our sakes."

Jennifer was not at all sure that she was understanding the coded messages written into all this but Christine was obviously keen to help in the kindest possible manner. It was time to repay some of the confidences.

"I met David on a flight to Nairobi. We sat next to each other but only spoke in the last half-hour or so. Silly, isn't it? He then left a message in a hotel that he recommended to me, but wasn't anywhere near to my itinerary. I did go there and got the message, in both senses of the word, but he didn't leave any address or phone number. Nothing, not even his surname."

"Typical," muttered Christine.

"The best the hotel could do for an address was Carlisle and a name that was spelt wrong. In the end I came to Carlisle and found him. That was when Muriel threw me out, metaphorically speaking, and the guy over the road in the tyre place told me I might find him here on a Sunday morning. I did."

Christine nodded.

"I went home and was beginning to think I had offended him or something because I heard no more. Then a phone call the night before last – could I come and help? There you have it. Sum total of my life with David," she finished.

Christine nodded again. "Good luck," she said, and once more became all official. "Now here are some papers David needs and some cheques to be signed if he is capable of that. Also, the figures for last month which are just about passable although they will depend finally on work in progress figures. He needs to work that out, if he can."

She handed Jennifer a clutch of papers to add to the ones she had already been given.

"Hang on. Let me give you a folder to put them all in or half will be missing by the time you get back to Brampton."

She did just that and Jennifer got up to go.

"Oh, by the way which are your days in here, it might be helpful to know for future reference?"

"Monday, Wednesday, Friday mornings, occasionally Thursday instead of Friday if I'm busy at the weekend."

"Fine, thanks, I'm sure we shall meet again," answered Jennifer as she let herself out into the passageway. She didn't see Christine settle back into her chair and say to herself, "If she and David get together, there will be changes around here and not before time. You mark my words." The latter directed at the light fitting on the ceiling. Christine wasn't yet sure what, but something was bugging her and this new development made her feel happier than she had been for some time. Progress in a funny sort of way.

Jennifer drew a deep breath and opened the door into the general office. Miranda was still at her keyboard and Muriel appeared to be doing something with hers.

"I'll be off then," she said.

Miranda looked up but no response from Muriel.

"Am I allowed out of the front door or is it to be the tradesmen's entrance again?" she enquired.

"Thought you'd go as you came but I suppose you can go this way if you want. Where's your car?"

"At the back but I'll go this way if I may, please."

"Frightened of the works are you, dearie?" intoned Muriel.

"Not in the least, the odd wolf whistle does wonders for my confidence," Jennifer replied with a smile.

Muriel hrrumphed out of her chair and grudgingly unlocked the door.

"And let's have it open and in use next time I come, shall we? I'm sure I shall be back. Goodbye, Miranda, goodbye, Muriel."

There was a faint "Bye" from Miranda but pointedly nothing at all from Muriel. She walked out of the door and then through the double swing doors into the sunshine. She did deep breathing exercises as she walked along the wall to the rear car park and her car.

Oh dear. What have I done? she thought. *Was that really me in there?*

She felt a bit wobbly as she drove out. She would have liked to have sat there for a while and let herself come down to earth, but in full view of the open doors of the works and with what felt like every pair of eyes inside it boring into her, she just could not. She suddenly realised it was just about lunchtime which was something of a shock as she did not think she had been there anything like that long. It also reminded her she was supposed to be doing some shopping for herself and David. She managed to find her way out of the city and called in at one of the supermarkets he had mentioned. She got them the ingredients of a stir-fry for the evening and some snacky things for what would be a belated lunch, that is if he hadn't already found something in his flat. She didn't remember there being much for him to find. She heard voices as she climbed the stairs to the flat and rounded the corner to find an elderly lady hovering rather nervously in the room, talking to David.

"This is Mrs Colmer," he said. "If you remember she's the one who cleared me up off the pavement. Mrs Colmer, this is Jennifer."

"Good to see you, Mrs Colmer," replied Jennifer. "I've got my hands rather full at the moment, let me dump this lot in the kitchen and then we can be introduced properly." With that she went to the kitchen and did just as she had said, dumping her carrier bags on the worktop and returning to the living room to shake Mrs Colmer's aged hand.

"Ooh, 'e was a mess," she said, "blood all over the place, 'tis a wonder 'e weren't hurt much more than 'e seems to 'ave been. Look after 'im, luv, if 'e'll let you. You know what men are." She looked at Jennifer sideways. "By the way I've left an apple pie in fridge, thought it might be useful. Bye for now."

"Thank you very much, Mrs Colmer. That will be most acceptable. But be careful, we don't want you falling down the stairs now, do we?" Jennifer said as the old lady started down the stairs.

"Certainly not, but then I'm not trying to carry too many things, now, am I?" the good lady called as she reached the bottom.

"She seems a dear," said Jennifer.

"One of the best," replied David. "But now I have to be serious while it's still in my mind. What sort of a rumpus do you think you've been causing in my factory?" he demanded.

"Muriel's been on the phone then?"

"She has."

"Oh dear, I thought she might."

With that Jennifer got up and went to the kitchen returning with a sandwich and a pasta bowl each together with the sheaf of papers from the office.

"Here, have a sandwich, it'll make you feel better."

"Don't try and get round me like that, this is serious. I seem to have a mutiny on my hands and all you can do is give me a sandwich, like a monkey in a cage. That's about

137

what I feel like at the moment too." Plainly, he was not pleased.

"Calm down, you haven't got a mutiny when it's only one person who's upset."

"Well, it sounded like it on the phone. Muriel's hopping about, shouting at me down the wire, she's not going to be treated like this, I should know better, my father would never have sent in some unknown hussy to collect his messages, why couldn't she bring them out, etc., etc.?"

"She was a bit upset then," said Jennifer with a perfectly straight face.

"You could say that," said David and was about to launch off again when he began to see the funny side of it.

"Yes, you could say that," he grinned in a calmer voice. "And by the way I also had another irate person from Cirencester on the phone this morning also looking for your blood by the sound of it."

"Mr Halliwell, I presume."

"That sounds right."

"Oh dear, again."

But the telephone rang before he could pass on this latest disaster. He answered it.

"Hello, Roger, and how are your problems, if you've got any… Yes, I'm on the mend. I shan't be going far for a bit but at least I'm feeling more like a human being. …Yes, you had better do that one the way you suggest, it's only for occasional use so the loading won't be great on it… And the UJC one, yes, do that the same way… That was easy then… Yes, I've had Muriel on the phone, spitting blood..." Long pause. Jennifer began to panic. Was there really a mutiny? It sounded as though there was more than one person involved now. And who was this Roger anyway? "OK. Don't worry. I appreciate you ringing me. I'll pass the message on... Excuses. Excuses...! Yes. OK. Don't worry. Bye for now."

David put the phone down and looked at Jennifer.

"Well, you've collected one fan on the field of battle then," he said.

Jennifer looked at him in surprise.

"What are you talking about? I never met a Roger, who's he?" she said.

"Oh, but you did even if you didn't speak to him."

"The man in the white coat?"

"That's him, Roger Wildsmith, works manager. Now he really is indispensable. He doesn't say much but he is a perfect judge of people. Picks them without fail and always gets the best out of them. He was impressed by you, even if he didn't speak to you personally. It's what you said to Muriel that seemed to impress him, even her version of it! He's a taciturn man and he must have done a bit of soul searching first before ringing me. The questions about a couple of jobs was just a blind, he knew perfectly well what to do, it was the barney with Muriel that mattered to him; he wanted me to side with you not her. Now there really is an accolade for you."

Jennifer was embarrassed. She had been determined not to be browbeaten by Muriel but she had not intended to create such a disturbance in the ordered calm of T.H. Wear & Son Ltd. First Christine, whom she was not going to tell David about, and now this. Justifiable praise it may have been from Roger, but she felt contrition was more what was required.

"I'm sorry," she said. "I didn't mean to cause so much trouble."

David laughed. "Don't worry, I've known for some time that one day I would have to face this one. Muriel has background knowledge which can occasionally be vital but the occasions are getting less so all you've done is to bring the day of reckoning forward."

"I'm sorry," was all she could think of to say again.

"And now what about your Mr Halliwell?"

"Oh, what do you have to remind me about him for?"

"Well I shall probably get the call when he rings again."

"I suppose so."

But Jennifer was not convinced. She really did not feel like bringing that day of reckoning forward. She really did not know what she would be doing. How long was David expecting her to stay and look after him? She would have to go home very soon anyway; she needed some more clothes if nothing else. Underwear especially. Was she going back to her job or was she just passing through on her way back here? Reluctantly she would have to ask him, even if it meant bringing a beautiful episode to an end. No time like the present she supposed.

"My answer to Mr H depends entirely on you, you know. Is my usefulness over? Do you want me to stay on? What am I supposed to be doing if I do?"

David thought for a moment.

"Yes, I guess it does. No. Yes. We'll talk about that tomorrow."

"You're getting at me," she smiled, remembering being on the aircraft with him. "But if Mr H rings then it's down to you."

"OK. I can tell him any old tale that you've been eaten by dragons or whatever."

"Please make it at least plausible if you're going to invent something preposterous."

"I'll try."

"No, not just try. Promise?"

"Promise. Now I've got work to do."

"You're getting better."

"It's having you here," he grinned.

She made a face at him but relaxed all the same. Even if it was only mid-afternoon, she was tired. One way and another it had been quite a day. Mr H could look after himself and she would worry about that tomorrow or whenever David got round to telling her his plans for the future and, just at this moment, she really couldn't care less what he had in mind just as long as it involved him and her.

Chapter 4

In the big Victorian house, it was conference time. Gerry was at school. Henry, unusually, came home for lunch. and this gave Muriel and Millie time to get their stories 'straight' before they had to, not so much confront Henry, as make him realise that it wasn't entirely a put-up job and that he would survive the trauma he was trying to make out of it. Most especially how it was going to affect his 'image'.

"How do we get away with this without the world guessing what happened?" was his opening remark.

"That's easy," said Muriel. "I'm only employed here to look after Gerry and naturally I'm allowed some time off."

She looked at both of them.

"You know you're free to come and go as you like."

"Yeah, well I had a one-night stand with this fella and look what happened! I don't know who he was or where he came from, now do I?"

"Perhaps ought to have some sort of name for him," suggested Millie.

"I think his name might've been Rick, or it could have been Thomas."

She giggled and Henry blushed.

"And we're being the kind-hearted people who are accepting your unfortunate situation and continuing to employ you. Is that right?"

"Spot on."

"And eventually whose baby is it?" broke in Mrs Wear.

"That's the one thing I'm not sure about."

"I'm glad there's something," said Henry.

"You see, although I love looking after Gerry, and I did my brother too, I'm not sure I'm cut out for motherhood. Although Gerry runs to me, I think I'm too hard, too practical to be a good mother so maybe he, or she, should be yours!"

She looked from one to the other of them.

"That, I shall definitely have to think about. It's one thing being mother to one's own child but being mother to someone else's – that could be different."

"The child will be half yours, if you see what I mean." She looked at Henry.

"Hmm," was all he would say.

"We shall have to see how that works out. How Gerry takes to a brother or sister and maybe then it can just be 'our' child."

"And you go to all the antenatal classes or whatever under this same alias," said Mrs Wear.

"Of course."

***

And so it all came to pass. Muriel stuck with her side of the bargain. She did all the right things. She accepted with equanimity various jibes about being caught out having a good time. Possibly because she had been this way herself her own mother was the one who took the most convincing and was the most reluctant to accept the situation. Given the opportunity she would have guessed the situation exactly right. As it took a long time before her pregnancy showed she even began to wonder whether she and the doctors had got it right but, eventually, her belly grew and something was kicking inside her.

Both Millie and Henry were excited with her progress although neither could share it with anyone else. They were simply doing the right thing by her. Because she was suffering high blood pressure the medics decided that she should have the baby in hospital and in due course Henry and Millie took her to Cumberland Infirmary one Thursday afternoon. Millie stayed but Henry claimed to have 'things that had to be done'.

"Anyway it's women's work," he said. "They don't want me cluttering the place up."

"Squeamish," said Millie.

Under duress he admitted she was right.

"And make sure you're back in time to pick up Gerry from school."

He waved acknowledgement as he walked away.

It was not an easy birth but after much pushing and encouragement twin baby girls were produced, much to everyone's surprise, both with their mother's jet-black hair and coal-black eyes to go with it all set in faces, that, even at this young age looked very much like Henry.

"Dianne and Daphne," breathed Muriel when she was in a state to say anything at all.

"That's nice. I like it," said Millie. The Wears had not discussed the child's names and deliberately left it to Muriel to make her own choices in the hope of improving her mothering instincts. They had certainly been unprepared for twins.

Once home there had to be one further life-changer for Muriel and it was Henry who brought it up.

"Your hair," he said in a tone almost as blunt as Muriel could be, "will have to change its colour on a permanent basis from now on."

"You're quick!" Muriel cast him a sly look.

"No, don't be silly. Anyone looking at those babies will know instantly that you're their mother."

"I am their mother."

"Yes, but if Daphne and Dianne are to be part of this family then it shouldn't be quite so obvious."

"But she looks like you."

"That's allowable."

Muriel mulled this over.

"I suppose," she said. "So what colour would you like me?"

It was Millie's turn to comment.

"You look nice as a blonde but for this purpose, any colour except black!"

"What about Gerry? He knows I'm black."

"He's used to you being a rainbow of colours so I doubt he'll take any notice. He possibly doesn't know what your natural colour is anyway and, being male, is likely to forget even if he ever knew!"

"I'll think about it."

"No, you'll do it."

Henry could be tough when the occasion demanded.

***

Dianne and Daphne began their lives as they were destined to continue it and that could be summed up in one word – belligerent. In their early months the twins were sticklers for routine. If Muriel didn't feed them or change them at the appointed time, they would yell at a decibel level enough to shatter the windows.

"I told you I wasn't a mother," she grumbled to Millie.

"They'll get over it," soothed the latter.

"Huh!"

They both knew that their joint experience in child rearing had been with Gerry, who, whilst never a placid child had at least been fairly obliging and generally nice with it. But Daphne and especially Dianne didn't get over it. They continued their opposition to the world and all that it held for them. They seemed to sense that the routine that had been built up for them was too convenient and changed tack, allowing themselves to be fed only when it suited them and making a mess of a clean nappy as soon as it was put on.

"It's a good thing there are two of us to cope with them." Muriel and Millie consoled each other. Henry kept his distance but was mollified by comments from his cronies about 'having proved himself a man' by producing not just one daughter, but two. Their waywardness also gave him a topic for conversation and he compared notes with his friends as to the awfulness of their respective children.

It was a common enough and a chance remark to Gerry from several people that was ultimately to prove fatal.

"Now, Gerry, how do you like your little sisters?"

Gerry would shrug his shoulders and say, "They're OK," without really understanding what was behind the question or even if he had any thoughts on the subject at all. However the upshot was that he started to call them both 'Little Sister', soon corrupted to 'Li'l Sis'. At the time everyone thought this was rather sweet and a sign of affection from one small boy to his recently born sisters. That is until Dianne became of an age to realise that Gerry was her brother and that he called her by a name different to that used by everyone else. Even at that age she managed to pick up the slightly disparaging way that he said it. Daphne, being slightly thicker skinned, took it in the manner in which it was given,

"Not Li'l Sis," were not quite Dianne's first words but fairly close to them, which of course only made Gerry worse at poking fun at her.

"Gerry, you must not call her Li'l Sis," Millie would remonstrate with him. "It upsets her."

Gerry would grin and say, "But she is my Little Sister," with logic wholly behind him.

"But she hates you calling her that. Dianne's her name and you know that perfectly well."

"OK," he would say resignedly and peace would reign for a few weeks until she provoked him in some other way and he would get his own back by reverting to the 'Li'l Sis' moniker. Then the whole process would start all over again.

Worse still was the fact that despite the five-year gap between them Dianne and Daphne had no intention of being left out of anything that Gerry was doing. Initially this could have also been treated as sweet but, once they were able to climb onto chairs and thus onto the table, it became all a step too far. He would push them off and instead of crying their eyes out, they would just laugh at him and thus become even more annoying. A big sigh of relief was given all round when they were old enough to go to playschool and the house could be quiet for a few hours. To everyone's surprise they took to this easily, possibly because there were more people to annoy than just their brother and, by spreading the annoyance, they were not seen to be quite so devilish.

"Where do they get it from?" bemoaned Henry when tales of their latest exploits were told to him upon his return from work. "I'm sure it's not from me so it must be you, Muriel."

"Not really. I can be pretty horrible at times…"

"You can indeed."

"Thank you, but I'm not vindictive with it."

"That's true, I'll allow you that."

"And they can't have got it from me, whatever the appearances and, besides, I'm not like that," chimed in Millie.

"Right on both counts," muttered Henry.

"Could have been my mum," said Muriel.

"Was she like that?"

"Not really, or not as I remember. Might have been my dad, whoever he was!"

"Better blame him then as he's not here to argue!"

Although it did not stop them arguing and on occasion coming to blows with it, a sort of a truce came to exist between Gerry and the twins. After all they all knew they had to live under same roof, eat the same meals, cope with the same parents – all three of them – and generally live a reasonably peaceful existence. But life was about to change again.

***

Coffee time had become confidence and confession time between Millie and Muriel so it was nothing unusual when Millie coughed and said, "Not sure what you're going to think about this, Mu."

Her using the shortened 'Mu' was a sure sign that something serious was on the cards. Muriel looked at her but could read nothing into her eyes. It was the wrong way round; it was mostly she who had an outlandish scheme or a confession to make.

"Spit it out then."

Millie hesitated.

"I've taken a leaf out of your book," she said.

"Which book?" Muriel wasn't just playing hard to get; she simply didn't know what the other woman was talking about.

"The twins' book."

"I wouldn't take any leaves out of that book if I were you! Ooh, do you mean…?"

"Yes. I do. I'm pregnant again after all these years."

Millie hunched her shoulders and smiled broadly right across her face, causing Muriel to rush round the table and give her a huge hug.

"Does Henry know?"

"Not yet."

"How did you manage it?"

"I did what you did. I came off the pill and it all happened. Much quicker than you too."

There was a tiny note of triumph in her voice but Muriel missed it.

"When are you going to tell him?"

"Have to be tonight. Now you know, one of us is bound to say the wrong thing and then he'll be upset and with good reason."

"Will he be pleased?"

"I think so and there won't be quite the complicated storytelling to do that there was with you."

"All legal and above board!"

It sounded like a jibe but Muriel did not intend it as such, more as a statement of fact.

"And no need to change the colour of my hair!"

Henry was not just pleased but very pleased with the news and not only for the purely practical reasons but because, as he said, "Let's hope it's another boy to even things up."

"It's a big age gap," said Millie.

"Not really, plenty of people your age have babies," he pontificated.

"Not that. There's going to be better part of eleven years between this one and Gerry. How's he or she going to cope, and what about the twins?"

"Gerry'll manage. He's coped with his sisters. Probably never notice!"

"Don't be silly, of course he'll notice."

"I know that but the age difference will be so much that they will almost grow up in different worlds."

Muriel thought about her own much younger brother.

"You're right," she said. "Once my brother was past being a baby I had virtually nothing to do with him. Not sure if I'd even recognise him now if I met him when I wasn't expecting to!"

"Same rules," said Henry. "All the antenatal bit, exercises and so on and so on!"

Both women groaned.

"I guess so."

Millie suffered all the rigours of pregnancy without too much complaint and Muriel rose to the occasion by relieving her of anything she didn't actually have to do. It wasn't until the end that it got complicated. Fortunately, Henry was in bed with her on the night that she had to wake him.

"I've started," she said, "I think we need to get to the hospital quickly."

She sounded and felt remarkably calm although she had this premonition that time was of the essence.

Bleary-eyed Henry said he would get dressed and then go and tell Muriel.

"And hurry," said Millie.

But Henry was being ponderous.

"No need for your suit. Any old clothes will do."

She was content to throw a dressing gown over her shoulders. She wouldn't need clothes to restrict her where she was going.

"Hurry," she said again when next she saw Henry, but he was gathering up keys to get the car out of the garage. Muriel appeared.

"For God's sake, Henry, get a bloody move on. I'll shut the garage doors behind you if you insist."

This outburst had an effect on Henry who finally seemed to get the message that his wife needed to be got to the hospital pronto. He realised it even more when Millie started to yell at him, "It's coming! It's coming! Get me there quickly. It's coming!"

Driving fast and then an abrupt stop outside the A & E Department was the final straw. The baby slipped out of Millie into the footwell of the car. Henry was aghast but he was fairly good in an emergency and rushed through the doors shouting that his wife had had her baby in his car and was outside. From there on the medics took over and he could relax. And contemplate the mess in the front of his beautiful Jaguar.

As if in compensation – it was a boy!

David proved to be an ideal baby for a household fraught with the rancour and competitiveness fostered by Gerry, Daphne and Dianne. He was quiet, even withdrawn, adored his mother, was happy in the hands of Muriel and apparently unaffected by the mayhem that could be going on around him. There were times when Henry wondered if he was even a bit backward, but a natural curiosity shone through from an early age.

***

"Frosties this morning, Sis?"

"Not if you're having them."

"Whatever's that got to do with what you have for breakfast, Li'l Sis?"

"Nothing."

"So are you having Frosties? Where's Daphne?"

"No. Mum's taken Daphne shopping for new shoes."

"You're daft, you know that? Li'l Sis of mine."

"Why do you always call me Li'l Sis when you know I don't like it? You never call him Li'l Bro!" She pointed a spoon at David who was by now a toddler and sitting on a blanket with his head turning to each of them as they spoke, just like someone watching a tennis match.

"He's not a Li'l anything yet. He's got to grow a bit!"

"So why me?" Dianne shouted at him.

"Because, Li'l Sis," he rubbed it in by saying it slowly. "You always get tetchy about it."

Dianne was about to throw a plate at him, and damn the consequences when Muriel walked in.

"Dianne!" she shouted. "What are you doing?"

"It's Gerry," she said. "He's Li'l Sis'ing me again. He knows I don't like it."

She was on the verge of tears.

"Gerry!" said Muriel severely. "If I've told you once I've told you dozens of times not to call her that."

"I know, but it's great to watch her be a cry-baby!"

Muriel was speechless, but Gerry was gone before she could speak her mind to him. Instead she took her frustration out on Dianne.

"No Dianne, don't you rise to him all the time like you do. It only makes him worse."

"I hate, hate, hate him."

"No you don't really. You know that."

"I do."

"OK you do, but he's got Jamie coming today and I don't want you and your tantrums spoiling their time together like last time he was here."

Now this was something to stop crying for. She could get her own back later on. David continued to sit and watch, and learned when to keep quiet and out of the way!

Dianne knew that when Jamie was there, they always had at least one session kicking a football about in the garden and that this was her chance to upset both of them. To go and play with another ball of her own was her favourite ploy.

"Oh no," groaned Gerry as she appeared nonchalantly and prepared to kick her ball into their goal.

"I know," he said. "Why don't you go in goal and see if you're clever enough to save our goals."

He knew this was touch of brilliance. She would be unable to avoid the challenge and the possible slur on her abilities despite the obvious age difference. He whispered something to Jamie and they played gently for a start.

"See," she said, "I can stop all your goals."

With that goading him Gerry took a mighty kick at the ball. He hadn't expected it but it hit her right in the midriff and she doubled up, winded. When she could breathe again, she looked venomously at Gerry but took the hint and went off to the house to nurse her wounded pride. Gerry was quite unrepentant.

"Is she always like that?" asked Jamie.

"Yes."

"She was last time, too."

Gerry looked all around to see if the garden had ears and then said quietly, "She's a bastard, a real bastard."

It was perhaps fortunate that neither boy knew the full meaning of the word or just how close to the truth Gerry was in saying it.

***

There were no tantrums with David going to school and in truth he may have found it a relief from the ups and downs of his home life. This once again left Muriel without a job but she was certainly not going to have another baby. Dianne and Daphne were quite enough to last her a lifetime. Nevertheless she was bored. Millie seemed quite happy to potter about the house and garden all day but that wasn't Muriel's scene. She was definitely bored. It was time for Henry to come to the rescue again.

"I'm fed up being here all day with precious little to do. Have you got anything I could do in the factory?" she said to him when they were alone together one evening.

"Think you'd be good with a welding torch, then?" Henry had scoffed.

"I might be but I don't intend to try. No, something in the office. I could learn to type, keep the books even. I can make tea and coffee!"

"I'll think about it," said Henry. "No promises though."

Muriel knew better than to press him and even then she didn't hear directly from him.

"What's this I hear about you working in the factory?" said Millie a month or so later.

"Not actually in the factory, I hope, in the office perhaps. It would be nice as there's not enough for me to do here nowadays."

"Henry tells me that the office junior is leaving. Got a better job or something so he's going to give her job to you."

"It'd be nice if he had told me."

Muriel was miffed at getting the news second hand.

"That's what he told me but you never know. It may not happen. You know what he can be."

Muriel nodded her head in agreement. You never did know with Henry but this time it did happen. The first intimation from him was when he told her to learn to type and fast, both the typing and the learning. He seemed amused by his own joke.

"And where am I supposed to learn that?"

"Lots of secretarial places in the city. One of them must be able to teach you to type. Take your pick."

"And that's all you're going to do about it?"

"Yes."

"Gee. Thanks."

Henry became a bit more conciliatory.

"Look, Mu, I'm offering you a job in the office, possibly against my better judgement, and that's going to cause a bit of a flutter in the traditional dovecot. So it's down to you to prove that you can do what's required of you without coming wailing to me. You've got to stand or fall by your own efforts there. Get my drift?"

"I suppose."

"You know, you're getting to sound just like Dianne!"

"That proves something at any rate. Daphne's getting to sound just like you."

But Henry wasn't rising to the bait. He was in business mode.

The Albion Secretarial School was in a back street but, yes, Miss Frobisher would be pleased to teach her to type and use a word processor. It would be done on a one-to-one basis and she should be proficient in a few weeks. She didn't ask Muriel any questions about previous experience, schooling or even why she wanted to do this. Muriel had some rather thin answers to those questions up her sleeve, but was glad not to need them.

Within a couple of days, she was thoroughly depressed and was shouting at Henry that she would do better to go on the streets that put up with that bloody Miss Frobisher. "And I know I'd earn more than you're likely to pay me!" she added for good measure.

Henry was unmoved.

"You want the job, or don't you?" was his comment.

Reluctantly Muriel had to admit that she did want the job. It was all very well being a kept woman but with each of them getting a bit older life could become very monotonous. So she persevered. She'd get her own back one day.

It took her a while to realise that one of her principle problems was that her education, such as it had been, was very basic and she had done little over the years to improve matters. After all, she could get by so why bother to read all those books that would so-called improve her mind? She'd done all right so far, hadn't she? She mastered the mechanics of touch typing quite quickly, something that Miss Frobisher assured her a monkey could be taught to do, but it was after that that it went wrong.

"Did they never teach you to spell at school?" was a perpetual refrain from Miss Frobisher. "Even the easiest words you get wrong."

"Of course they did," retaliated Muriel. "It's just that when I'm having to think about which key to press. I can't think how to spell as well."

"Now that's a man argument," said Miss Frobisher in a rare show of humour.

"It's true," said Muriel sulkily.

"And we haven't got to punctuation and editing yet." Muriel had heard of punctuation but, wasn't sure what editing was, but didn't like to say so. Her tutor read her mind.

"Your boss will scribble something illegible on a piece of paper and expect you to turn it in to an official letter to whoever it is. That will mean finding the address, because he won't know it, and probably rewriting the document so that it will be intelligible to the recipient."

Muriel was getting in at the deep end. However, once she could type and spell reasonably proficiently, she decided the niceties of letter writing could wait and be learnt at her convenience. It was more important to get into Henry's office while the opportunity was still there.

"Start next Tuesday then," Henry said. "Always start office staff on a Tuesday. Monday's too busy with timesheets, wages, etc. plus whatever may have happened over the weekend."

If Muriel thought that she was going to work with Henry in his big car she was again mistaken.

"Why are you humiliating me like this?" she complained. "I am the mother of your child and you treat me like dirt."

"No, Mu, I'm not. If we are both not to look too silly you've got to be seen to be doing this yourself. Tongues are already wagging or I'm mistaken and we've got to keep our distance for a start, at least."

Eventually she made her way to the factory for eight thirty a.m. on a Tuesday morning wondering what she had let herself in for. She had, of course, been there before but as a guest, not as an employee. Her instructions were to report to Mrs McTaggart.

Mrs McT, as she was known to all and sundry, summed Muriel up in about three seconds flat. She was going to find it hard until she proved if she was any good or not!

***

"That bloody woman. I swear I'll kill her. Poison her coffee or something."

"Don't be silly, Muriel. You know you won't."

Millie was getting tired of having to cope with Muriel's tantrums as well as those of the twins, and to a lesser extent Gerry. She was not at all sure that Henry taking Muriel into the factory had been a good idea, but then he had always been impulsive and she had no complaints of that. Like getting hold of her in the first place.

"You know what she called me today?"

"No," said Millie judiciously, even if she had a good idea as she had been privy to a conversation with Henry when the expected epithet had cropped up to their mutual amusement.

"She called me Henry's bimbo."

"Well?"

"Well what?

"In the nicest possible way, you are, aren't you?"

"Don't you start."

"But seriously Mu, anyone looking at us from the outside would be shocked, and Mrs McT is one of the old school, remember."

Muriel was only slightly mollified.

"Anyone would think I was only a sixteen-year-old."

"In her eyes you probably are."

"I can do the job, well, just about anyway."

"Ah." This was beginning to tally with what Henry had said. "I'm told she's a bit of a perfectionist.

"Comma in the wrong place, word spelt wrong and you'd think the end of the world had come."

"Sounds like her."

"I'll get my own back on her one day, you mark my words."

"You know the best way to do that, don't you, Mu?"

"Tell me."

"She's due to retire in the not too distant future. Between you and me I think the office will breathe a sigh of relief, but that's not the point. If you're half good enough Henry'd probably give you her job."

"I'll think about it."

"We'll both think about it and work on Henry together."

Millie hunched up her shoulders at the thought of the fun that would be. Muriel was studiously unconvinced, but she could see a way of getting back at all of them.

Chapter 5

The rest of the day passed agreeably enough. Melanie passed through and did the necessary with David's leg and pronounced that he was getting better.

"I never feel it after you've been," he grumbled.

"Och, ye'll bless me soon enough when ye're up an' aboot an' runnin' aroond like a young 'un. Sue'll be in tomorrow an' if she thinks fit, we'll leave you in peace till Monday," was all the sympathy he got.

"Well, that would be something, I suppose," he said through gritted teeth.

They watched television that evening and found they were able to have a mutual grumble about the lack of anything interesting or informative on a Friday evening. Jennifer phoned her mother to report progress, although she didn't enlarge on her experiences at the factory. She said she would be back on Monday afternoon or evening but was not sure for how long. She was told that Mr Halliwell had been on the phone there too and didn't sound too pleased. She was happy enough to let life drift for the time being and see where she finished up. David seemed to be waiting for something that appeared to be going to happen the next day, but she had no idea what. Well, tomorrow could look after itself.

The night passed easily as well. David certainly had a less disturbed night and she had rather got used to the idea of there being someone else in the bed. What was she talking about? She had only been here two nights and that was the only two nights she had spent like this; but it was rather nice. The thought had had her giggling when she washed in the morning. Breakfast was toast and coffee and made both of them feel like an old married couple. Finally, Jennifer had to get some idea of what was in store for the day, and what, if anything, was expected of her.

"So what's the plan today?" she asked tentatively. "How do you usually spend your Saturdays? Not that that there's much chance of you being able to do it this Saturday."

"True," David replied. "I usually spend Saturday along with ten thousand other people doing my weekly shop and then I like to get out for some fresh air. A walk on the fells or some such. Generally, quite domesticated. But now I'm just an invalid in bed," he finished bitterly.

"You're not in bed," was all she could think of to say, but at least it broke the despondency. She added, "We do have to eat. Anything particular take your fancy? Takeaway, Chinese, Indian, fish 'n' chips, if Brampton runs to any of those."

"Chinese or fish and chips is about the limit of it. Fish and chips tonight, Chinese tomorrow. How about that?"

"Fine by me. I ought to busy myself doing something useful like a bit of cleaning, or be rash and check what we have in the way of mundane things to eat like cereal, milk, etc., etc."

"Don't panic for a minute, because I'm pretty certain Mother will call this morning." Jennifer felt a real panic rise inside her. "And there's a good chance she'll bring enough to feed an army."

And as though on cue, there was a knocking on the door and the sound of someone coming up the stairs. Jennifer was not sure what she had been expecting when and if she had to meet David's mother. Whatever it was, it was not what she got. It was only with difficulty that she did not burst out laughing when someone looking like nothing so much as Beatrix Potter's, Mrs Tiggy-Winkle, came round the corner into the room. She was very short and very round, with snow-white hair and a slightly surprised look on her face. A light-coloured dress and wholly 'practical' shoes added the finishing touches but the pièce de résistance was a large and well-loaded shopping basket. A genuine wicker one, Jennifer noted. She stood looking from one to the other of them as though she was short-sighted, which she may have been, without knowing quite either what to do or what to say.

It was David who rose to the occasion, even if his bonhomie did sound slightly artificial.

"Hello, Mum, I thought you'd be here this morning. This is Jennifer, Jennifer Suffram, who I told you I met in Africa and who's kindly come to look after me. Jennifer, this is my mother."

Jennifer took up her own cue.

"It's a pleasure to meet you Mrs Wear, I think David is getting better. In fact he certainly is: he's beginning to think about work."

Mrs Wear was a bit dismissive, but she had half expected that.

"Well, he would, wouldn't he?" she said, and turning to David carried on, "I've brought you some things to eat because I don't know what, if anything, you've been eating these last few days."

There was a certain accusation in her voice, probably due to Jennifer's presence and, if truth be told, the older woman's feeling that her role had been usurped. Again, David came to the rescue.

"Not at all. Jennifer's a good cook and her mother sent a huge shepherd's pie made of home-grown lamb."

That was perhaps not the most politic thing to say. Mrs Wear stood up very straight but said nothing although Jennifer could almost hear her mind saying, "Who is this hussy, whose mother sends my son, yes, *my* son, shepherd's pies?" Jennifer coloured slightly and decided it was time not to be there. She gathered up her handbag as she spoke.

"I'll leave you two for a while. I could do with some fresh air. I'll go and explore the delights of Brampton. See you in a bit."

"That shouldn't take long. See you," he called after her as she went down the stairs.

***

Had Jennifer been able to be a fly on the wall she would have heard a conversation initiated by Mrs Wear: "Who's that and what does she think she is?"

To which David replies, somewhat wearily, "Mum, I did explain all this to you. I met her on my last African trip. I was attracted to her and obviously she to me as she came and found me, God knows quite how. After my fall I knew I didn't want to be mothered, least of all by Muriel…"

"I know. I've had her on the phone," cuts in Mrs Wear.

"I can guess…"

"Not best pleased with little Miss Whatshername trying to lord it about the place, is Muriel."

"I know that too. As I was saying, in a fit of feeling sorry for myself I rang her to see if she would come and help me. I never expected she would, but she did. And a good thing it's been too."

"That's not what I heard from Muriel. Walked in as though she owned the place. No by-your-leave or anything. Just came in, and through the factory too, just as though she belonged there. You need to be careful with that one. She's a gold-digger, you mark my words."

"Not a chance. The other way round if anything. Her family own God knows how many acres of the Cotswolds and a large manor house to go with it."

It is a good, if specious argument, for David does not yet know the sometimes-precarious state of the Suffram finances. Mrs Wear is impressed but turns the argument to her own advantage.

"Well, what's she doing up here then? What's she know about business? Born with a silver spoon in her mouth no doubt. You be careful, young man."

David is shocked. He has never seen his mother so bitter about anything. But then she has had to come out of her shell in recent times and he supposes this is the effect. Again, he makes the wrong comment:

"Roger was impressed with her anyway, even if she never spoke to him." Adding, as he realises where this might lead, "But you better not tell Muriel that."

"Roger? What's Roger got to do with it?"

"You know as well as I do that Roger doesn't get on the phone unless he has to, but he cooked up some cock and bull excuse to ring me that was really to say how impressed with Jennifer he had been. You also know that he never fails when it comes to judging people."

It is a clincher of an argument, but Mrs Wear is not going to show that she approves, so she changes tack. She grunts and says, "Anyway, where's she staying? You haven't room for her here."

"We're managing," is all David will reply.

If looks could indeed kill, the piercing look that Mrs Wear gives her son would kill half the population of Brampton, but she says nothing, and David happens to be looking the other way, so does not notice. They move on to more mundane subjects.

***

Meanwhile, Jennifer walked the few streets of Brampton trying to look as though she had a purpose in her walking. She felt that everyone, but everyone, knew who she was and what she was doing. More particularly she was sure

167

that they also knew that David's flat only had one bedroom and therefore… She knew this was all totally irrational and felt herself visibly jump when some kind person passed the time of day with her. She walked up the hill and a little out of town, if you could call it that, and felt better with some fresh air in her lungs. At the top of the rise there was a seat, and she sat, reminding herself of the time she had sat on that decrepit seat on the point at Tanga.

Once again she had to take stock of what she was doing. Why did everything seem to happen so quickly? She had struggled to realise she wanted to find David. She had struggled to find him. Now that she had, she seemed to have become part of his life, and that in less time than it took to think about it. She wasn't complaining, far from it, but it did rather take her breath away. And added to everything else she did actually have a job to which she should be going, and from all appearances Mr Halliwell was getting more than a little fed up with her sudden disappearance from his well-ordered office. She had to decide about that as well. And it wasn't as easy as just taking off for home as she had done in Tanga. She knew if she went home, as she very soon would have to do, she would equally soon be back here again, and then what? She would have to give up her job if David wanted her to come back. That wasn't the end of the world anyway. After all, being a receptionist was hardly a career. She could find a similar job anywhere, even here if necessary. There was, however, the small question of money. She had taken a large chunk of two years' holiday in one go, and it just might be that she would owe Halliwell & Stoddard rather than the other way round if she left just now. Fortunately, she had not overspent whilst she was away, so her bank account wasn't quite empty. But if she was coming up here consistently then that was a lot of petrol. Oh well, she would have to worry about that when she knew better what David was expecting of her.

But what was she thinking about? It wasn't up to David what she did. She was her own master – well, mistress if she was to be pedantic about it. She lived in a different age. She wasn't some Victorian wife who was duty-bound to do just what her husband said. Besides, she wasn't even his wife – even if she hoped that one day she might be! She could do as she liked. She could go home now and leave him to it. Let his mother and Muriel look after him. She didn't have to put up with his grubby factory with its noise and smell of oil. She didn't have to get involved in the politics of his life. That brought her up with a jolt. From what deep instinct did that idea creep up on her? There seemed to be something slightly mysterious in the background all the time. There appeared to be a connection with Muriel, and it was here that her negative determination asserted itself. She was not going to be pushed about or even out altogether by that woman. She had been very deliberately snubbed by her once. It was not going to happen again. Most assuredly it was not. And that decided her course of action for the immediate future. She would no doubt be running errands for David on Monday morning. She would return home in the afternoon, but she was pretty sure she would be back again by the end of the

169

week. And Mr Halliwell? "Sod him," she said to herself; most unladylike and most uncharitable.

With immaculate timing, as she rounded the corner back into the square, she caught a glimpse of what she thought was Mrs Wear driving out of the other end of it. This was confirmed when she arrived back with David. He was slightly on edge and somewhat over-jolly but she presumed not to notice as he enquired where she had been. She explained she had been sitting on a seat admiring the view and taking stock of what she was doing here.

"And what mind-blowing conclusions did you come to?" David asked, half seriously and half facetiously.

"In a nutshell, I'll run errands for you on Monday morning but on Monday afternoon I must go home."

"Why?" he asked bluntly, and before she had a chance to continue.

"Because," she continued caustically, "one, in case you hadn't noticed I only have one change of clothes with me, and two, maybe you have forgotten, I do have a job I'm supposed to be going to every day."

"Clothes, maybe, but the job; well that doesn't sound too important. Get another one up here or come and work for me."

"Hang on a minute, David, just what are you saying?" Her mind began to whirl.

"Well, anyway, how am I going to cope without you?" he added slightly peevishly.

So that was it. Typical man. Needed someone to look after him. Got used to her being around and at his beck and call. It was possibly a compliment but she wasn't quite ready to view it that way.

"You'll cope the same way you did before. Your leg will soon be, is nearly now, usable and you'll just have to get used to living with only one arm and the other as a prop. You've got your mother and Muriel to look after you in the short term, and then you'll be up and away. It doesn't have to be me, that's for sure."

He grunted and was quiet for a moment. Had she said too much? When he spoke again the bluster had gone and been replaced with the voice of a small boy. It wasn't a wheedling tone, just one which came from the heart.

"But, Jen, it does have to be you. You don't know my history and don't want to for a long time yet, but it does have to be you. You're the first person I've ever felt at all permanent with, more so than even my parents."

She couldn't maintain the stern tone. Despite the ongoing mystery she had to give in to him.

"OK, OK, but I do have to go back on Monday."

He nodded.

"And I have to do a deal with Mr H. I may well have to work out a week's notice at minimum. Then I'll be back."

"Atta girl," David said, using his good hand as though to punch her on the arm had she been near enough. "I knew you wouldn't let a wounded soldier down."

"Don't push your luck too far." Her anger was about to rise. "I really don't know why I'm doing all this, I really don't."

171

She did actually. It was because she loved him, but it was too soon to admit to that.

"Well, I expect I shall survive, but don't be away too long."

"As I have tried to get across to you," she replied, "that depends on my job, if I've still got one. I do have to work you know. Don't be deceived by the Valley Court, Valley Farm bit. Money has always been at a premium in our establishment."

"Join the club," he said, adding enigmatically, "But that can all be overcome."

He wouldn't say any more and there, matters were left, somewhat in limbo. Jennifer wanted more but had to be content to let it ride until next time and enjoy David's company for the rest of the weekend. She also felt frustrated at being cooped up in his flat; she was after all used to the wide-open skies of the Cotswolds, but she was determined to cope.

And so Monday morning came round with something of a sinking feeling for Jennifer. She was going to have to leave being with David, which, despite her bravado, was not something she wanted to do. She had to go into his office again and face the certain wrath of Muriel and who-knew-what obstructions to what David wanted of her. Hanging over all of that was the prospect of having to face up to Mr Halliwell when she reappeared in his office on what was now only tomorrow morning. On the latter front she knew she should not have ignored his phone calls. He was not going to be pleased, and that would not make reaching a resolution any easier. Oh well, as always in her rather happy-go-lucky world, tomorrow would have to look after itself. Therefore, she set off into Carlisle in some trepidation with a long shopping list that she and David had compiled so that he would not be skin and bone by the time she got back (still with the proviso of 'if' she came back). She was also returning all the papers she had brought back previously, duly signed and dealt with. Added to that was another string of queries for various people from him. He was definitely getting better. There was no doubt about that. So why did he still want her, she mused. She hoped it was for the same reason that she wanted him.

She was not sure whether she was going to be expected or not and because she had no wish to be snubbed with a locked front door again this time, she drove straight into the works car park. In any case she wanted to see Roger both on David's behalf and her own. She hoped he might be in his office as she had deliberately timed her arrival for what she guessed would be morning break time. She got it right and he was.

"Hello, luv," was his cheery greeting. "Somehow thought you might be in this morning. Have a seat, although you're a bit smartly dressed for the sort of chairs I have about."

In order to maintain appearances, especially with Muriel, she had 'office dressed' again. She laughed.

"I do feel a little bit like a new girl at school in my new uniform but these genuinely are my working clothes so they will just have to get used to a new environment. It's me that has the problem, I'm quite simply out of my

173

depth with all this." She gestured vaguely in the direction of the works, with its machines and tools apparently randomly scattered about.

"Don't worry, you'll soon get used to it," he replied in a kindly voice. But why was it that everybody seemed to presume she was here for keeps? It was all a bit mysterious and to cover her confusion she produced a note of what David had wanted.

"David wants to know how you're getting on with the two emergency pump sets for Tesco and the special for the RNLI. He seems to be fussing about them but I'm afraid I don't know quite why."

Roger got up and shuffled through some grubby bits of paper in what looked as though it was meant to be an in-tray, then sat back in his chair for a moment looking blankly into space.

"Tell him not to panic about Tesco, we've run them up and all's OK. Now we're only waiting to tidy up the wiring, complete some panel work and the soundproofing for the cabinets. Should be out on time. Now, the RNLI, that's a bit more difficult. The coupling that was on two weeks' delivery is now suddenly on six weeks when we start to chase it. If I can't get that improved, we shall be late on delivery and I know we shan't be popular. Tell him I'm twisting a few arms about the place and although we may be late, I hope we shan't be that late."

"Good. He'll be pleased."

Suddenly there was a mighty increase in the noise level as the works went back to work after its morning break. A man in oily overalls walked into the office and, on seeing her there, started to back out again in some confusion.

"No," she said, "come on in. What Roger and I have to talk about can wait. You have first call on his time."

The man grinned and entered into a long conversation about pipe sizes, threads and fittings. It went right over her head, but she did know from life at the farm that it was important not to hold up employees unnecessarily. It had been drilled into her from childhood as being common courtesy if nothing else. The financial implications of not wasting their time she only realised later. Roger was obviously impressed and said so.

"Well done, lass, you'll definitely do."

Jennifer coloured slightly and said, "What I did want to say to you was to thank you for your call to David the other day. He might have got the wrong end of the stick if he had had to choose between what I said and what Muriel had told him.

"Silly old bat," said Roger. "But don't tell him I said so, mind. Thinks she runs this place, used to very nearly when his dad was here, but since –" That pause again. "Since he left, she's lost some of her clout and doesn't like it. I think David's eyes may have been opened now, but time will tell. I guess you've got to see her as well while you're here?"

"Yes," she answered. "And Christine, who should be in today."

"Yes, she should, although I haven't seen her myself yet. Have you met John, the design man, yet?"

175

"No," she replied, "he wasn't in the other day when I was here."

"Had a day off, I think. Come on, I'll introduce you."

He led the way down the works towards the office door but then diverted off sideways.

"So you can tell him what you've seen, these are the two Tesco pumps."

She looked rather blankly at two large engines mounted on steel frames with what she presumed were the pump units mounted to them and wires in all directions for their control. She guessed that these were the wires that needed tidying up, and tried to look intelligent as Roger continued to talk.

"Going in one of their stores where the storage area is liable to flood. Only happened once, but they have to have two in case the first one doesn't start. Probably never ever be used, just started up twice a year to test them." He shrugged his shoulders as he moved on. "So who are we to argue? It's all work."

They went up the steps to the office corridor. She missed the wolf whistle she got last time but perhaps that was because Roger was with her or maybe someone had been told off. He led the way this time and then turned into an office that she had not been into before. This she had guessed previously to be some sort of drawing office not least because it was light and airy. A large drawing board stood in one corner but had been superseded by an equally outsize computer screen on a desk. On this she presumed that the many coloured lines meant something to someone. For reasons unknown she had been expecting an elderly person here, but found herself meeting a youngish man with sandy unruly hair and piercing blue eyes. Her first impression gave her the feeling that she might have trouble creating any sort of rapport with him, but he seemed pleasant enough at this brief meeting, although he wasn't afraid of coming straight to the point.

"Caused a bit of flutter in the dovecote, you have, you know," he said after the initial introductions were over.

"Sorry," was all she could think of to say whilst trying to look contrite at the same time.

"Don't be sorry, had to happen sometime. And sooner rather than later has to be better."

There was a finality to his terse Yorkshire accent that she did not quite know how to deal with. She changed the subject. "David didn't mention anything for you. Do you want anything from him? I'm only the messenger, you know," she said brightly.

"Naw, 'tis detail work I'm on the minute, no grandiose schemes to dream up just now. I'll give him a bell if I need anything."

"OK. Now I must catch up with Muriel."

"Ah, and good luck to thee."

"Thanks," she said with feeling and left.

Jennifer moved on down the corridor. Christine was not in her office, although she was obviously here as her bag hung over the back of the chair. She must be in the front office for coffee. Coffee time in the office was no doubt deliberately at a different time from the works. She opened the door and walked in. Except for the cream cake the tableau was almost exactly as before. The silence was not quite so deafening, possibly because she was at least half expected, but it was there all the same.

"Huh, creeping in the back door again. Why can't you come through the front like any normal person?" cried Muriel in exasperation.

Christine jumped from her perch, saying, "I'll get you a coffee. How do you like it?"

"Thank you. Black, one sugar please." She turned back to Muriel. "David wanted some information from Roger, so I thought it best to get that direct from him. Anyway the door might have been locked. It often is, you know."

Muriel coloured very slightly under her make-up.

"Thought there was a chance you might turn up so I unlocked it."

"Thank you," Jennifer cut in before she got too far into her stride.

"And I could easily have found out whatever it was he wanted from Roger."

"True, but now I've got it straight from the horse's mouth and there's no chance of anything being forgotten or misinterpreted."

Muriel coloured a bit more and changed the subject. "Have you brought back all those papers I gave you the other day? Some of them are becoming urgent."

Christine appeared with the coffee. Jennifer thanked her and said she would be with her in a few minutes. Christine nodded and left. She's not getting directly involved, thought Jennifer. Turning back to Muriel she said, "Yes, I've got them all here. In case you don't think

178

they're genuine, it's my writing on them. David can't write himself yet."

Muriel looked up sharply.

"It's his right arm he's broken and I presume he's right-handed," Jennifer said patiently.

Muriel harrumphed and said, "I suppose so." She took the papers and looked briefly through them. "OK, I can deal with those now. There's some more here for him. Particularly these two top faxes need some prices working out."

"I'll take them but he may have to phone the answers through to you as I don't know when I shall be back."

"Thought you were getting your feet well under the table," Muriel said sarcastically.

With infinite care Jennifer spelled it out for her. "No. I'm going home this afternoon and I'm not sure when I shall be back. I do have a job that I'm supposed to be going to."

This seemed to surprise Muriel and she seemed almost at a loss for words, so Jennifer rubbed it in a little harder.

"I'm not one of those people who can just take off whenever and wherever they fancy. I do actually need the money."

"Well, we won't hold you up here then," Muriel said out loud, while thinking to herself, *Good riddance and get out of my hair.*

All this time Miranda had been typing away with her eyes glued to keyboard and screen but with her ears very much elsewhere. Jennifer could not ignore her.

"How are you today then, Miranda?" she asked. Miranda visibly jumped.

"Ohh, fine, thanks," she replied, looking briefly at Jennifer and then returning to her typing.

"Good. Well I'll see you both in due course. Now I'll go and catch up with Christine." She gathered up her coffee mug and the papers before smiling encouragingly and leaving the room. She didn't see Muriel make a hoity-toity face at her as she went through the door.

She sat down with Christine and handed over another batch of papers together with the cheques that had required a signature.

"He says his signature is a bit odd because of only having his fingers stuck out of the end of a plaster. He hopes the bank will accept it. Maybe you should warn them in advance."

Christine nodded her agreement to the idea. The atmosphere was calmer in here and less highly charged. However she had barely passed a few conventional remarks with Christine when all that changed as Muriel came storming in. She was shaking a piece of paper at Jennifer as though it was a snake caught by its tail.

"What does he mean by this?" she shouted. Jennifer was nonplussed.

"By what?" she asked.

"This request for a quotation from Simmons," she carried on in a high voice. "He says I'm to decline to quote. They're one of my best customers and he says we're not to quote." Her voice was rising with the repetition. "What is he thinking about? You've gone to his head, my girl, and warped his mind."

Jennifer, for her part, really was at a loss and it must have shown, because Muriel visibly cooled.

"All I can tell you is that he took an awfully long time thinking about that one, and I didn't actually write his note to you until this morning, literally just before I left. I'll ask him if you like," she added helpfully.

"Don't bother, I'll stir him up myself, broken arm or no broken arm. Young idiot! He can't do this." And with that she went grumbling out of the room.

"What was that all about?" queried Christine.

"No idea. Truthfully, I haven't. Like I told Muriel, David spent a long time thinking about it and only at the last minute did he decide on what was written for Muriel. He didn't enlighten me at all. Is there something I should know then?"

"No, I don't think so, but it is odd. David doesn't usually miss a chance to try and sell somebody something. But that's by the by. Did you two have a good weekend?"

"Yes. Obviously couldn't do much, but he's due to get the stitches out of his leg in a day or so and then at least he should be more mobile. Wouldn't mind betting that he'll be back in here in no time at all."

"True," admitted Christine, adding, "And where does that leave you?"

Jennifer, to her annoyance, blushed. Was it that obvious?

"Don't know. I've got a job to go back to. That is if I've still got a job and haven't given myself the sack by

181

taking off up here the way I have. The boss has been phoning for me and I'm beginning to regret not having been a good girl and ringing him back."

"Tut, tut," said Christine. "But don't worry too much. My bet is that you'll find yourself back here before you've had time to think about it."

"Here's hoping," responded Jennifer, but in reality, she wasn't so hopeful. There had been talk of her coming back but it was not as positive as she would have wished, and for sure she wasn't looking forward to having to return to her old life. What did she mean her old life? She had only been away from it for four days. Even if it did seem like a very happy eternity, she thought wistfully. But Christine was moving on to other things and she had to catch up quickly.

"Tell him there's been some useful money in the post this morning and if he signs this batch of cheques he can send them off himself. If you get some stamps from next door all he has to do is put them in the envelopes. He should manage that."

She did as she was told and Muriel laboriously stamped an exact number of envelopes for the cheques and payment slips she had been given. She also looked hard at each one as though it needed her approval as well. She had in the meantime sorted out another batch of messages for David. Once she had these, Jennifer found there was but one option, and that was leaving. Much as Muriel intended, she guessed. She walked out of the front door with a deliberately cheery goodbye, to which she heard a grunt from Muriel, a squeak from Miranda and a distant goodbye from Christine. *That about sums it up,* she thought. To this was added a cheerful wave from John 'over the road' as he continued his apparently endless sweeping of the forecourt.

She returned to Brampton laden with shopping of a kind that she hoped David would be able to cook for himself, and with enough office work to keep him going for at least half a day.

"I've brought a sandwich and a pasty for my lunch and then I'll need to be on my way if I'm to get back at anything like a sensible time," she announced, rather too loudly it seemed to her. But she had to keep her spirits up somehow. It was not what she wanted, but for a whole host of entirely practical reasons there was no alternative.

"And be back when? Thursday? Friday? Or will it be sooner?" said David as casually as if he were asking the time of day.

Jennifer was stunned. Love, wishes and anger fought inside her and it was the anger that won.

"You're impossible. You know that," she stormed. "You know I have a job to go to, at least I hope I have. And if I haven't it'll be your fault. And it's quite likely I haven't. I hope you know that as well. Here we are, been talking all weekend about my leaving this afternoon, and there you are expecting me back before the week's out. Indeed before I've even gone."

"But I need you," was all he said.

"You don't need me, you just need a nanny. Well, get that bloody woman in your office to nanny you. She seems to know all about you and know what you should be doing

183

and how you should be doing it." She knew she was venting her wrath at Muriel on him and that it was not entirely fair, but she couldn't help herself. She knew she didn't want to go but quite simply had to, and she also knew that he knew all her reasons as well. It made her sadder than it should have done and a scene was the last thing she wanted just now.

"That's why I need you," he said.

"What do you mean? Why you need me?"

"Listen, my love…"

"Don't you 'my love' me in that patronising way!" she shouted at him, knowing full well that she did not mean it. "Just tell me why you need me."

"I'll start again," he said, in the same patient tone that she had been using on Muriel. "Listen, Jennifer, if you prefer that." She nodded and he continued. "I'm not going to say any more for now than that you've opened my eyes to Muriel in the short time you've been here, but that is not entirely the point. On a purely practical level I am going to need help for quite some time to come. Actual, physical help. To get me about, for instance. I shan't be able to drive until I get this plaster off, in fact not even immediately after that. But more to the point, much more to the point, I desperately wanted you before all this happened." He raised his plastered arm and winced with the effort. "And I have reason to believe that you wanted me, but whether so desperately, I don't know. You, God bless you, found me and I'm not going to let you go again so easily. How we work it out remains to be seen but I want you back here."

It was quite as speech. Romeo would have done justice to it. Jennifer was floored. This roller-coaster life was becoming too much. It was what she wanted to hear but why, oh why, could they not have discussed it rationally over the weekend rather than in this storm of accusation just as she had to go? She collapsed onto the settee beside him and, putting her head gently on his shoulder, cried. She cried as much from nervous exhaustion as anything else. It had all been quite a strain, even if exhilarating at the same time.

Within an hour she was on her way. She noted as she drove off that David had got to the window and was standing to wave to her. She knew just how much effort that had cost him. She was honoured.

Her journey back was uneventful except for a severe delay north of Manchester, but at least the traffic kept moving, even if only very slowly. She began to realise how tedious this journey was going to become if she had to make it regularly, but it did give her time to think about what she was going to do next. David was expecting her back, and soon. There was no doubting his determination about that. But she had not committed herself to giving up her job. This had become almost an obsession with her, almost as though it was her only link to reality. As she had told herself many times, she could find a similar job almost anywhere, anytime, so why hang on to this one? She supposed that she didn't want to throw everything away just in case she and David didn't work out. But they would, she knew that equally positively. So why? Subconsciously she guessed it was a last link with home and the world she knew so well. However, now she had not only looked over the horizon, she had actually been there for a spell and liked what she had found. In due course she would no doubt give up her job, but that would have to wait until she saw how the land lay. Despite his best efforts to persuade her differently she hadn't actually promised anything to David.

And so she arrived home. Although she had only been away a few days she found herself akin to a stranger there. She had felt a little like this on her return from Africa, but this time it was worse. She really and truly felt that she did not belong. These last few days had changed her life, there was no doubt about it. For all that, life was very normal. Her mother was expecting her and was cooking supper for all the family as usual. The farm looked unchanged. The house looked unchanged. She could only try and fit back into this normality herself. After initial greetings she busied herself sorting the clothes she had brought back into the washing machine and then finding a better selection from her wardrobe to take back. She wasn't sure why she was doing this if she wasn't going back straight away, but it gave her something to do and she knew it was a waste of time talking to her mother whilst she was cooking. That would all have to wait until they sat down to eat, or even until later in the evening.

"So how was bonny Scotland then?" It was her father who opened the batting.

"Dad, I haven't been to Scotland and you know it," she scolded.

186

"Damned close to it though. So how are your nursing abilities? Never saw you as a nurse."

"Too right. I'm not."

It was her mother who called them to order.

"Stop sparring, you two. Now, darling, just tell us what you've been doing and all about David and how he hurt himself."

So Jennifer filled in some of the blanks on what she had said on the phone. She explained about her trips to the factory, adding, "And I had a blazing row with the silly old fool that runs his office." This brought both parents up with a jerk.

"I shouldn't think he was best pleased about that," commented her father.

"Well it was strange, he said something about opening his eyes to certain things but wouldn't enlarge. What is even odder is that he wants me to go back again before the end of the week." She knew this would be a fairly large bombshell to throw into the family scene but she could see no easy way of leading up to it gently, so jumped in with all four feet. The effect was immediate and as she might have expected. Astonishment and anger. Her mother got in first.

"But you've only just got back. Why does he want you to go rushing back up there again? Can't he manage on his own now? You must be mad to even think of such a thing."

To which her father followed through with, "But what about your job? You can't go gallivanting off just like that as and when it suits you. Mr Halliwell won't like it. He'll more than likely give you the sack, and I wouldn't blame him."

Jennifer raised her hands in mock surrender. "I know. I know. I haven't actually promised that I will go back immediately."

"That's a relief, at least," said her mother.

"But I haven't ruled it out either," Jennifer added, knowing that she was twisting the knife.

"Oh, for goodness sake," exploded her father. "What are you thinking about? This young man – at least I presume he's young – comes along with some sort of injury and you drop everything to run round after him like a poodle on a string. I say again, whatever has come over you?"

Jennifer's antagonistic temperament was about to flare up big time, but her mother, having seen it coming, said, in a voice as smooth as silk, "Now let's not get heated and all say things we shall regret. Come on, tell us all about it and how you are thinking and I'm sure we can all see sense." She looked hard at her husband, ensuring that he did not wade in with any further unnecessary remarks.

Jennifer thought for a moment or two, marshalling her thoughts as to how best to approach this. She had hoped it would not all have to come out quite so quickly, and then preferably only with her mother. She decided to play for sympathy.

"You have to bear in mind that he hasn't just fallen downstairs, he's injured himself quite badly. If he'd done it any other way you would be very sympathetic rather than just laughing at him."

188

"For goodness sake, we weren't laughing at him."

"No. I know you weren't actually laughing but Dad was close to it." She ploughed on before he could say anything. "He's not only broken his arm pretty badly but he's got a black eye that would do a boxer proud and a cut on his shin that required a good many stitches. In practice he can hardly walk although once the stitches are out and the leg healed, he should be mobile fairly soon."

Simon looked a bit startled. "How on earth did he manage all that just falling downstairs?" he asked.

"He fell through the glass door at the bottom and out into the street. Frightened the life out of a little old lady who happened to be walking by."

"I bet he did." Perhaps sympathy was working.

"I still don't quite understand why he called for me. After all we'd only met for a few hours up to that point and still less do I understand why I went, but I did and that's all there is to it. Actually, I enjoyed it. It was a whole new scene. Somebody actually making something. People beavering away in his factory, doing things I've never seen before. A whole new set of priorities I've never come across – sales, deliveries and things like that."

"Sounds awful to me," muttered her father. Her mother said nothing and let her muse on.

"I suppose it's not that much different from us: sending sheep to market, waiting to see how much we get for them, and then waiting for the cheque to come in before we pay the bills." She was being deliberately naughty because she knew that she was not supposed to realise how often this had been the case in their lives. Her father coloured slightly. Again, her mother said nothing.

"I shouldn't think he has those sorts of problems," he said.

"I think he does, and possibly more so. Anyway, that's not our problem. Going back to where we were, he seems to need me to act as 'Mr Fixit' between him and his office until he's fit enough to get back there himself. His mother seems pretty useless." She glanced at her own well-organised mother. "Perhaps that's not quite fair as I only saw her for a few minutes. I didn't see his father, who was described as 'having withdrawn from the business'. What do you suppose that means?"

"No idea."

"Nor me."

"Perhaps he's retired."

"But then you'd think they'd say so."

"True."

"Again not my problem at the moment. Once he can get about, he's going to need someone to drive him and maybe that's the other role I shall be playing – chauffeur, or rather, chauffeuse."

"That's going to look a bit odd."

"It's all going to look a bit odd," she said, but she was dreaming out loud again. "But then I like him and he appears to like me." She hesitated to use the word love. "So I suppose we can make a sort of business relationship if nothing else." And she added for good measure, "I am old enough to make my own life, you know."

It was her mother's turn to explode. "Just hang on a minute, Jennifer, darling. If you want to go back up there because you want to and because you like him and because you want to help him, that's one thing. If you're going back because he wants a personal assistant to help him out of a hole, that's entirely another matter and although it may sound much the same, it very definitely isn't. You can get that sort of job down here or he can find someone up there. It's how you feel with him that counts. To put it bluntly, if you want to test the water with David, then go back but do it with your eyes open. Wide open. As to your present job, well, in truth that's neither here nor there."

"Now you know why I married your mother," grinned her father. "Always gets straight to the nub of the problem in one easy move."

"Nonsense," said her mother, but knowing full well that he was being honest.

Jennifer was relieved. She had won her battle and could do what her heart and her conscience told her with at least the tacit approval of those who loved her. "So where do I go from here?" she asked.

"Carlisle, I imagine," said her father.

"Bed, I think," said her mother.

"Yes," said Jennifer, "And I've got to make my peace with Mr Halliwell tomorrow morning. That's not going to be fun."

"No, I should imagine it's not," responded her father.

Chapter 6

Tuesday morning dawned dank and dreary and not at all conducive to helping Jennifer overcome what she foresaw as being a very difficult session with her boss. She really should have let him know what she was doing and when he could expect her back. At the very least she should have responded to his phone calls. But she had been in a dream world with David and at the time she could not have cared less. Oh well, this was where she was going to get her comeuppance, no doubt about that. She was more and more certain that she would not have a job in an hour's time, but she had to try. It was not exactly a happy drive into work.

She drew a deep breath and pushed open the front door of the office in some trepidation to find that Julie was sitting at her desk.

"What are you doing here? I thought you'd left," was her first comment.

Jennifer was taken aback.

"I know I've been absent without leave but I haven't left, unless he's sacked me without telling me. And that's quite possible as well."

"Well, that's not what he told me," Julie replied. "Called me in yesterday and told me you were leaving and that I'd be doing your job from now on. He knows full well that I don't like it but he buttered me up good and proper. Told me what a good job I'd been doing and all that bullshit."

Jennifer was now aghast, not just taken aback. For Julie to break into even mildly bad language implied a serious situation.

"But what's going on? Here I am coming back full of apology with my tail between my legs, only to find that I've given up my job. If it wasn't so serious it would be funny. What's the man thinking about?"

"You'd better ask him: he's just coming through the door."

On cue the door swung open and Mr Halliwell strode through it. He looked at Jennifer, who tried hard not to cringe under his stare.

"Ah, Jennifer," he said, "so you've deigned to come back. Better come up to my office."

So this was going to be it. Curtains, no doubt about it. She said nothing, but grimaced at Julie as she followed him towards the staircase. Julie looked blank and she felt like a girl waiting outside the headmistress's study anticipating certain retribution for some infringement of school rules.

With studied deliberation he put his briefcase on the side table to his desk, gestured that she should sit in the chair usually reserved for clients and then walked across to look out of the window at the street below, where life was just starting into another day. He was a tall man and although not small herself she felt intimidated, which was no doubt what he intended. But what he said floored her completely.

"That young man of yours – David is it? You want to be careful of him. He's got a very silvery tongue. Do you know that?"

"I'm sorry?" she stammered. She wasn't sure she had heard him right.

"Rang me up yesterday, he did. We had words."

Jennifer was speechless.

"I was pretty cross at his having dragged you off the way he did, and I said so. He did apologise and explained his situation and in the end we had quite an amicable chat. Turns out we have the odd mutual acquaintance, which is surprising, to say the least. Anyway, the top and bottom of it is that we've agreed you can go up there and help him out of his problems. Against my better judgement I have agreed to hold your job open for a month to see how it all pans out."

He smiled, which could be something of a rarity for him.

"I don't know what to say," she said. It was lame but had the merit of being absolutely true.

"Not much to say," he said gruffly. "Come back within a month and the job's yours again. After that, well, I shall have to find somebody else and you'll be out of luck as well as a job. I know Julie won't do it indefinitely."

Jennifer rallied. "How on earth did he manage to arrange that with you?" she blurted out.

"In a way it's the old story of not what you know but who you know." He was becoming quite animated. "I spoke to one of our mutual friends and got the rest of the story. He's got a lot to tell you, but – and this is my very sincere advice – don't press him for it. He'll tell you in his own good time. He's said to be shy, although that's not quite the right word. Reserved might be better. You and he could be good for each other but that's for you to find out. I'm going to wish you well. Now get out before I change my mind, and anyway I've got work to do."

It was an abrupt finale and Jennifer rose, thanked him and left before he could, as he had warned, change his mind. It was a wonder she didn't fall down the stairs, her head was in such a whirl. She flopped into a chair beside Julie and just looked at her.

"Whatever happened? You look as though you've seen a ghost."

"I think that would have been easier," Jennifer whispered.

"So what did he say?" Julie was all business-like and curious.

"He knows you don't like this job."

"Too right," interjected Julie.

"But he's holding my job for a month while I go and sort David out. And myself too. After that; tough, he'll get somebody else."

"That's a relief anyway."

"But Julie, you're missing the point. David rang him yesterday and talked him into all this. And they know some of the same people. And he knows more about David than I do. He says, well no, he didn't actually say so, but apparently there's some sort of a skeleton in the cupboard somewhere and that David will tell me about it in his own good time. I'm definitely not to press him. What do you suppose that's all about?"

"Search me." It was obvious that Julie was not really interested.

"But who do you suppose they both know?" Jennifer persisted.

"Bill Godsell, probably. Didn't you say David was into pumps?"

"Of course. How stupid of me not to think of that straight away. David was down here to see him whilst I was in Africa and even had a peep at the farm."

"Well there you are then."

Jennifer could not understand how Julie was still not interested; just couldn't see how curious it all was.

"I need a coffee, even if it is early and even if I don't belong here any longer."

"Help yourself, you know where it all is."

Jennifer did just that, but already she felt out of place in this office that was going about its daily business and in which she had worked for four years or so. She clutched her mug in two hands and avoided, or was monosyllabic with, any other members of the staff she met. In the end she was glad to escape and she knew in her heart that she would never be coming back whatever happened with David. She walked out into the drizzle of rain now falling, feeling very lonely but at the same time somehow exhilarated.

She did not go straight home, she was not expected in any case, but drove out to one of the local lakes, old gravel pits really, where she could sit by herself and get her breath back. She had to think a bit. She realised that she seemed to spend an awful lot of her life 'thinking' at the moment. She had been to Africa to 'think'. She had sat on benches in Tanga and in Brampton 'thinking' and now here she was doing it in the rain in her car. And the outcome of all this thought? At face value, not much, but she supposed her life was working its purpose out.

Idly looking at, but not really watching, a few people messing about in boats, she felt able to relax. She hadn't realised how keyed up she had been over her expected dismissal from her job. She had put a blasé, couldn't-care-less face on it when in fact she had been worried silly once back in this part of the world. Now she could sit back in the continuing drizzle and fogged-up car and let it all wash over her. At least she had a clear conscience with which to return north. She valued what her mother had to say and she had said she must do it with her eyes open, wide open. That was easy down here but, and she knew this for sure, much more difficult when she was with David. David, there was something odd there. What was it Mr H had said? He, David, had a lot to tell her but not to press him for it. Well, she hadn't. Though more by instinct than conscious thought, it had to be said. But then one never quite knew what David was thinking. Shy, reserved, according to Mr H, but were devious, withdrawn, even cunning better words? Only time would tell. So what was she going to do now? Go back to Carlisle, just as her father had said! Yes, but when? Today: too late. Tomorrow: maybe. Thursday: she didn't think she could wait that long. Hey, Jennifer, you're acting like a teenager; can't wait to see the boyfriend! She made a face at herself. She sniffed and decided that she would get herself properly organised with what she needed to take with her and then go in a cool, calm and civilised manner.

"Some chance," she said out loud, knowing full well that as soon as she was ready, she would want to be off, teenager or not. She wiped the fug off the windows and found a watery sun had appeared as if to confirm her decision to go and go soon. She started the car and drove slowly home wondering just how she was to break all this to her mother.

It was easier than she expected.

"Had a feeling that you'd soon be back. How did it go? Has he sacked you?"

"No. Given me a month off!"

Her mother whistled in a very unladylike manner.

Jennifer explained.

"This David I have to meet," she said. "To talk your boss into doing that is quite something. So what are your plans? I guess you're moving out, then?"

"Hey, Mum, that sounds awful. I'm not moving out. Just going to Carlisle to help David."

"So, what's that if it's not moving out?"

Fortunately, her mother grinned or Jennifer would have thought she was being serious, which of course she was. While she had the opportunity, she continued to be so.

"Now one thing, Jen, and I am being serious. I gather his flat's quite small, so what are your sleeping arrangements."

Jennifer had been half expecting this one at some stage and had her answer ready.

"One bedroom. One large double bed. But the state he's in he's not going to be doing anything he shouldn't for a long time to come."

What she did not expect was her mother's answer.

"Don't you believe it. Men, when they're injured, seem to have an irrepressible urge on them. Perhaps it's something to do with continuing the species in case they don't survive. You remember that time when your father had a poisoned leg? He was supposed to sit with it up all day long and I was running the farm. Never worked so hard in all my life; day and night it was." A sort of dreamy faraway look came over her face.

Jennifer was quite shocked but her mother was too far away in a world of her own to notice. "You be careful. You know what I mean?" she said as she came back out of her reverie.

"Yes, Mum. I am on the pill you know."

"I didn't."

"You must have."

"No, I didn't know, although I guessed you might be. So that's all OK then. Now when are you going?"

She's always the same, thought Jennifer. *When the going gets tricky, change the subject.* Although she said out loud, "I don't know. I need to sort myself out and what I'm taking. Then I might be able to tell you when I'm going. But I need to talk to David first to find out what he has in mind." She retired as far out of earshot as she could.

"And how's the son of the Blarney Stone then?" she began. "You know what I mean… Yes, I've got a month's grace… How on earth did you get that out of him? … Well it seemed to work. Listen, I presume because of all your backroom work you want me to come back up your way… Yes, of course, don't be silly… No, I can't come today… Tomorrow, perhaps, if I'm ready in time… Yes, but I need more than the one change of clothes that I had last week… You start saying things like that and I shall know my mother was right about men… Ha, ha… No, seriously it isn't quite as simple as that. I've been accused of leaving home and on reflection there's some truth in it… It's a long way to come back for something I've forgotten, and you can't pop back for me… Yes, OK, all I wanted to know was that you wanted me… Of course I want to come… Now give me a chance to get on with it and I'll be there all the sooner… See you, want you."

Jennifer sat open-mouthed with the phone still to her ear. It was all happening too fast. Her mother was right. She did have to have her eyes open and her wits about her, but it was all rather deliciously exciting, wasn't it? Nothing even remotely like this had happened to her before and she was loving every minute of it. So much for her supposedly racy friends and their rather staid and very county boyfriends. Just like Richard! That was below the belt but it was true. Her life with him would have been wholly predictable. This was better, and different. Someone who actually needed and wanted her for what she could do for him. And that wasn't just in bed either. It was to help him with the affairs of his business. To somehow cope with the likes of Muriel on his behalf and to get to know a whole range of new people who viewed the world entirely differently from those she had known up to now.

Her mind raced on and then came up with a jerk. Leaving home, her mother had said. She had said as much to David. Somehow, she didn't see it that way. She was going to help David. She was coming back, wasn't she? Well, was she? That was actually quite a good point. If she did as she was proposing, was she ever going to come back? She was sure she was. Anyway, his arm would heal and then what was she going to do? Oh, to hell with it, as usual she would take one day at a time and see what happened. Now she had to get ready to go away and as it was for more than just a day or two that needed thinking about.

She departed to her room and stood looking around her as though she was seeing it for the first time. This had been her home, her room, her anchor, her place for a very long time, since at least when she was about ten or twelve and now, she was just going to walk out of it as though it had never been.

"Don't be silly," she scolded herself. "You've left it before. You did when you went to Africa. You did last week. You're just doing it again but maybe, just maybe, for longer."

With that she straightened herself up and started to throw clothes out of cupboards and drawers onto the bed. She soon had a pile that looked more like a jumble sale than anything else. That was all too obviously no good so she started to sort the pile into some kind of order. Underwear, bras, pants, slips, vests and so on in one pile. Day-to-day wear, jeans, sweatshirts, T-shirts, everyday skirts, big jerseys and their ilk into another, because it was colder Up North, not to mention it being winter anyway. Then some office clothes in a third. She didn't need to be as smart as at Halliwell & Stoddard but she needed to keep up standards and appearances if nothing else. The hair pricked on the back of her neck when she thought of her overdressing for David's office last week, but it had perhaps made the point that she wasn't to be trifled with.

Next problem was what was she going to pack it in. Her rucksack that had taken all her possessions to Tanzania was fine for the common or garden items but her better clothes needed something better. There was a pretty battered common user suitcase around somewhere that she had used occasionally when sleeping over with schoolfriends, but when she found it, she decided it was far too tatty for someone who was ostensibly leaving home.

"Mum," she called downstairs, "have we got a half-decent suitcase I can borrow for my decent clothes?"

Clattering noises coming from the kitchen were followed by her mother obviously deep in thought.

"How big?"

"Not too big, I can use my rucksack for most things. Just want to keep my Sunday bests tidy."

"There's a bright blue one I use on the rare occasions when we get away."

"But Mum, that's your best one. I can't take that."

"Why not? I'm not going anywhere that I know of and if I am, you'll have to bring it back – which will be a good excuse to see you again."

"Oh, Mum, don't rub it in, but thanks anyway." And she was off up to the attic to fetch it before her mother could make any more snide remarks.

With her father out, lunch became a somewhat subdued meal. Jennifer was not normally at home at lunchtime, simply having a sandwich and coffee in the office, so she found she was something of a visitor in her own home. They found themselves reduced to making polite conversation and that was no good to either, as Jennifer wanted to be happy and her mother wanted to be sad. Finally, Jennifer had to take the bull by its proverbial horns.

"Come on, Mum, let's take our coffee into the snug and talk this through properly and then you may see where I'm coming from."

The snug was a room they used as somewhere to sit where the furniture didn't mind what clothes you were wearing. It was, as its name implied, cosy, with old chairs that were well worn in and in which you could slouch in great comfort. It didn't matter if one of the dogs wanted to sit beside you with its head on your knee while you watched television. During the day the sun shone in for a high percentage of the time. In short it was quite simply – snug.

They settled in their accustomed chairs but her mother wasn't saying anything.

"What's eating you, Mum?" Jennifer implored. "I do know what I'm doing, you know."

"Do you?" her mother shot back, almost viciously.

"Yes, for once in my life, possibly for the first time ever, I do know what I'm doing. I'm positive about that."

"But it's all so sudden, and you're going so far away." Her mother was almost wailing which Jennifer found very disconcerting. It was children, even ones as big as she was, that cried. Mothers were there to put a stop to them, doing it either by brute force or by making soothing noises.

"Yes, it is sudden. I will admit to that. I had hoped something like this might happen but even in my wildest dreams I never expected this." Jennifer could sense that this conciliatory explanation of the situation was helping so she hurried on. "I had hoped to have time to get to know him better and then take it from there, not to find myself nursing him and sharing his bed because it was the only one available. He had made arrangements for me to stay in the local pub – did I tell you that?" Her mother shook her head. "Yes, but I opted to stay with him. Like I said, he isn't capable of much." She was getting close to deep water again. "Anyway, he blames me for the fall – did I tell you that as well?" Another shake of the head.

"How so? You weren't even there." Her mother seemed to have perked up a bit.

"Says he was thinking about me and not what he was doing!"

"Well, I suppose that's something," her mother conceded.

"Yes, he said he was carrying too many things balanced together, thinking about me and stumbled, or whatever, and, well, you know the rest. I guess it's a compliment really."

"Mmm, maybe."

Jennifer needed to keep this conversation going.

"You know, Mum, there is one thing that worries me."

"I'm glad something does." The words were acid but the tone wasn't.

"Yes, I'm not sure about being cooped up in a small flat. I had to get out for some fresh air last time. Here, well, even though I'm in an office all day we seem to live half out of doors. And there's always space, either outside or somewhere in this great big house. You know what I mean?"

"Hmm. Actually, it's the reverse of that which worries me," said her mother in something like her normal tone of voice. Jennifer felt she was perhaps getting to the bottom of whatever it was that was bugging her mother, but said nothing: just looked up in some surprise. "I'm going to be left on my own in this great big house as you call it. I'm going to rattle like a pea in a pod without you here."

Jennifer looked more closely at her mother and saw someone who was feeling extremely sorry for herself. It was a new experience, along with all the others.

"Oh, but Mum, I'm never here anyway. I'm out all day and quite often in the evening as well. Dad's here more than I am. And Paul; Paul's in and out half the time it seems to me. You'll never know I'm not here."

She knew the last remark was trite but she had to say it somehow, even if it was a bit harsh.

"But you're different," came the reply. "You're a daughter. No, I don't think you should stay here to look after your parents like in some Victorian melodrama but… but I shall miss you. OK, yes, Paul and Simon are here all the time but they're both their own independent selves and just think of me and the house as a source of food when they're hungry."

"Now that really is rubbish and you know it," exploded Jennifer and then regretted what she had said.

"Yes, I know it is, but there are times when it seems that way to me. You'll find out for yourself one day. They don't take me for granted all the time but for a good lot of it they do, especially Paul and definitely at certain times of the year. But I guess that's the penalty of being a farmer's wife and having a nice, if great big house like this to live in."

"Oh, Mum," was all Jennifer could say but they both seemed to have got something off their respective chests. Her mother came back to being her normal, practical self.

"So when are you going and what are you taking with you?" And thus they moved onto purely mundane matters, which was a relief for both, even though both knew that the subject was not finally closed.

In the end it was agreed that Jennifer would go the following day, leaving after lunch, but she thought it would not be the end of the world if she left it another day and went first thing in the morning. She knew David wanted her as soon as possible and, if she was honest with herself, she badly wanted him. In the event it was the latter course that she took. David seemed understanding about it and she hoped he really was. It wasn't the packing and getting ready that held her up; she could be as organised as her mother when the need arose. It was having to explain and justify her actions all over again to both her father and her brother, both of whom seemed to find their own set of objections for which she had to find answers. Her mother continued to come up with yet more conundrums, as though she thought that if she kept at it long enough, she would find something that would put a stop to the whole grand scheme. All this creating of problems also made her keep thinking of extra things she ought to take so that by the time she did finally leave, her car was loaded with more loose things than packed ones and she was totally shattered by the whole experience. She really did hope she was doing the right thing.

"Don't be silly, Jennifer, you know you are," was her response to that.

***

Leaving on the Thursday morning was a most odd feeling. It was akin to the loneliness she had felt when she walked away from the office on Tuesday, and yet it had the same exhilaration as well. There was something different this time. Her mother had actually been in tears and her father nearly so but putting a brave face on it. Only Paul managed to be facetious. Once she had got everything into the car, she too had needed to don the traditional stiff upper lip, and she had left rather more hurriedly than she would really have liked. No matter, now she was on her way. The M5/M6 beckoned. The open road North, to who knew what adventures?

Except that it was not so open. As she was to learn, the traffic round Birmingham could be horrendous and also at various other points along the way, but it gave her time to reflect on what she was doing, and even why. She began to feel sorry for her mother, left alone in that great big house as she had called it. She nearly turned round and went back but knew that was no good and not what she or David, or her mother for that matter, wanted. She surprised herself there with thinking of David first in front of her family. Yes, indeed, life had moved on and she with it.

The journey was slow and she was getting bored and blasé about driving up the motorway. She clicked through the various radio stations and stopped at the latest news bulletin. Police had begun operations at 25 Cromwell Street, Gloucester and the newsreader droned on dispassionately about a series of horrible murders. Jennifer felt horrified and quickly found a local music station playing *Love is All Around* by Wet Wet Wet. This was more like it and she allowed herself to be caught up in the song by joining in the chorus at the top of her voice as she drove. Paul had informed her somewhat portentously that this came from a new movie, *Four Weddings and a Funeral* that he had taken his latest flame to quite recently. It had obviously had the desired effect as he had a stupid grin plastered across his face. She wondered if she might persuade David to take her to see it.

She waited in the queue for a phone box just once to report progress to David and eventually drew up in the square outside his flat in the middle of the afternoon. She gathered up her handbag and some provisions she had bought along the way, just to add to supplies that her mother had insisted she take with her. As she walked through his door, she noticed that it had had the glass panel replaced with a wooden one. At least he wouldn't now land in the street if he fell down the stairs again.

"Hi, Jen," said his voice from the top of the stairs, and there he was standing – yes – standing there. Well he was standing on one leg and supported by a crutch under the shoulder of his broken arm, but it was great to see him standing. She bounded up the stairs and threw her arms around him, careful not to knock him over but complete with handbag and shopping.

"Hey, hang on. You could do me an injury like that."

"I'll risk it. According to you I've done you one already." It was just so nice to be here again. "And anyway, when did this sudden mobility start? You don't need me now then?" she teased.

"Yesterday and oh yes, I do. I've only just about managed this thing. I've been practising all morning so as to surprise you. And you're about to push me over if you're not careful."

She let go, again carefully, and he slowly, so very slowly she noticed, moved himself back into the living room and to his accustomed corner of the settee. The effort had cost him more than she would have dared ask.

"I may be mobile after a fashion," he said, "but it's a hell of an effort."

"But well done," she encouraged. "You have to start sometime. Tea?"

"Please. I did manage to go to the kitchen and make myself coffee this morning. First time for ten days, can you believe? It tasted great just to have done it but it nearly killed me."

"Well done again," she said and gave him a long kiss just to confirm it – and to confirm to herself that she was really and truly back with him.

She made tea for them and they sat together drinking it.

"You know," she mused, "I almost feel as though I've come home. I've only been here a few days but it feels sort of comfortable, if you know what I mean."

"Hey, that's great," he replied. "It's sort of nice just having you there."

"Mmmmm," she breathed in reply. But it was time to be business-like or this might get out of hand.

"Also, you should know, I've got a car full of belongings and I have no idea where I'm going to put them. I think I somehow imagined more cupboard and drawer space than there actually is."

"If I was even remotely capable, I would clear out some space for you but you may have to do it yourself, under instruction from me. I don't want you prying too deeply even if inadvertently."

There seemed something almost like fear in his voice. Whatever might she uncover? Girlie magazines, condoms, perhaps. The former she somehow doubted, the latter was always a possibility. And it seemed to have brought a hard edge to his voice.

"No problem," she said quickly. "I'll only do just what I'm told. Now, I'll go and get the first load."

David seemed to relax.

Jennifer disappeared downstairs and struggled back up with her rucksack and a gift-wrapped parcel.

"My that's a man-sized rucksack," commented David. "Everything including the kitchen sink by the look of it."

"It took all my worldly possessions round Africa, but now it's only got day-to-day clothes, underwear and suchlike in it. There's a proper suitcase for respectable clothes. I told you there was a lot."

"Think I prefer the underwear and suchlike to the respectable clothes," he quipped. "But what's in the parcel?"

Oh, my, he's getting better, she thought, but said, brightly, "No idea. Mother gave it to me with strict instructions not to open it until I was with you. Muttered something about I might need your help."

"Well come on then, especially if it's for me as well."

"She never said anything about it being for you," she countered. "Just that I wasn't to open it until I was with you."

"Same thing."

"No."

"Well, nearly."

"No, nowhere near nearly." But she could see the twinkle in his eyes. It was good to see him not feeling so sorry for himself.

"Well, get on and open it then!"

She sat as far away as the settee would allow and pretended to open it very slowly, peeking under the paper as she did so.

"Ah, now it all makes sense. Look." She held up the unwrapped box.

"A mobile phone. Now that is what I call sensible of your mother. I've been worrying about your driving up here and getting delayed or having any problems."

"My mother is a very sensible woman," intoned Jennifer in a mock announcer's accent. "She is too. Renowned for it, Dad would be totally lost without her."

"And I guess my job is to set it up for you and show you how to use it, if you don't already know."

"I don't. Apart from being a bit behind the times on the farm, people who do have them, reps and such, say they are totally unusable in the valley. No signal or something."

"That figures. They can be very patchy round here. It'll get better in time and it will be OK all the way up the motorway, which is what really matters. Now, first thing to do is for you to get all the bits out of the box and get the battery on charge. Sorry but we, you, can't do anything until that's charged up."

They fiddled around with all the components and she was very appreciative of David letting her do it all under his instruction rather than just taking it out of her hands and doing it for her. In reality though, she reflected, with one arm in a plaster he was a bit restricted in what he could have actually done. Anyway, it was a nice thought. After that she made three more journeys to the car, one for the suitcase, a second for food and sundries that her mother had sent, and the third for all the odds and sods that were otherwise unaccounted for.

"Your mother doesn't plan on us starving, does she?"

"As I said, my mother is a very sensible woman."

"I shall start to get frightened of her in a minute even though I've not met her yet."

"No. No need. She's great – but very sensible!"

Jennifer removed the suitcase and rucksack into the bedroom and surveyed the wardrobe and chest of drawers without opening either. Unless David had an unusually large selection of clothes – and if her brother Paul was anything to go by, she considered that unlikely, she thought there was every chance of getting what she had brought in somewhere. She went back into the living room.

"Think I'll start on the good stuff first, mostly on hangers. How's the wardrobe for space?"

"Work from the right-hand side and you should be OK. You may have to flatten out some boxes and things. Shout if it's not obvious. In the meantime, I'll think about the chest of drawers. Roughly how much space do you think you'll need?"

"Don't know, drawer and a half perhaps."

"I think we'll cope then."

"Good." And she returned to the bedroom and gingerly slid back the door of the built-in wardrobe. She found it slightly embarrassing to be opening somebody

213

else's cupboard. She was half expecting something to jump out at her. Silly – she felt as if she was prying into David's innermost secrets, but it was only a wardrobe after all. He had been right. Well, of course he would be. The rail was only half in use, she could see a couple of suits, a jacket and several pairs of trousers in the dim recesses of the other half. As he had said there were a collection of nondescript boxes piles up her end. Her end? What was she thinking about? Her end? It was his wardrobe and his things in it. It might become her end of his wardrobe.

She moved the boxes down to make only one layer on the floor and then opened the suitcase. It looked as though her clothes had travelled well and they shook out without too much creasing when she hung them up. They really looked quite smart hanging there in 'her' side of the wardrobe. A couple of pairs of shoes she put on top of the boxes.

"Any thoughts on the chest of drawers?" she called through to David.

"Yeah, the bottom drawer is nearly empty. If you transfer everything from the drawer above then you can have that. Next time I'm on my feet I'll sort through one of the top ones for you. How's that?"

"That's fine," she replied. Remembering her feeling from the wardrobe she was glad not to be sorting through his more intimate clothing. Again, there would be time enough to get used to that idea. She hoped. Doing as bidden she emptied most of the rucksack into that drawer and just left her underwear and immediate items for the small drawer. She went back to sit with David.

"You look dazed, shocked, surprised or something I can't quite place. Are you OK?" he asked. He sounded concerned.

"I am all of those and more besides." She turned to look at him. "Do you realise that in just about a week I have chucked up my job, left home, moved in with a man I hardly know, including sharing his bed, not to mention creating havoc in his well-ordered business to boot. I think I've an absolute right to look dazed!"

"It's not that bad," he said, extending his better arm towards her. She took his hand without realising that it was the first time she had done so without it being to help him do something.

"It is. Just think about it, David. Here I am… No, correction, there I was; a nice country girl with a steady if unexciting job waiting for my life to take its appointed course, and now look at me!"

"I am," he said with a twinkle in his eye.

"Stop it," she shouted. "And wipe that grin off your face for a start."

"Why? Now let's be logical."

"Because it annoys me, OK? But let's be logical," she said in a sing-song voice.

"Yes, let's," he said. "First," he began, marking things off with the fingers sticking out of his plastered hand, "you haven't lost your job, you're just on sabbatical for a month, if you want a big word for it."

"Oh, come off it, David, you know, I know, everyone knows that I can't go back to Halliwell's. OK, you negotiated a month, but I can't go back. I'd be a laughing stock."

"Perhaps. Well, second, you haven't left home. Valley Court is still home, that's where you come from," he said.

"I know that too, but it feels like I have left home. If I go back, I shall be like a dog with its tail between its legs. Yes, I know I should always be welcome but I should also know, always know, that the one positive decision in my life had been wrong."

"Rubbish, but we shall have to work on that. Now, three. We've known each other for quite a long time…"

Jennifer cut him short. "Yes, we've known *of* each other for quite a long time, if you call six or seven weeks that, but as to knowing each other it's really only a matter of days. But I'm not complaining," she added in a small voice.

"I rest my case on that one then," said David. "Four, 'sharing his bed'. Well I seem to remember it was your choice when you did have the option."

"And I'm not complaining about that one either," she said in an even smaller voice.

"And as for creating havoc in my business, I think you may have opened my eyes to a number of things, but that's not for now. So where do we go from here?"

"We have to work it out somehow," she said as she moved up the settee and snuggled under his arm. She began to feel secure again with strength of purpose returning.

"Atta girl," was all he said.

The rest of the day and evening passed pleasantly enough in what might have been termed domestic bliss but there was just a certain something in the air and Jennifer was pretty sure she knew what it was. Her mother, as always, had been right.

When they were settling into bed, David said, "Jen, do you think…?"

Quick as a flash she cut him off and, looking under her eyelashes at him, said, "Do I think what?"

He was embarrassed and he blushed, but she had intended that.

"Do you think we could manage… it?" he said.

"It? That could be all sorts of things you know," she said archly.

And it was his turn to cut her off. "You know perfectly well what I mean," he answered peevishly.

"Yes, my darling, I do know what you mean, and my mother, being a very sensible woman," they both intoned together, "warned me about injured men like you."

"Did she now?"

"Yes, she did."

"And what was her advice?"

"She went all dreamy talking about it."

"Did she indeed!"

"Yes, she did," said Jennifer very quietly.

"And do you think…? And are you…?"

"Yes and yes. Just like the old days, isn't it?" she said brightly.

"Not quite sure, well, how good I'll be though," he said, giving himself a back-out if necessary. "Or how much you'll enjoy it."

"My love," she said, "if you can manage it without actually making yourself a lot worse, I'm sure I shall cope somehow."

And she wriggled down the bed and out of her nightie and knickers. And manage it they did. It could never have been called a night of passionate lovemaking. It obviously cost David a lot in pain and effort, and Jennifer could but do her best to help him.

Spent and exhausted she muttered dreamily to him, "I may not have known you long, but that really has made this feel like home."

"Amen to that," he answered, and they slept.

***

David and Jennifer looked at each other a bit sheepishly as they surfaced the next morning, but then both grinned broadly. It was David who spoke first.

"Are you OK, Jen, I mean really OK?"

"Yes, I'm fine," she replied. "More to the point are you still alive?"

"I feel better already. Perhaps that's the sort of medicine I really need!"

"Maybe, but too much of any drug can be deadly you know."

"Hrmph," was all she got for an answer but she laughed all the same.

218

"Now you stay there and recuperate while I get us some breakfast."

It was around half past nine that there came a ringing of the bell to the flat door.

"A good thing we're both decent if we've got visitors," muttered Jennifer as she went off down the stairs to see who it was. She opened the door to find Christine from the works looking bright, rather serious and a bit flustered to see Jennifer. More surprisingly she was carrying a briefcase.

"Oh dear, sorry to disturb you. I didn't realise you were back," she said. Jennifer instinctively looked for a barb in her tone but failed to find one.

"No, no problem. You obviously want to see David, so I can make myself scarce," she said as she led the way up the stairs. "Look he's getting better. Soon be back to see what you're all at."

"Good to see," Christine said a bit vacantly as if pondering something. "No, on reflection Jennifer, I think it might be best if you were in on this. It could be said to be your fault anyway, although I should probably have got there in the end."

"Everything seems to be my fault around here at the moment, even if I only appeared on the scene five minutes ago," she laughed.

"My, this sounds serious," intervened David. "But whatever brings you out here at this time in the morning? You're only just about due in the office by now. Anyway, take a seat. Coffee?"

"No, not yet, thanks. I'll sit at the table if I may, then I can spread papers if needed."

"So," said David, "what's eating you?"

Christine looked confused again, visibly wishing she was anywhere but here.

"I'm sorry," she said, "I don't quite know where to begin."

Jennifer went and sat at the table as well in an instinctive bid to give her confidence in whatever it was that had brought her here. Perhaps two women together would help.

"Try starting with me," she said, "if I'm the problem."

"Oh, no, you're not the problem," said Christine hurriedly. "You're the catalyst that's brought it all to a head."

"Now, come on Christine, no more mystery. What is this all about? Please." David was being formal and business-like and it seemed to have its effect.

"It's Muriel," Christine blurted out. Jennifer stiffened and noticed David flinch as he did the same.

"What about her?" David asked in a perfectly level tone of voice.

"I think she's defrauding the company. There, now I've said it." She seemed relieved.

David's voice remained wholly neutral. "That's quite an accusation. Can you prove it and what makes you think she is? And for good measure, where does Jennifer come into all this?"

"The last bit's easy. Jennifer here and Muriel are like a red rag to a bull to each other, as you may have heard."

220

David grinned. "Well I know, don't ask me how, that Jennifer is as straight as a die. And Roger thinks so too." David grinned again remembering a previous telephone call. "And I reckon Muriel can see it too and it doesn't suit."

"I would agree with all that," said David, "but it proves nothing. Nor does it suggest fraud."

She turned to Jennifer.

"Do you remember that first occasion when you walked into the front office from the works? The first time you and I met?"

"How could I forget? It's imprinted on my heart!"

"I'm not surprised." Christine managed a small laugh. "But more importantly do you remember Muriel's accusation that you might be a spy!"

"This is news to me. I'm all ears," chipped in David.

"We all thought she was talking about T. H. Wear and more or less said so, but I think she thought you might have been sent to spy on her and she was in a sudden flap about it. When she realised our line of thought she backed off and became quite reasonable."

"For her," said Jennifer. Christine smiled at her.

"But it still doesn't prove fraud," persisted David.

"I know." Christine sounded irritated. "I've read somewhere that fraudsters are usually caught out on something quite insignificant. Often by pure chance. Well, I was checking some illegible figures on a faxed copy invoice from PenR Factors. Now as you know I go one day a week to Railston Engineering, and quite inadvertently I gave their name not ours. The lady I spoke to ran down the part number prices. These were all completely different from the few that I could read on our invoice. Then she realised that this was a Wear invoice not a Railston one and there was much confusion. After some pushing and an almost visibly red face at the other end of the line it transpired that all prices to us are plus 10% or discounts reduced accordingly. Now you are aware that all orders have to go through Muriel and how insistent she always is about that: costing jobs, etc., etc., any excuse will do. We've all heard it. I made some enquiries elsewhere under an assumed name and found a similar situation. I think, but as yet I can't prove it, that she's skimming a profit for herself off some of our suppliers."

Jennifer was aghast but said nothing. David leant back in the sofa with a totally poker face.

Christine bit her lip, all too obviously thinking about something further.

"There's more, isn't there?" David said quietly.

"Yes," said Christine, blushing scarlet.

"It's better if you tell me what you think rather than that I jump to conclusions," said David. gently.

"Yes," said Christine again, visibly gathering her courage around her. Jennifer found herself grasping her hands together until the knuckles showed white, willing Christine to continue. Almost in a whisper Christine said: "And I think your father knows, or knew, that this was going on."

"That's what I think too, which leaves us all with a problem," said David, recovering his composure. The relief of Christine having said this rather than him having to articulate it seemed to be palpable.

"Yes," said Christine, for the third time, as the responsibility started to ebb away from her.

Jennifer looked from one to the other with some sort of wonderment on her face, waiting to see what would happen next. Not much. There was a long pause and Jennifer knew instinctively that it was not for her to break. Finally, it was Christine who broke it.

"What do I do now?" she wailed.

"Nothing," said David with considerable finality.

"Nothing?" Christine looked astounded.

"Nothing," reiterated David.

"But I can't just let her carry on as though nothing has happened. As though I, we, don't know what she's doing. I'd be an accessory, or whatever the word is, after whatever it is that she's doing."

"You can and you will do nothing, although ultimately you may be needed as a witness," commanded David, in a manner that smacked of a parade ground sergeant major.

"I think I need that in writing," said Christine looking straight at him.

"Then you shall have it in writing. Typewritten if I can organise Jennifer here into doing it, or in my own crabby left hand if not."

Jennifer came out of her reverie with a jump at the mention of her name.

"Oh, yes, of course," she said, although she wasn't at all sure how she was going to do it. There didn't seem to be any sign of typewriters, computers or printers in the flat.

David's tone softened. "I think it's time we had some coffee, and possibly with something stronger in it. Jen can you oblige?" he said.

"Oh, no, just coffee, thank you," said Christine hurriedly. "I know what you Wears can be."

There was a trace of a smile on her face, partially reciprocated by David.

"No problem," Jennifer said as she went to put the kettle on.

"I'm sorry if I was a bit imperious just now," began David. Christine smiled weakly. "I know it's not going to be easy for you but you just have to keep on as though nothing was happening. She will hang herself eventually. These people always do. Usually they get greedy and go for just that little bit extra, and especially so if they get wind that they may be found out."

Jennifer produced coffee and biscuits, and Christine clasped hers as though her hands would never be warm again.

"What do you want me to do, if anything? I can't just let it carry on. It's against everything I've ever been taught or believed in."

"You can and you will." David was commanding again, but then changed his voice almost to a wheedling tone. "But you will try to keep a record of where you think this is happening. Don't, for all our sakes, try to play the detective, because Muriel isn't silly. She'll realise all too

224

soon and then anything could happen. I can't do much until I'm fit again and properly back in harness and that's going to be a while yet. Keep some copy invoices and let me have them via Jennifer, and then we shall see. I know it will cost us a bit but we've survived this long without noticing it, so a little longer won't hurt. Softly, softly, catchee monkee. Yes?"

"Yes," said Christine. She didn't look convinced, but at least she relaxed enough to drink her coffee.

"And don't be afraid to come and see me again if you think it necessary, but don't do it too often or she'll twig," he concluded.

"OK, I think I get the picture. I'll do my best.

"Well done. More coffee?"

"No, thanks," she said. "I ought to be getting to the office although I must admit I don't feel much like it. Would it matter if I went in this afternoon instead? Just to give me time to adjust."

"Might be better to take the whole day off. Phone Muriel and tell her you're not well or anything you like."

"Thanks, David. I might, no, I will do just that."

She gathered her papers up and prepared to leave. Turning to Jennifer she said, "Look after him. Get him back on his feet again – for both our sakes. Don't come down, I can find my own way out."

And she was gone.

Jennifer found herself staring vacuously down the stairs after her, alternating this with looking at David as well.

After a long pause it was David who spoke. "What do you make of that then?"

"If I was a car, I'd say I was in need of new shock absorbers!" she said.

Chapter 7

The teenage years for Gerry, Dianne and Daphne were riotous and wearing for both themselves and for all those around them. If anything, Gerry was a bit late deciding that the good-time life, along the lines that his father led, was for him but Dianne and Daphne were hardly into her teens before the tragedy struck. Whilst Gerry was happy to party his time away without necessarily getting involved with girls and the sex bit, Dianne was after nothing else from the moment her breasts started to show and she began to menstruate. In all probability Daphne would not have been far behind and Dianne missed her not being there as co-conspirator. Meanwhile David was left somewhere in the background as a seven- or eight-year-old and that suited his nature just fine.

"What's the matter with those two that they must always be arguing?" he would complain to his mother.

"It's just the way they are," she would answer, subtly dodging the true answer to the question.

Millie was much more au fait with what was going on than either Muriel or Henry. She was far from silly but even then it was more by intuition than anything that she knew that for both Gerry and Dianne it was their method of blanking out the loss of Daphne who, in spite of it all, had been very dear to both of them and especially all three 'parents'! Therefore, Millie understood and could forgive them, whereas Muriel and Henry in their various ways were immersed in the affairs of the factory and merely saw the worst side of it all. She realised that Gerry had done a good job of entirely blanking out the whole Daphne tragedy and that he often thought of it as something that had happened to an entirely separate family. It was his way of coping. The love of a beery lifestyle was probably nothing to do with it and likely to have happened anyway. *Like father, like son,* she thought and was entirely correct.

Not so Dianne! She was completely unable to forgive and forget, no doubt exacerbated by their having been twins. She blamed Gerry fairly and squarely for the whole incident and in that, strictly speaking, she was correct. There were only two bits that she had blanked from her mind. One was that the two girls had egged Gerry along, when they should have done their collective best to have stopped him. The second was that, caught up in their own distress, they had done nothing to find Daphne when they were on the upturned boat. This last would have changed little but nevertheless she blamed Gerry and would continue to blame him for what had happened. And despite Millie's remonstrations he would persist with the 'L'il Sis' bit as though it was some uncontrollable tic.

She took out her frustrations very largely on boys of all ages, at least one of her teachers and any other man who would turn a blind eye to her young age. She liked boys best because they were mostly virgins and did not know what they were doing. She would titillate them along and they were embarrassed when it all happened too quickly.

She would then laugh and humiliate them. Word soon got round and she found she had no takers, so had to resort to older men. The problem with them was that they did know what they were doing and it hurt both mentally and physically. She didn't always have the upper hand!

***

Whilst Gerry and Dianne caught the same bus to school it was some time before Gerry realised that she didn't always get off it when they got there. He started to keep a watch on her but nothing untoward appeared to happen. He forgot about it and was more interested in discussing the merits of different brands of beer with his mates than in what his little sister was doing. Then he noticed it again. She was not always there. She was playing truant!

This left Gerry with a dilemma. He was not dishonest by nature, as he knew she could be, and whilst he was willing to go along with her tantrums this was different. By the same token he was not willing to give her away of his own free will. He would tackle her about it.

"Hey, Sis," he said in his jovial manner when they were alone at home, "are you playing truant from school?"

Dianne went white but as always, she deemed attack the best form of defence.

"What if I am?"

"You'll have us all in trouble, Mum and Dad too, if you are."

"Am I supposed to care?"

"Yes," said Gerry, and he meant it. Home was home and he for one didn't want it upset. There had been enough trauma recently.

"Why?"

Gerry hadn't got an answer for this one, but Dianne was carrying on.

"Are you going to tell on me?"

"No. Not unless I have to."

"Good. You better not."

"And what you going to do about if I do, Li'l Sis?"

She came very close to him and hissed in his ear, "If you do, then one day, I will assuredly kill you! Just as you killed Daphne."

Gerry was unfazed and laughed it off. She had threatened to kill him before, increasingly since Daphne's death, but more recently for some minor transgression of her own warped code of ethics, but it hadn't happened yet.

Dianne had not yet learnt and understood that retribution catches up with those who think they are being clever and her truancy caught up with her in due time. The family were convulsed by the affair and Gerry had no choice but to tell what he knew about it, which in truth was not much more than that it was happening.

He knew nothing of the petty thieving. This was something of a side line of Dianne's and was really no more than 'getting one over on the world in general'. It was a measure of her innate skill that she was never caught. In her wilder dreams she even considered making a career of it! The way she carried on with boys had reached Gerry but he kept that to himself. He did wonder if she was really out to kill him but hoped she was not. Life returned to a sort of normality.

***

Gerry saw himself as the natural successor to the Wear crown to follow on from what his father and grandfather had created. He had worked in the factory in his school holidays and was well known amongst the works staff. However, like Muriel before him he was surprised to discover that, whilst his father had a place for him, it was up to him to get there.

"The old adage is that if you want to be a master of craftsmen then you must be a master of their crafts," Henry had said when his official entry into the business was being discussed. "Whilst perhaps not strictly true nowadays, the principle still holds good."

"But, Dad, I can't go in there and just work with them. I shall be a laughing stock."

"You may be but that's for you to get over. They'll think all the more of you for not just swanning in as the high and mighty son of the boss and you just might learn something along the way. Find out what makes the working man tick, if nothing else."

Gerry was appalled. This did not fit with his bon viveur lifestyle at all.

"And start and finish with them?" he asked tentatively.

"But of course."

It was bad enough having to drag himself out of bed in time for school at nine o'clock but to be working at seven thirty was impossible.

"And sober with it," added his father as though his thoughts were an open book.

This was not quite what Gerry had planned for himself. Perhaps he should re-think his options? He had written off the idea of going to university in part because he doubted his A-level grades would be good enough but also because he was fed up with being educated and wanted to get out into the big wide world and stamp his mark on it. Maybe a few cushy years at university would be a good idea? After all, from listening to his friends talk it seemed as though it was just one long party; he never heard of them actually doing any work! No! He couldn't face all that and, in any case, he was too late for this year's intake so he would have to spend a gap year doing – what? Probably working in the factory. So he might as well start now and get on with it.

"Ah," said the foreman when Gerry presented himself on that first Monday morning of full employment. "At least you know where the mess room and toilets are so I don't have to show you those. 'Fraid you'll not have a lot to do for a couple of days. We've got a bit of a panic on to get a job out."

Gerry grunted. He wasn't used to being ordered about. He also felt a complete lemon mostly just standing around when everyone else was knuckled down to the job in hand. He did wonder whether it was done deliberately in order to put him, the boss's son, in his place but then things did get better.

"Putting you alongside Derek," he was told on Wednesday morning. "Good fitter, probably forgotten more than you'll ever know so you listen to what he tells you. It'll give you an insight into how all these bits we make go together and how essential it is that they're all made correctly."

"Don't mind him," said Derek when they were together, "Barks worse than his bite but he is fair; I'll say that much for him."

"I'll get used to it."

"You'll have to. That right you're t' gaffer's son?"

"Yeah."

Gerry had hoped to avoid this issue until he had to. He now had to.

"S'pose I could call it promotion having you under my wing."

"I doubt it and I shouldn't think there's any extra money in it."

Gerry knew from his school day experiences in the factory that the men were only interested in money and sex, usually in that order.

"Sure not to be. Just hold me up you will, but we all have to learn some time, so let's be getting on with it. Can you read a drawing?"

"Maybe."

"OK. See all these part numbers down the side here?"

Gerry nodded.

"Go and see that miserable old git in the stores and tell him you want all that lot. And here there's a list of all the nuts and bolts we shall need. If you lucky an' he's pushed he might let you sort them out yourself, but then again he might not. 'Pends whether his missus let him have it, last night or not."

The storekeeper had obviously been deprived last night as Gerry had to wait while he ponderously sorted out all the items, including the bolts, but he did eventually return with a trolley load of bits that he hoped were correct and what Derek wanted. Then they could get down to the assembly work. By lunchtime Gerry was feeling a bit more as though he belonged and thoughts of mutiny were banished. As previously he found the factory staff a decent bunch to whom he could relate and all of them seemed to accept the slightly difficult position he found himself in.

***

It had taken a bit longer than Muriel had hoped but, as predicted, Mrs McTaggart did eventually decide to retire a couple of years before Gerry joined the firm on a permanent basis. Before she did so she had an embarrassing, for him, chat with Henry. She had never been one to mince her words.

"I don't know and," she stressed, "don't want to know what the relationship is between you and Muriel."

Henry looked alarmed.

"Yes, you're right to look alarmed, but I think she's up to no good."

"Come again!"

"I reckon she's after my job as office manager, now that I'm retiring."

"What makes you think that?"

Henry was playing for time.

"Mr Wear, humour me by not pretending that I'm stupid."

"I was suggesting no such thing."

"Huh."

Mrs McTaggart could put all sorts of emphasis in that simple word.

"So, Mrs McT, just what are you saying?"

"Several things. First, I don't think she's up to the job. She came here as worse than a complete rookie and in fairness she has got her act together and copes pretty well. Second, and this is between these four walls only, I'm not sure just how honest she is."

"That's a big accusation."

"I know and I've got no real reason or evidence for saying it. It's a gut reaction and hopefully wrong; but I thought you ought to know."

"Thank you for that. I shall bear it in mind."

"Bet you don't!"

Mrs McTaggart had left before Henry could think of a suitable riposte and after she had gone, he spent a lot of time staring vacantly at the wall thinking over what she had said. He was under considerable pressure from both Millie and Muriel, both of whom he loved in equal measure, to promote the latter into the position of office

235

manager and like Mrs McT he had his doubts about it. Also like her he could give no concrete reason for those doubts.

He discussed it with Millie. He discussed more about the business with Millie than anyone would have thought as he found she had a surprisingly incisive brain underneath the fluffy exterior. In this instance he got exactly what he expected. Muriel was expecting the job, so go for it. It might go some way towards helping her overcome the loss of Daphne. Despite her avowed aversion to being a mother she had mourned Daphne long after the rest of them and also long after what seemed a decent period of mourning. This was real and not to be confused with the anger that had invaded Dianne's life.

Instead Henry dithered.

There was something of a celebratory party when Mrs McTaggart left but whether it was in thanks for the work she had put in over the years or because she was finally going was hard to tell! Either way Henry said all the right things but said nothing about a replacement. In truth he wondered if a follow on was absolutely necessary now that a good deal of the work was computerised.

A fortnight later with Muriel having been in a non-stop sulk, both at home and in the office, he had little choice but to make the appointment she had been waiting for.

***

A spin-off from Gerry starting work at the factory was that it acted as a catalyst for Dianne to sort her life out.

236

Although she would never have admitted it to a living soul, she was becoming bored with the music, disco and boys scene. What had seemed so glamorous when she ceased to be a child was now starting to be tawdry and superficial. She wanted more.

With the long age gap between them she had never really been able to compete directly with Gerry at school. In sport she was always in a lower age range and in school he was always those several years ahead of her in the natural order of things. Now that Gerry had gone to work and was prepared to get his hands dirty for the sake of the future, she was going to leapfrog all that.

"I'm going to go to university," she announced to everyone in general but aimed at Gerry in particular.

He was the first to respond.

"Bully for you, Li'l Sis," he said.

"And when I've done that there'll be less of the Li'l Sis bit, in fact none of it at all."

"We shall see," grinned Gerry, gratuitously adding, "Li'l Sis."

If looks could have killed, Gerry would have died just then. Millie came to the rescue.

"That's marvellous but you're going to have to work a lot harder than you are now if you want to do that."

"I know and I shall."

Muriel was daydreaming and not listening attentively. The mere thought that a daughter of hers, a granddaughter of her mother's, might go to university was almost unimaginable.

"Do you think you can?"

"Course I can. I'm not going straight into that silly old factory of yours. I want to see the world, experience it, feel it, know about it…" She was getting carried away with herself and she knew it, but she had seen a vision of what might be possible and she wanted it.

"I'd have thought you'd felt quite a lot of it already," said Gerry mischievously.

"Shut up," she said and stuck her tongue out at him.

"So which university do you have in mind," said Millie, in a further effort to defuse the situation.

"Don't know," she said. "Haven't got that far but as far away from you lot as possible so that I can live a life of my own."

"We shall miss you," said Muriel.

"We shan't," said Gerry.

"Well, you've got plenty of time to decide about that! It's years away yet but I'm going. Yes, I'm definitely going."

As was his wont David sat and watched the argument ricochet to and fro without fully understanding what it was all about. It was obvious that if you went to university, you went somewhere else and the possibility of Dianne not being here to argue about every tiny thing was a cloud with a silver lining indeed.

Dianne was as good as her word, to the astonishment of her family and even more so of her teachers and school. No longer the truancy. No longer the couldn't care less attitude. No longer the mini-miniskirts, the yawning cleavage and boys on demand. She was there to learn and learn she was determined to do. For once she had an aim in her life, and with that she was unstoppable.

Chapter 8

There was a further knock at the door and his mother was coming up the stairs laden with her basket and a variety of supermarket bags. David raised his eyes to heaven and Jennifer went to welcome her.

"Ah, you're back, are you?" Mrs Wear said as she arrived somewhat breathless at the top.

"Yes, I am that," said Jennifer but without the heart to make any reciprocal comment. She looked over the top of her at David and said, "I need to go along to the shop, I'll just pop out now." And disappeared down the stairs before any more could be said.

She felt it best to leave mother and son to sort themselves out. She did need to go to the shop and that was soon done, but the centre of Brampton was small and never exactly crowded. She soon felt conspicuous just drifting around, so she walked purposefully back up the hill to where she had sat last time when she needed to think. Fortunately, the sun was shining or she would have needed a coat on this January day. She felt she was beginning to make a habit of sitting on public benches when trying to assess her life.

By the time she got back, his mother's car had gone and so had most of the morning. David was in grumpy mood.

"What made you disappear like a fox with the hounds behind it?" he grumbled.

"Well it was pretty obvious she didn't think much of my being here. 'Ah, you're back, are you?' is hardly a 'pleased to see you' type remark."

"She can often be like that. Take no notice."

"I don't yet know her well enough to know that, now do I?"

"I suppose not," he continued to grumble.

"So I thought I was best out of the way. Anyway, I did need to go to the shop."

"Took you a long time."

"Well I didn't know how long a mother and son tête-à-tête was going to last, did I?" She was beginning to get cross now. He took the hint and relented.

"I suppose not," he admitted grudgingly. "Sorry."

"OK," she allowed. "Where were we?"

"You needing shock absorbers." And he grinned.

She was relieved but she wanted to move on. "So what happens now?"

"Nothing." He spat the word out and the hard look returned to his face.

"Nothing? You can't just sit back and do nothing. Goodness knows for how much she's robbing you. And spare a thought for poor Christine who's having to work in the lion's den as though nothing were happening. For whatever reasons, you may not want the police, but do nothing? No way."

"I can and I will. Christine will cope. She will have to."

"Maybe."

"I know her better than you do."

"Maybe."

The air was electric and the silence intense but it was down to David.

"I need to see Dad before I do anything. Another day, another week, won't break us and, in that time I should be able to hobble about a bit, and you can chauffeur me to the family bungalow. Now there's a jolly prospect for you." The sarcasm in the last sentence was apparent.

"Always ready to oblige, sir," she said in mock humility. "It will be a pleasure to meet your parents at the ancestral home. Would sir like me to obtain a suitable uniform in the meantime?"

"Huh, that would be fun but for entirely other reasons." There was a lecherous glint in his eye. "But it won't be necessary. And don't expect to enjoy it."

"Why ever not? Seems perfectly normal to me."

"Normal it is not, but that's enough for now. What did your shopping bring us for lunch?"

It was obvious that Jennifer was not going to get any more out of him. Once again, she was going to have to possess herself in patience until he chose to tell her more. Or until she managed to glean it from him little by little. She thought that was unlikely but she would pigeonhole away the odd snippets and one day they might all come together and make sense. Ignoring the question about lunch she carried on:

"Unless it's absolutely vital I don't think I should go into your office this afternoon. It would make it difficult for Christine, if she did decide to go in today after all. It will be easier for her once she's got used to this crazy idea of yours to do nothing, when I'm sure all her instincts cry out for some action to stop it. If she hasn't gone in, there's the further snag that I should have the undivided attention of Muriel, although I expect I could cope with her."

"I know damn well that you could," said David. "No, it isn't one hundred per cent vital even if desirable. No, Monday will do. I can gather my thoughts a bit more in the meantime."

During Saturday David made valiant efforts at making himself mobile on his crutches. On Sunday he finally overcame his fear of the stairs when Jennifer was able to help him down and out to her car.

"Boy, is that nice to get a bit of fresh air," he said as he came out into the street.

With some difficulty she got him into the car complete with stiff leg and arm in a sling.

"Getting you out may be entirely different," she joked. "You may have to eat you lunch sitting in there."

"I'll chance it," he said. "I'd prefer to be doing something more exciting with you but at least I shall see that the world still exists."

They drove with his window wide open 'to get some fresh air', as he said. Jennifer wished she had put on a thicker coat. With David's directions they drove up to the bungalow that she had seen during her first foray around Carlisle. What a good thing she hadn't called. The mere thought raised the hairs on the back of her neck. She was quite sure she would not be where she was now if she had.

Somebody had been out and opened the gates and on David's instructions she drove in as though she owned the place. As compared to Valley Court, driving in was a misnomer. The driveway was short, not much more than a large car's length and finished in front of a double up and over door to the garage that was itself attached to the bungalow. With a path straight from the front door to the gate the front garden was made up in wholly traditional suburban style. Her first instinct was that it wasn't much like David, but then she supposed that whilst it might have been David's home it was certainly not how he chose to live now. Mrs Wear appeared from the front door to greet them.

"Front door treatment, eh? Didn't know it still worked," David whispered to her.

"Sounds just like home," she whispered back, and with that they proceeded to the delicate but strenuous task of getting David out of the car. With David upright, if a bit wobbly, they could both turn to greet Mrs Wear properly. With difficulty they negotiated the front door and its steps and made it into a large lounge overlooking the back garden. David's father struggled up out of a deep leather armchair and took a tentative step towards them. He had greying hair and a slightly vacant look to his face. He was about the same height as David and wore a green tweed suit for which baggy was an understatement. He certainly looked older than Jennifer guessed his years to be. After making sure David wasn't likely to fall over, she went forward to meet him.

"I'm Jennifer," she said. "I fear you may have heard a lot about me."

"Indeed I have. All good though. Pleasure to meet you." It was the voice that took her by surprise. She had expected an old man's thin reedy voice but this was a sonorous deep tone, almost military, more like the local nabobs she had heard at her father's pheasant shoots.

"All good?" she queried. "There must have been some bad bits somewhere."

"Don't recall any. Now Millie, get us some drinks will you. What do you drink? Jennifer, is it? Not Jen, or Jennie, or something?"

"I answer to all three but prefer it in full if possible and a whisky with some water would be fine." She didn't often drink whisky but it seemed the right thing to ask for.

"Ha, now there's a drink for a lady," he crowed. "D'ye hear that, Millie? I'll have the same, so will David, even if he shouldn't with whatever pills he's taking. And get whatever you like for yourself. Make it the Jura, will you? That's a malt you know." He said the latter in her direction whereas the rest was as though he was on parade in the officers' mess.

"I know and I like it," she responded.

"Ha," was all he said before collapsing back into his chair and resuming the 'elderly gentleman at his club' stance. The silence that followed was like that said to follow a catastrophe before the screaming and wailing starts. Once again it was David who came to her rescue.

"If I get down into one of those," he said indicating the deep armchairs and sofa, "you may never get me out

245

again. Can you pull out that chair in the corner? If the shock of using it doesn't cause it to collapse."

His father grinned a bit sheepishly at the joke but said nothing. Jennifer was a bit lost at the change of tone after the initial banter but did as she was told and carefully installed David in his chair. If it was needed, and it was, the ice was further broken by the return of Mrs Wear with the drinks set out on a tray. She had a gin and tonic for herself, Jennifer noticed. Polite conversation followed, with Mrs Wear going off twice, very apologetically, to look at the lunch. David's father hardly spoke. It was all very odd.

Lunch followed a similar pattern except for a lively outburst when Mr Wear wanted to know more about the farm, its size, crops and stock all in so much detail that Jennifer found it hard to produce all the relevant facts from memory. And then came a return to the vacant old man syndrome. At the end of the meal David said, "Now, Jen, if you can get me into the study and sitting comfortably in a chair there, then Dad and I can talk about what we need talk about."

"All very mysterious," boomed his father and set off into a room on the opposite side of the hall. So Jennifer did as she was bidden, although she had a funny feeling that David was putting on a bit of an act for his parents' benefit. He seemed to be managing remarkably well, even if the effort was obviously taking it out of him. Study was not quite the right word for the room she took him to. It was set up and equipped very much more along the lines of a business office, but it was patently not used very often.

There was a generally musty smell, the calendar on the wall was a year out of date, and there was a sort of *Marie Celeste* feel to the place.

When she came back Mrs Wear was clearing the table and appeared flustered to see her. Each looked at the other in a nonplussed way, each apparently waiting for the other to speak first. Jennifer opened the batting.

"Come on," she said, "I'll give you a hand to clear this lot away and help you wash up."

An expression of relief came to Mrs Wear's face which said as clearly as though it was written down, *Gosh, you are normal, after all; not some high and mighty squire's daughter*. But she said, "That's kind of you, my dear, but most of it will go in the dishwasher. There's only the oddments will need washing."

"OK. Then they won't take us long. You stack the dishwasher as you know how you like it and I'll carry from here." She felt she sounded just like her mother.

Mrs Wear went off happily into the kitchen and Jennifer took her time gathering up some plates before following her. After the typical farm kitchen at Valley Court with its Aga, uneven stone-flagged floor, immense table in the middle, large dresser along one side, dog baskets, cat beds and all the detritus lying around that had not reached the farm office or someplace else, this was an eye opener. It was obviously Mrs Wear's pride and joy and was spotless to boot. Operating theatres or a space ship control centre came into her mind.

"My," she said, "this is quite some kitchen. I've never seen anything quite like it."

"Do you like it?" said Mrs Wear happily. "I had it done last year. It was a sort of anniversary present to ourselves. We needed something to take our minds off things." She suddenly looked fearful as though she had said too much but added wistfully, "He didn't take much interest though. Left it all to me; said I could have whatever I wanted; he would just sign the cheque. So I did!" She hunched her shoulders and grinned with her eyes.

"I shall never be able to look our kitchen in the face again," laughed Jennifer. "It looks just like the ones in the catalogues. All this stainless steel, and are these real marble work surfaces?"

Mrs Wear nodded her head vigorously in affirmation. "But I don't think he realises!" Again, she hunched her shoulders and grinned with her eyes. Jennifer suddenly realised the attraction of this Mrs Tiggy-Winkle of a woman. She must have been quite a stunner in her youth. They carried on clearing and washing up the few remaining pots and pans, and every comment that Jennifer made further endeared her to Mrs Wear.

"And do you do the garden as well?" she asked, looking out of the kitchen window at an equally immaculate garden.

"Well, nearly. Somebody comes in to mow the grass, but I do most of the rest of it."

"Can you walk me round it?" Jennifer asked, knowing full well the pleasure it gave her mother to walk visitors round her garden.

Mrs Wear beamed. "Would you like me to? Really?" Almost as though she couldn't believe her own ears.

"I'd love to. I'm no expert, mind. I just about know a rose from a pansy and that's it," she joked, well knowing that this was actually very near to the truth.

"Just minute while I put a coat on. Do you want something?"

"No, I'll be OK for a bit. If I get cold, we'll have to come back indoors," she said, thinking that it might be a good excuse if she got out of her depth.

They went out through an equally catalogue-style utility room and again Jennifer inwardly shuddered at the thought of their chaotic 'mudtrap' back at Valley Court. But then she reflected that it was just a simple difference in lifestyle. Almost everyone else she knew had a room full of dog baskets, spare bits of tack, wellies, coats and all the other paraphernalia of living in the country. Here they emerged onto a paved patio still wearing their indoor shoes.

"Oh, that's good to get some fresh air," said Jennifer, echoing David. She breathed deeply. "You know I love helping David and being in his flat but I miss being outside every other minute. Even in the office I seemed to be being sent on errands round the town several times a day." She breathed deeply again.

"I know what you mean. That's one reason why I love my garden so; always a reason to get outside. And since Dad's been at home we don't go anywhere much now." Again, Jennifer could almost feel the brakes come on as they moved into the garden proper. But Mrs Wear was not to be put off entirely.

"You've been a great help to David. I don't fully know how you came across each other, still less how he persuaded you to come all this way to look after him, but – " and she paused. "I think he loves you. Do you love him?"

Jennifer blushed and coloured to the roots of her hair and probably all over, she thought.

"Oh, sorry love, I shouldn't have said that. It just sort of came out."

Jennifer drew herself up, breathed deeply again and gave the only answer she could.

"Yes," she said.

"Ooh, goody, goody," said Mrs Wear and shrugged her shoulders so far up that Jennifer thought her head might disappear altogether like a tortoise. Then she became all serious. "Now we must look round the garden so that we can talk intelligently when we go back in, and you must lose that colour from you face."

Jennifer laughed and breathed a sigh of relief for this common-sense approach. Taking the opportunity given to her, she said, "I love your yellow daisies; there're making a splendid show."

"Yes, it's been a good year for them this year," replied Mrs Wear. They carried on walking round the garden as she extolled this or that plant and commented on where it had come from and whether it liked the soil or not. Jennifer found herself calming down and not having to say very much to keep her prattling away about what was patently a large part of her life.

They were back in the house when the study door opened and David's father came out looking even more vacant than before. Indeed, so much so that even Mrs Wear seemed taken aback. Before flopping down into his accustomed chair he gestured with a languid hand towards the study saying, "I think he needs some help."

Jennifer rushed in to find David sitting in the chair she had left him in, but with a face like thunder and staring fixedly at the spot behind the desk where his father had been sitting. She stopped in her tracks.

"We're leaving; help me up," was all he said. Obediently she did and they struggled into the hall, where his mother was waiting.

As he was not going to say anything, Jennifer felt she must. "I think David wants to get home," she said.

"Pity, but OK," said Mrs Wear, at the same time raising one eyebrow as much to say, *You sort that one out and I'll cope with this one*. She really had a most expressive face.

They struggled to the door and into the car without David saying another word. The pleasantries were left to Jennifer.

"Where do you want to go?" she asked after they had backed out of the gate. "Back to the flat? Do you want to drop into the office? Where?"

"Just drive," he said through gritted teeth. "Turn right at the end of the road."

And so he continued to dictate monosyllabic instructions, but they were given in good time. This took them out of the city and down smaller and smaller lanes with worse and worse surfaces until they finally wound up in a bleak area of saltings and wheeling gulls beside the Solway Firth. It suited David's mood but she did notice that the peremptory nature of his instructions modified as they progressed and, by the time she switched the engine off his voice, at least, sounded back to normal.

She leaned back in the seat.

"And what was that all about?" she said.

Silence.

More silence.

"All right then, I'll start guessing. I know you needed to see your father about the Christine/Muriel bit. Christine's in the clear as she found the problem. That leaves Muriel, and for whatever reason your father wants it all left alone. Now let's think why that might be…"

"OK, OK. If I leave you to it you might just guess right, if it's that obvious. First things first: would you marry me?"

She noticed immediately the *would you marry me* rather than *will you marry me*. He was wholly matter-of-fact about it. It seemed to have nothing to do with his actually wanting to marry her.

"Yes," she said, equally matter-of-factly.

"Foolish but fine. Then you can have some of the story. The rest will have to wait another day."

The gulls continued to wheel and scream, and scudding dark clouds were being driven in from the west. It seemed an appropriate setting for family confessions.

"Surprising as it may seem I had no inkling of this. Naivety, innocence, mental blockage, not seeing what was under my nose, whatever? I claim total ignorance." He tried to raise both hands as in surrender but winced at the pain in his broken one. She sat silent.

"It seems that my much-loved father has been having an affair. No, that's pussyfooting around it. My father has been keeping Muriel as his mistress for years, and I mean years, and my mother has been fully aware of it. Altogether in the same house I suspect, although he didn't actually say so."

Jennifer blanched but remained quiet.

"A ménage à trois?" he muttered to himself and then shook his head in disbelief.

"Anyway, be that as it may, it seems that one way Dad supported his mistress was by employing her in the firm and allowing her to pick up what perks she could along the way over and above her salary. Now Muriel is pretty shrewd and I wouldn't mind betting she's doing very nicely thank you out of T.H. Wear & Co. Ltd. And Dad will have me do nothing, absolutely nothing, to stop what's going on. For old times' sake, you understand. Huh, more likely she's got him by the balls and is blackmailing him over some other bimbo that we don't yet know about. Sorry for the language, by the way."

Jennifer shrugged.

253

"So what do we do about Christine?" he asked, again almost to himself or as though he was thinking out loud.

"We?" she queried.

"Yes, we," he growled.

She wanted to stay quiet but the urge to help overcame her.

"How bad is it?" she asked.

"I don't really know," he answered more reasonably. "I suppose it could be just pin money but somehow I doubt it. She could be doing it just for the hell of it, just to see if she can, but again I doubt it."

He shook his head from side to side as he continued to think it through.

"For what it's worth, Dad says we're insured against employee theft."

"But that's not much use if he won't let you go to the police. The insurance company would never pay up just on your say-so."

"Exactly. Which makes it odd that Dad doesn't consider it a problem and that '*Oh, just claim it on the insurance!*' is all he says. We damned well can't, or rather, he's effectively preventing it."

It was Jennifer's turn to ponder out loud. "It seems a slightly odd thing to insure against in your sort of business. I could understand it in a place like a shop with a lot of cash about and casual employees, but I guess you're like the farm. It's all cheques. There's never any real money around unless you go to the bank and get it."

"You've hit a nail very firmly on the head there," said David. "But I'm not sure it helps us any. How do you manage to think of all these things? I'm sure a farm doesn't have this sort of problem."

"True, but Halliwell's are often on the periphery of them when their clients get caught out," said Jennifer. "Being only a lowly receptionist, I've been even further on the edge, but the office gossip used to keep me up to date."

"I see."

"Now, let me keep guessing for a moment. Did your father carry on a lot of his business from the so-called study at the bungalow?"

"Yes. So what?"

"Hang on a minute. Why did he?"

"I don't really know. He always said it saved him the chore of being like everyone else and going to the office every day."

"Therefore, was Muriel effectively in charge of the admin, at the very least, back at the works, even if she didn't actually run the place?"

"Yes."

"Well? Doesn't that explain a few things? She had free rein to do as she liked, run whatever scam suited her, knowing full well that as long as she didn't get too greedy and create problems for the firm your father, tacitly perhaps, wouldn't mind."

"Steady on, Jen, that's a bit strong."

"Maybe, maybe not. Now going back to where we were, have you actually noticed any shortfalls in cash? Well not actual cash, but receipts generally. Business short of money when it shouldn't be? Anything at all, other than what Christine told you about?" She ran out of suggestions.

"No I haven't, but you could just have a point. Where there's smoke there's usually fire. Actually now, come to think of it, we did have a crisis earlier in the year when I wasn't expecting one but that turned out to be us having seriously over-ordered on a lot of things we didn't immediately need." He seemed relieved by the explanation.

"Hey, but David, that's exactly what I'm talking about. Those were probably the things where she got a good kickback and at the same time she needed the money. Did she go on holiday or anything soon afterwards perhaps?"

"Yes. I think she might have done. You're right. You really are. See how I can't cope without you!"

She ignored the compliment, keeping her mind on the ball.

"Then that's one for Christine to sort out and find out what was what. I presume she worked for you, then?"

"Oh, yes."

"Then she can see what was bought at that time and you can determine whether it was needed or not. Then maybe, just maybe, Christine, using one of her hats can find out what the price differences are. Hopefully, bingo, you'll have something to nail her with."

"Fine, but Dad won't let me."

Jennifer's enthusiasm was deflated. "Well, at least you'll have facts and figures for him."

"Might help," he bemoaned.

"It should, and can we move on? I'm getting cold sitting here."

He shivered. "Yes, so am I. I hadn't realised. Back to the flat I guess."

"Well, you'll have to direct me out. I've a reasonable sense of direction but we might spend the rest of the day getting away from here. Do you come here often?"

"Used to as a kid. Especially on occasions like today. I could get away from it all and let the wind blow my troubles away. It's within cycling distance of home, you see."

"Was life that bad?"

"Sometimes." But he didn't say any more and she left it at that. He didn't say any more about marrying her, either.

Chapter 9

Jennifer was surprised to discover how long it took David to recover from the revelations about his father. Despite the sometimes abrupt and brusque exterior she was finding a sensitive and diffident person inside. She could almost watch his pondering for some days before he made the decision to take her at least partly into his confidence.

Eventually and quite unexpectedly one breakfast he said, "I need to tell you a bit more about Muriel."

"That's a good start to the day then," she quipped.

"No, it's not at all but I'm serious."

"OK, if you must."

"I don't honestly know when Muriel first appeared on the scene but she's certainly been around as long as I can remember. Part of the family. Always there, slightly shadowy, somewhere in the background. More like an *au pair* or a nanny. I suppose she was young once when I was little. I suppose also she was probably very attractive or at least to my father and, it would appear, also, to my mother." He grimaced.

"And so one thing led to another as they say," said Jennifer, intrigued. This was the stuff of novels, not real life. Not her life anyway.

"I guess so. The strange thing is that I never cottoned on to it. Never. Not until now when Dad literally spelled it out. I can only suppose it was just that she was so much part of the family that she became actual family, at least as far as I was concerned. Just what the three of them got up to I shudder to think but it must have worked somehow, probably because she was willing and managed to be very discreet. As I've told you my childhood was a bit miserable at times and anyway, I tended to be a loner. Always doing my own thing, not being part of a gang or anything like that."

"Sounds a bit like me. Never wanting to be part of the big picture. Always knowing what I didn't want to do rather than what I did."

"I can't quite imagine that," said David. "You seem, you've proved even, that you can fit into any scenario."

"Depends whether I want to or, more usually, not want to. I suppose I do need to know all this?"

"Yes, then it won't come as too much of a shock because I fear Christine is going to need some explanation."

In due course that did indeed prove to be the case, or at least David made it work that way, because following the passing of a surreptitious message by Jennifer, Christine was on their doorstep one morning shortly afterwards. This time Jennifer was ready and had the coffee waiting. Christine was patently nervous but not as bad as the last time and was prepared to wait for David to do the talking. Once the pleasantries were over and they had settled down to their mugs of coffee, David began.

"I have discovered what's been happening. It's not a happy story and I'm going to take the risk of telling you it as it is, or at least as much as you need to know. Quite where we go from there I don't know and to some extent that may depend on you."

Christine jerked her head up in surprise but said nothing.

"The long and the short of it is that Muriel and my father have been having an affair for years and one way he paid for it was to give her a job in the firm and let her make a 'profit' for herself where she could. When I taxed him, he knew all about it but not all the gory details."

Christine's mouth had dropped open in total astonishment although she was completely unaware of the fact. She let out a long "Aaaah." David hurried on.

"The bad news is that he won't let me do anything about it. Nothing at all."

Christine's body language was working overtime as she accepted this piece of news and Jennifer felt decidedly sorry for her.

"So, my initial instruction to you to do nothing still stands and very much so," he emphasised, "but so does my need to know just how bad the situation is. Without that I don't know what, if anything, I can do about it."

Christine seemed to come out of a trance.

"So you're telling me that this has been going on for, well, years and your father and you are going to do nothing about it?"

"That is just what I am telling you."

"Why?"

The question was shot out as though from a gun and both David and Jennifer jumped. David seemed prepared for it.

"Because, and this is the galling bit, my father says so."

Christine looked at him through narrowed, questioning eyes but he didn't notice. He had to take the next step.

"Again, put quite simply, he holds the purse strings. He has a total controlling interest in the company and is prepared to use it to enforce his wishes. I have always been very much a minority and whilst I may have done the outfit some good he is not prepared to recognise that where this is concerned. He even threatened to kick me out if I didn't agree."

It was Jennifer's turn to look aghast.

"So what happens now?" they both asked more or less together.

"Military planners say that information is everything. The more you can find out about what is or has been happening can only help. If it really is peanuts, which I doubt, then I may go along with it. Only may, notice. If, as I suspect, it is serious, when I know how bad the situation is, then I can make a decision as to whether I have another go at Dad or I go to the police and damn the consequences. But, and it's also a very big but, Muriel is not to know that we know. Nor is anybody else for that matter."

"You mean all that, don't you?" said Christine.

"Yes, I do, I'm afraid."

"I'm not entirely sure I can go along with it. I ought to resign."

It was now David's turn to blanche. He had not bargained for that possibility.

"Now, Christine, please…" he began.

Christine smiled.

"Don't panic. I'm not going to. It could be very interesting, who said bookkeeping was a chore? I'll do the best I can and, believe me, I can be very discreet."

"Phew, that's better. You had me worried there," he said and as an afterthought, "And thank you."

Christine seemed to have made up her mind and be satisfied with the situation and changed the subject.

"You're looking remarkably fit compared to when I last saw you. When are you coming back into the office? I know you can't drive like that but I'm sure Jennifer here can drive you."

"No, I can't and she can, but to be honest I've been using it as an excuse to sit tight and think about you know who and plan some possible course of action."

"You mean that despite what you have just said, you actually have a plan?"

They all laughed. It lightened the mood and acted as confirmation that Christine was very much on their side.

"And it also allowed me to see you away from the office without it being an issue if she happened to find out you had been here. Give it a few more days and I shall be back to see for myself what you have all been up to. But I have to say that I am appalled how doing anything seems to take it out of me. But I shall be back and soon."

"Good. Speaking of which, I must be elsewhere too. I'll do the best I can for you. Both of you."

She glanced at Jennifer, smiled, then rose and gathered up her bag and the few papers she had got out of it.

"Thanks," he said and they heard the street door close behind her.

They sat and silently looked at each other. The conversation had taken a turn that Jennifer had been waiting for and she leapt at the opportunity to get something off her chest that had been bugging her for some little while but she did it in some trepidation. She did not want the answer she might well get.

"Speaking of which," she began, "were you serious about getting back to the office?"

"Yes," he said.

"Then what about me?"

"What about you?"

"Well it's one thing while I'm here looking after you and chauffeuring you around but, once you're back at work, I'm redundant. And anyway, I've got a job I'm supposed to be going back to."

David went pale again.

"But you don't have to," he said ingenuously.

Jennifer felt herself getting cross and she didn't like the feeling.

"Aside from the fact that the end of my sabbatical, which you so neatly organised for me, whilst not quite in sight is not that far over the horizon, there is the small matter of money. I was just about skint when I got back

263

from Africa and you going and breaking your arm and then my hurtling up and down the M6 hasn't quite given me the chance to refill the coffers, you know."

David considered.

"I suppose you have a point," he said. "I guess the firm will have to pay you for services rendered in some way or another. I can't let you up sticks and leave."

"Now hang on a minute, David, we've just been through how your father has used the company to maintain his mistress. You don't seriously think I'm going to put myself in the same situation, do you?"

"You're not my mistress."

"Do not split hairs." She articulated the words very slowly and carefully. "You know perfectly well what I mean."

"It's not the same."

"Yes, it is. Or at least it will be in the eyes of most other people. Especially those who know and there's bound be some out there who do."

"Well you can't just up sticks and go, can you?"

"What else am I supposed to do? No way am I going to be the little lady back home or more likely your bit of stuff on the side."

This really started them shouting at each other.

"Now you just hang on a minute, Jen –"

"Don't you Jen me. You know I like my name in full."

"OK. Miss High 'n' Mighty Jennifer Suffram. We can work this out. There's no need to fly off the handle."

"Yes, there is when you suggest that I should follow in your father's footsteps. Who's the third one going to be. Eh? Let's make a threesome of it. Come on who is it?"

They were both appalled at what they were saying but neither felt able to back down.

"Well, you better get out then if that's what you want. I told you once before to bugger off back to your fancy Cotswold people but you didn't go."

This was too much for Jennifer.

"Well I'm bloody well going this time." And before any more could be said, or shouted, she flounced into the bedroom and started stuffing clothes into her rucksack with awe-inspiring savagery. Within minutes she was heading down the stairs towards the front door.

"Goodbye," she shouted as she went, "And you can take that stupid grin off your face before it sets."

She slammed the door behind her, threw her bags into her car, was for a split second surprised she had not damaged her car by slamming its door with such force, started the engine and roared out of Brampton in a cloud of pebbles and dust. She imagined David looking around the empty space in his flat, probably still grinning stupidly and wondering what he should do next. Silly she knew, but it gave her a childish pleasure. She stopped before she reached the motorway and phoned her mother.

"Hello Mum. As usual I've got it wrong. I'm on my way home. See you later."

"But darling..." began her mother.

"Stuff it," she said and cut the connection.

265

After staring at the gently purring instrument for a few minutes she said to the empty house around her, "Give her a couple of hours and she'll be on the phone for advice."

What Jennifer expected to be the return call from Valley Court turned out to be David. "And you can stuff it too!" she yelled down the line, with deliberate pleasure pressed the red button, slammed the car into gear and set off with total disregard for any speed limits. Her phone continued to ring at irregular intervals but she ignored it. Her mother or David she cared not. She had to stop at Killington Lake for petrol and it was here that the first iota of doubt began to infiltrate her mind. No. He had said bugger off and she was doing just that. She drove on. Her phone continued to ring.

By the time she reached Charnock Richard these small molehills of doubt were beginning to become quite large heaps of earth. She decided she needed advice. She thought about Julie back in the office but her time would be limited by work and anyway Jennifer knew she wasn't really interested. 'I told you so,' would probably be the maximum sympathy to be had in that quarter. It would have to be her mother, but how would she react after what she had just said? Should she, shouldn't she? In the end she dialled the number three times and rang off before it could ring the other end. Or she thought she had; in reality it had given the odd tinkle for no apparent reason and her mother, being a very sensible person, had guessed what was going on.

Finally, she let it ring but was all set to give up if any other member of the family should have answered it. She

266

needn't have worried. They all had strict instructions not answer when next it rang properly. When it was answered Jennifer was all of a rush.

"Oh Mum, I'm sorry for what I said just now but he told me to bugger off and I'm doing that but is it right? I'm halfway home, well, nearly, and I shall be back soon. Mum?"

"Now calm down, darling, and tell me what's happened."

"Well, nothing's actually happened."

"OK. So, what's the problem?" Her mother could have infinite patience.

"It's what's going to happen. Or rather what he wants me to be."

"And that is?"

"I can't tell you."

"Why not?

"It would be betraying family secrets."

"Does that matter if you're buggering off, as you so succinctly put it?"

"Yes. No. I'm on my way. See you soon."

She rang off and started to drive again. As she drove her molehill of doubt was beginning to reach slag heap proportions. She began to think that David was right. She was a spoilt brat whose life to date was not in the world as it was lived by most people. At a more mundane level she found she was also worrying as to how David was going to cope without her. She knew he was, as yet, in no state to look after himself on a permanent basis. Knutsford Services loomed and she pulled in. She had reached

267

decision time. Travel any further and she would have no choice but to go home complete with her tail between her legs exactly as she had foretold.

After an equal amount of 'shall I, shan't I?' she finally let David's number ring. There was no reply! She stared at her mobile in total disbelief. He had to be there. He couldn't possibly be anywhere else. She tried it again – same result. She rang Valley Court in a panic.

"Mum? I've got to go back. I've tried to phone him and there's no reply. I'm sure he must have fallen and hurt himself. He can't get to the phone or something." She ran out of breath.

"Now steady on, Jennifer," came the very sensible voice of her mother. "He could just be in the loo or out of arm's reach of the phone."

"I suppose so."

"Or he could simply be playing hard to get."

"Bastard."

"Jennifer, language, language."

"Sorry, Mum, it sort of slipped out."

"You couldn't blame him."

"Huh."

She then tried David again. Same result. She fumed and went for a cup of coffee. It was a long forty minutes later before she got a reply. It was such a surprise that the 'poor little me' voice that she had intended to use had deserted her. In any case, whilst the call was answered, he didn't speak.

"David. Are you all right?"

"Yes." Deadpan voice.

"You haven't fallen or anything?"

"No."

"David? Can I come back?"

"Perhaps." Again, without expression

This was too much. Frustration took over.

"What do you mean? Perhaps?"

"Just that."

"What?"

"Well I've no means of actually stopping you coming back to Brampton if you wish to do so."

"Are you saying you don't want me to come back? Or that you won't let me in if I do?"

"No."

"Then I'm on my way."

And following her newfound tradition of abruptly cutting off calls she phoned home to say she was going back causing considerable relief in that quarter. Lovers' tiff, her mother reported to Simon and Paul. Now as she retraced the miles her anxieties went entirely into reverse. Did David want her back? Should she have stuck to the original plan and buggered off home? She rang him again.

"Are you sure you want me to come back?"

"Yeah, if you like."

"Positive?"

"Yeah." Was he deliberately sounding doubtful?

"See you soon."

It was the best she was going to get. She had a nagging fear that she might be driving back down this way again in a few hours. She crept slowly into the triangular square hoping that there was no one about who might have witnessed her abrupt departure earlier in the day. All seemed quiet with no faces that she recognised. To her surprise the door was still in one piece – she had quite expected that she might have broken its remaining glass. She tried it tentatively and it opened. She went in and there was David standing at the top of the stairs and a smile right across his face and possibly round the back as well. She roared up those stairs.

"Oh David. I've been such an idiot."

"I'd agree with that."

"You're not supposed to."

"Always tell the truth, it's easier in the long run."

"I ought to hit you."

"No. The other way round. If I was able I ought to put you over my knee and spank you – hard – for being such a bloody fool as not to understand."

"Promises. Promises."

They both laughed and the tension broke.

"Honestly, David, do you think we can pick up where we left off?

"Well, I for one am going to have a damned good shot at it. I just hope you'll join me in the effort. Go and get your bags, sort them back onto the shelves, then we'll have something to eat and take it from there."

"You mean there's food?"

Jennifer was amazed.

"Oh, yes. But ask no questions."

"OK."

And she went off to get her rucksack and case. Trying to make her clothes presentable after the manner in which they had been treated before she left was another matter entirely, but she was sure that could wait. The continuation of the conversation that had brought them to this point was also for another day but inevitably it had to take place.

It was David who started it both very carefully and very formally the following day.

"You remember what we were talking about yesterday?"

"How could I forget?"

"Yeah, well I've been thinking. You gave me quite a lot of time to do that."

Jennifer smiled wanly.

"The thing is you could be right and I hadn't thought of it. They're not talking in the works are they, likening father to son and all that?"

"No, I don't think so. I think they just treat it as it is, but if you 'find a place for me'." She waggled her fingers to indicate the inverted commas. "Then, I think they might talk, and with good reason as I guess most of them know something of Muriel's position."

"Probably," he said morosely, "but I'm not like my father and nobody shall ever liken me to him. No, we have to find some other way round this. Anyway, in the short term I shall need a chauffeur if nothing else."

"And then I can go back to my proper job?" she deliberately taunted him.

"No, you cannot," he said loudly, but with obvious care not to shout. "Somehow we have to find a way round this one and we will."

271

"Oh, goody, I do love you," she giggled, kissed him and the tension that was starting to build again was over.

"I tell you what," she continued, "I'll let you hobble back into the office for part of a day this week. Then we will go south for a long weekend so that you can see Valley Court properly and meet my parents so that at least they can meet this man that I've run off with!"

"Might be easier to break the other arm," he said.

"I'll do it for you if you say that again. Parents aren't that bad. Mum, as we have repeatedly said, is a very sensible person and the last thing she will do is embarrass you. Me, maybe. But you? No. Dad will follow her lead. Brother Paul is the one most likely to put both wellie-shod feet into it."

"I capitulate and a change of scene would probably do us both good."

And so it was arranged. David did indeed have a hobble round his office and factory and was greeted effusively by all concerned. Telephone calls to Valley Court created a considerable tizzy there but Jennifer was blissfully unaware of all that.

The journey south proved very long for both of them. It seemed they stopped at pretty well every service area for David to stretch his leg, go to the toilets, re-sling his plastered arm or something. Both their tempers were frayed again by the time they reached Jennifer's home, egged along by both being nervous of the reception they might receive. They need not have worried. As expected, Jennifer's mother had risen to her reputation of being very sensible and had the whole household under control to say and do the right things. An evening meal that could have been very stilted passed off with aplomb and Jennifer breathed a large sigh of relief that they all, including Paul, seemed to have taken to David in the same way that she had. It had been a long day and David was glad to leave the family on their own and depart for an early bed, his only complaint being that he would be lonely without Jennifer to share it with him.

"You can't have everything even if I shall be lonely too!" was all the sympathy he got.

"I like him." Although said by her mother, she spoke for them all when Jennifer returned to the family gathering afterwards.

"Thank you," said Jennifer demurely. "I hoped you would." But she was very relieved nonetheless.

"And what do you plan for tomorrow?"

"Tomorrow," she said, "I shall pinch the Land Rover." She cocked a head at Paul, who nodded. "And we shall go for a tour of the farm."

"He seems surprisingly knowledgeable about farming," commented her father to no one in particular. "Especially hill sheep farms. Hadn't expected that."

"I plan to find out if he's just being clever or he does actually know. Knowing him, probably the latter," said Jennifer.

"Well, lunch is only bread and cheese so you can be here or not as it suits you," announced her mother. Jennifer doubted very much whether it would be 'just bread and cheese' but made no further comment.

She too was glad to get to bed in good time and she too was lonely in a bed all by herself but, unlike David, she had an answer to that.

Having shoe-horned him into the Land Rover they started by going away from Valley Farm so that she could show him the village, such as it was, and the immediate environs. He was surprised to find that it still managed a shop and a pub but less so by a rash of new, supposedly executive houses alongside an older council house-style development.

"We can't expect to keep a shop without some newcomers to help it along," said Jennifer.

She drove further out and then down a back lane that brought them to 'the Prairies' as her father called the big arable fields that were the backbone of Valley Farm. Fundamentally it was these fields that provided the wherewithal for the Sufframs to enjoy a comfortable lifestyle even if Jennifer's father's farming was not quite as profitable as that of some of his neighbours. The combe in which the farm lay and where they farmed in a more traditional manner with sheep and a cow for the house was to all of them no more than a hobby that just about paid its way. It also maintained a tradition. At the head of the combe was a small spinney and, by a slightly devious route, this was where Jennifer was headed.

"I'm glad you know where you are going," commented David, having completely lost his bearings.

"This is to me like your saltings except that I wasn't trying to escape from anything. I used to walk and ride around here on my own to my heart's content years ago. It makes me feel old to think about it," she laughed. But she knew exactly where she was going and why!

They had arrived at the back of the spinney in the front edge of which there was a slight hollow from which one could see down the valley to the house and farm. There was a low hedge because the ground fell away on the downhill side due to endless generations of sheep lying in the sun alongside the hedgerow. Behind and towards the wood were large clumps of brambles that shielded the spot from behind and any prying eyes that might come from that direction. Large clumps of brambles were a rarity at Valley Farm and it only occurred to a few of the users of the Nest as to why there were some here but nowhere else. The ground was in the form of a comfortable hollow, a miniature amphitheatre, and was a glorious suntrap at almost any time of the year. What had caused the hollow was anyone's guess. Maybe there had been a building there at one time, alternatively somebody had started digging for something. For those who knew it didn't matter. And a surprising number of people did know about it and most of them thought that they were the only ones that did.

Jennifer had been walked up here from an early age with her mother and had often wondered why her mother loved it so. When boys became interesting, she began to understand. It was a lover's paradise. See without being seen. It gave time and means of escape if anyone else happened in your direction. Blushing to remember, not to mention with whom, Jennifer had lost her virginity here. So had the boy she was with but it had served a useful purpose for both of them and put them onto the learning curve of life. Quite unspokenly each never mentioned it if they did chance to meet.

Whilst she did not consider herself in any way promiscuous, Jennifer did enjoy her sex and had used the Nest on a good many occasions since then for what was, she felt, its true purpose. She would, however, have been horrified to learn that her mother and father had used it in the same way in their youth, as had no doubt her grandparents before them. She would have been even more surprised to learn that they still did when the weather was nice and there was no one about. They in turn would have been equally put out to learn that some of the farm staff used it for the same purpose, with or without their own wives, and that a few of them also knew that the boss and his family did the same. It remained, again without a word being spoken, a closely guarded secret amongst all of them. So when Jennifer brought the Land Rover to a stand at the edge of the wood and only a few short yards from the Nest, all unknowingly David was like a lamb to the slaughter.

"This is where we get out," she said.

"Is this where you abandon me like Hansel and Gretel," he said.

"No. Silly. We're going for a walk, or in your case a hobble."

"That's what the gangsters say and then it's, 'Bang, bang, you're dead.'"

"Not dead, but bang, bang, maybe," she said archly, and watched doubtful realisation suffuse his face.

276

She led him through the corner of the wood and to the little path between the brambles and they stood looking down on Valley Court. David put his good arm around her from behind and she felt him hard against her.

"Now isn't this a splendid place to view it all from," she said. "But I'm not sure that you're concentrating," she added as she turned to face him and press herself into his body.

"The view is different from where I'm standing," he mumbled, "and I'm not sure I can cope with it."

"Then I'll help you cope. We'll manage like we have before," she whispered. She heard a faint 'Good' in reply.

Carefully, but with great urgency, necessary clothes were removed and love, ecstatic love in the fresh air, was made leaving them both flushed, exhilarated and drained all at one and the same time. Carefully, but in slower motion underwear was returned whence it came and they sat and looked at each other. Then laughed and cuddled.

"It's a good thing the sun was shining," said David, "or we should have suffered frostbite in embarrassing places."

"It always shines just here," said Jennifer, then realised she might have said too much but David appeared not to notice.

When they eventually got back to the house Jennifer's mother knew from the sparkle in her daughter's eyes precisely where they had been and what they had been doing but was much too sensible to make any comment. Paul fortunately wasn't around when they left the Land

Rover in the yard, but he was fairly sure they would want it again before too long.

Sunday morning found Jennifer realising she didn't know quite as much about David as she thought she did. The problem was church. The small Cotswold stone village church stood beside the entrance gateway to Valley Court/Farm and the land on which it stood had no doubt once been part of the estate. Her parents effectively 'ran' it. They had fought off various suggestions that it should be closed and had as good as picked up the bill when the roof needed major repairs. This just happened to be one of the two Sundays each month when there was a service and she knew that there was no way that she could avoid accompanying the family to that service, not that she really wanted to. Life had been good to her recently and she felt she had things to thank the Almighty for. But what about David? She was just not sure where he stood in these matters, if anywhere. He did of course have a perfect excuse but that was not the point.

Somewhat tentatively she had to enquire and was amazed by his reply.

"You try and keep me away. I haven't been in a church since I fell down those stairs and I should have been."

Quite improperly she started making excuses.

"You'll find it pretty deadly, you know, half a dozen people if we're lucky, and cold, there's no heating to speak of..." she trailed off.

"I know it's going to be a bit different from what I'm used to but, don't worry, I'll manage," he said. Then seeing the look of surprise on her face added, "I normally go to Carlisle Cathedral most Sunday mornings, that's how you found me in the works on a Sunday morning, I can call by and have an hour or so to myself without interruptions."

This explained a lot of things, like why he was looking smart and wearing a tie when she found him in the factory.

"But why don't you go in Brampton?" she asked, for something to say as much as anything else. "That would seem more sensible and nearer."

"You're being sensible like your mother!"

He laughed as she went to hit him.

"That goes back to the days when I used to go down by the Solway. An escape. On one occasion I cycled into town instead of out of it, came to the cathedral and crept into the back of a service. For reasons unknown it hooked me. Partly because I could be anonymous until somebody twigged I was by myself. The rest, as they say, is history. Somehow, I've never got round to doing the obvious and going to the local church. It'll make a change to come with you."

"And your parents, dare I ask?"

"Oh, them," he said, as though wishing he hadn't been reminded of their existence. "They couldn't have cared less where I was. For them Sunday mornings were for staying in bed." He added bitterly, "All three of them!"

He gave a hollow laugh. Jennifer knew it was time to move off that subject.

"Good. That's settled then. I shall break with the tradition of all my life to date and sit somewhere different. You shall sit with me and be exhibit 'A' for all the world

279

to see. Anyway, the pews are too short to be sensible with four people in them, especially with one who's a hospital case."

"I may need a bit of help," he said.

"You shall get it," she said, "like you have before." She winked.

She imparted this good news to her parents and David's stock went up several notches in their estimation. Especially for her father for whom the 'trade' epithet was beginning to dull as he came to know David better. She found that he had a good tenor singing voice and was quite unreasonably taken aback to find that he knew all the responses and his way through the service almost better than she did. He also said all the right things to the other members of the congregation, fourteen as it happened, and to the lady priest who had taken the service. The only odd part was that he had to stand at the communion rail, something usually only done by the very elderly, but there was at least an obvious reason for it.

"That will give them all something to talk about over their Sunday lunches," she said as they came away.

"Not half."

Jennifer found herself quite uncommonly relieved to have got this one out of the way. It had been subconsciously bugging her for some time. She didn't class herself as religious but going to church was part of her life and she didn't want to give it up. David had never mentioned the subject either which, to her surprise, had left a bit of a blank in her life. She had certainly never dreamt that he was a regular worshipper, least of all in the cathedral.

The call came late on Monday afternoon. Fortunately, David and Jennifer were back from seeing the local sights and had planned an evening eating out before returning north the next day. It was Jennifer's mother who took the call and with a meaningful look in her eye announced that there was a "Christine on the phone for David."

Turning pale, she said, "Oh, no, I wonder what's gone wrong now? It's got to be serious if she's phoned here."

For once her mother was completely mystified as Jennifer set off with the phone to find David. She gave it to him and was about to leave when he motioned her back whispering that she had better stay as they were in this together. She felt honoured. She didn't gather much from listening to his side of the conversation which consisted largely of 'blimeys', 'how much?' with the occasional 'bloody hell' thrown as though all else had failed. He assured Christine that he would be back the next day but insisted that she was not to alter her routine until he was back. He would phone her on the way. After ringing off, he slumped back in the chair and let out a long breath of air. Jennifer could hardly contain herself but knew she had better do so. He would tell her in his own good time, which, as it happened, was straight away.

"Muriel's done a bunk. Or at least Christine thinks she has which is a good as being a certainty."

"How much has she taken?"

"Just like your mother. Straight to the point."

Jennifer coloured. David noticed.

281

"Sorry, but seriously, not much idea of that either. It's seventy-five grand today anyway – but how much before that? Well, your guess is as good as mine, possibly better."

"How much?" Jennifer was aghast and showed it.

David spelt it out slowly: "Seventy – five – thousand – pounds.

"Today," he added, for emphasis.

"However did she manage it?"

"Again, straight to the point. Sorry," he grimaced. "As far as Christine can tell she had her own bank account in the name of THW Ltd and she would have people write out cheques to THW Ltd rather than write the whole T.H. Wear Ltd and then she would pay the money to herself. God knows how much she's skimmed off and no wonder the firm has been barely breaking even this last couple of years." As an afterthought he said, "Which happens to be about half as long I've been running the show. Not a coincidence, I suspect." He mused further. "I wonder if Muriel was clever enough to take just as much as she knew the firm could manage without us really realising it. Quite possibly. Clever, eh?"

"Police?" she queried.

"Father would never allow it, but he may not have the choice this time."

"And how much are we telling Mum and Dad?"

He thought about this for a while.

"They'll have to know sometime, yes, but we'll keep it to the bare bones for now. We don't know much more than that anyway."

"True."

They got a sympathetic hearing from the Suffram family although none of them had come across anything quite like it. They stuck to the fraud, deliberately keeping clear of more intimate matters. Jennifer's mother was relieved to discover who Christine was.

They did go out to the local Chinese restaurant and, whilst they enjoyed the meal and being out together in a different environment, the question of Muriel kept impinging on their conversation. They each had their own theories as to what, and exactly how, it had happened but equally both knew that it was only conjecture. Then Jennifer stopped with chopsticks halfway to her mouth.

"You remember that Simmonds order that you agonised over, then turned down and how Muriel went bananas about it?"

"Yes. So what?"

"It's just dawned on me."

"What has?"

"She said, and I more or less quote, 'He can't do that, they're one of my best customers!'"

David looked mystified.

"And?" he said.

"Don't you get it? 'One of *my* best customers.' Emphasis on *my*."

"I see. Yes. I do see. Slip of the tongue that meant nothing at the time but significant now."

"Did Christine know just whose money she's gone off with?"

"No. She thinks it's more than one. Doubtful if it's them as they don't usually owe that amount of money."

283

"Food for thought then."

And so their disjointed meal continued until it was David who finally said, "Do you fancy driving through the night so that we were back first thing in the morning?"

Jennifer thought about it. "No," she said, "I don't and I think both of us could do with some sleep so that we're not too jaded. Tomorrow's going to be a long day. Doubtful if either of us will sleep very well but the first awake after five o'clock wakes the other and we go early. Breakfast in a motorway café and back before lunch."

"Ever the sensible one." He grinned.

She made a face at him. "Depends on your leg and arm," she said.

In the event it was David who woke Jennifer and they were on the road before six. At around nine thirty David telephoned Christine at one of her other places of work to say they would be there be at the works around eleven thirty. Again he seemed to be listening rather than saying anything.

"How's she coping?" asked Jennifer.

"Afraid of her own shadow as usual," he said. "She won't be in till twelve but will phone us beforehand as she doesn't want us getting there before her. Working lunch I think so we need some sandwiches on the way."

"Always the important things first," laughed Jennifer. "Did she say anything else?"

"Yes, that she thought Miranda knew more than she was letting on. She thought keeping her in suspense overnight to think about it might become revealing, although Christine is sure that she is no more than an unsuspecting pawn in Muriel's game plan."

"I'd lay money on it. Although I don't think she's actually retarded, she's certainly not the world's brightest, but that probably suited Muriel just fine."

David thought for a moment and then said, "I think when we get there that I go and talk to Christine but before she has the chance to talk to anyone else and that you should talk to Miranda. She just might say things to you that she would be too intimidated to say to me, or even to Christine."

"You'd make a good detective but I'm not sure I'm cut out to be your partner."

"You'll cope. You always do. And be prepared for tears. She's been known to dissolve when I've barely said 'boo' to her."

"Gee, thanks."

He looked sideways at her and she thought she saw love in his eyes but perhaps it was just a reflection off a passing lorry.

In due course and by deliberate 'chance' they all met up in the office car park. Christine looked nervous. David struggled out of the car.

"God. I'm in agony. Hardly stopped. I shall be a cripple for life."

"No, but you are a cripple at the moment, and you need to remember that," said Jennifer.

"Yes, nurse," he said. It broke the tension and Christine smiled.

"You go ahead and get the kettle on; I'll bring the sandwiches and Jen is going to stop by and talk to Miranda on the way."

"That's if the door is open," said Jennifer.

"It will be. Muriel's not here," replied David with total assurance and he was proved right.

Christine passed through in front of them with a perfunctory 'Hi' to Miranda. David passed the time of day with her as he hobbled by and she responded in kind, but naked fear showed in her eyes when Jennifer spun Muriel's chair round and sat in it.

"I don't know nothing about it, miss. I'll leave if you want. I only come in this morning 'cos there was no one else to answer the phone," she said, all of a rush with the words spilling out like peas from a pan.

"Now don't panic, Miranda," said Jennifer in what she hoped were reassuring tones. "Nobody is accusing you of anything and nobody wants you to leave. And by the way, you're no longer at school, I'm Jennifer, not miss."

Miranda fumbled with her hands but said nothing, which did not help Jennifer much.

"I think you know that Muriel has in all probability gone for good and it looks as though she has taken a large amount of this company's money with her."

Miranda stared at her desk and nodded her head affirmatively. She still didn't say anything.

"Do you know anything about that?" said Jennifer gently.

She shook her head but continued to stare at her desk.

Jennifer decided to weigh in with shock tactics.

"Seventy-five thousand pounds – yesterday."

Miranda's head rose slowly as the figures registered with her and she stared at Jennifer.

"I could near buy a bloody hoose with that," she said.

"Yes," said Jennifer, "you could and you know nothing about that?"

She shook her head slowly. Then muttering something unintelligible to herself she got up, went to the bottom drawer of Muriel's desk and opened it.

"It's gone," she said, staring into the drawer as though that would restore whatever it was she was looking for to its rightful place.

"What's gone?" said Jennifer gently.

"Her file."

"Her file? What file?"

"Her file."

"Miranda, I'm the new girl here. Remember? I don't know what you mean by 'her file'."

"Her file. The one I was never to have anything to do with. Said she'd sack me if I did."

"What was it like? Do you have any idea what was in it? You're being very helpful, Miranda."

"I shall get in terrible trouble when she comes back if she knows I know about it." Miranda looked genuinely scared. "I don't want to lose my job. Jobs ain't easy at the moment."

"I think we can be reasonably sure that Muriel won't be coming back and even if she does your job is quite safe. I'll vouch for that," said Jennifer, adding to herself, *For what that's worth.*

Miranda looked doubtful, and still scared. Jennifer said nothing. Finally, Miranda moved, but not as Jennifer would have expected. She went to the large steel stationery cupboard and stood on tiptoe in order to see into the back of the top shelf.

"It's not there neither," she announced.

Again, Jennifer said nothing but waited for her to continue. In her own good time she did.

"It were a black lever arch file just like any other ones we have here." She waved a hand at a whole shelf of them. "But this one was special to her. She wouldn't let me see in it. Said it was special customer's details. But I looked one day when she weren't here. Just seemed like a lot of invoices same as in any other file." Again she indicated the shelf. "Nothing very big in it. Just a few spares now and again like. But the copies wasn't on T.H. Wear paper they was THW."

"Now we're getting somewhere," encouraged Jennifer. "Anything else you noticed? Any names you remember?"

"They didn't seem to be any of the usual names. I don't remember any. I didn't look too much, I were scared she'd come back, see?"

"You're doing fine. Give it a bit more thought and see if you can remember anything else. If you do, tell me, not anyone else, just me. But, as I said, your job's quite safe."

Miranda looked relieved. "I will," she said, "and I'll only tell you. Thank you, miss."

Jennifer hadn't the heart to correct her again.

In Christine's office the gloom was unrelieved. The hurried trip north was plainly causing David considerable pain in arm and leg. Christine had handwritten figures across sheets of A4 and it didn't take more than a glance at both of them for Jennifer to realise that the results were not joyous. Tentatively she said:

"I'm not sure whether I have good news or bad."

David drew a deep breath.

"It can't be worse than what Christine's dredged up," he said.

Christine just looked at her hopefully.

"Well," she began, "Muriel has patently put the fear of God, or at least of her job, into Miranda and she's scared stiff of what she knows. By the way I've promised her that her job's safe whatever happens." She looked at David, who nodded. "But I think first, what have you got?"

"The big one seems to have vanished into thin air. Christine, just tell Jen how much it is, I'm not sure that I can manage it."

"Seventy-five thousand, six hundred and eighty-two pounds plus the VAT, which comes to a further," she bashed figures into a calculator, "thirteen thousand, two hundred and forty-four pounds, thirty-five pence but we might get that back eventually. Say £89,000."

Jennifer whistled.

"You may well whistle," said David, and winced but whether from pain in his arm or pain from realisation of the amount involved she did not know.

"I think what I've got is very small beer by comparison unless it's been going on for a very long time.

To look on the bright side it could be the start of finding out what's been happening."

"Don't kid yourself,"

"It could well have been going on a long time," said Christine.

Before anyone could comment further there came a tiny tap at the door and Miranda came round it, looked at Jennifer and said in a small voice, "I found this, miss, if it's any use." She handed Jennifer something and was gone before she could be detained. It was a paying-in book, completely unused, but in the name of THW Partnership and for the Isle of Man bank.

"Good girl," said Jennifer to the space where Miranda had been.

"Come on, don't keep us in suspense," growled David.

"It seems that our Muriel had a nice little system whereby she sold small items to non-regular customers. Probably all non-account customers, now I think about it. The monies from these were invoiced by THW Ltd, or, more likely, THW Partnership by the look of this paying-in book, and banked by her personally into an Isle of Man bank account."

She held up the book as proof of what she was saying.

"If Miranda is to be believed, and I think she's too scared to do anything but tell us the truth, she had her own complete system alongside T.H. Wear Ltd."

It was David's turn to whistle but before he could say anything Christine had cut in.

"That possibly explains what David and I were talking about whilst you were in conference with Miranda."

"Miss," said David with a grin on his face.

"I'll kick your bad leg," she answered.

"Children, children," admonished Christine, though amused nevertheless. "I have been chasing through some of the works records and been unable to find any invoices for a steady trickle of jobs that have gone through. They've all been completed, despatched and, again, vanished into the ether."

"Any idea how much?" asked David.

"None and it would take a lot of finding, especially if this goes back a long way."

A sudden thought struck Jennifer.

"Do you think your father knows about this?"

"I wouldn't be surprised, but possibly not the scale of it. Unless of course he's the 'partnership' bit!"

Jennifer slumped back in her chair.

"I wonder if we're insured for this as well," mused David, as much to himself as anybody else.

Chapter 10

David kept himself to himself and let the shenanigans of Gerry and Dianne wash over him. Millie was the anchor in his life and the high jinks that his father and Gerry enjoyed were not for him. For a growing boy his outlook on life was almost puritanical. He could not make sense of his siblings that they always had to argue. His mother would only say, 'that was the way they were,' which didn't help him much. In truth she was probably no wiser than he was although he did not realise it.

When life got too difficult, he would get on his bike and go somewhere, anywhere, for peace and quiet. As a consequence, he knew the city and its environs better than anyone else in the family, from the back streets of its middle with their small shops and alleyways to the wide-open loneliness of the salt marshes adjoining the Solway Firth. He would occasionally call in at the factory where Muriel would welcome him as royalty, which he hated, and the works staff would treat him as one of them, which he loved.

It was at about this time that there came a new manager to works of T. H. Wear & Co Ltd, one Roger Wildsmith, with whom he found an instant rapport. He soon overcame his nervousness about walking into the working end of the factory as though he owned it to sit quietly in Roger's office until the latter had time to chat.

"Get me shot, you will," he would say, "sitting here talking to you when I should be chasing the work round."

But there was a twinkle in his eye that David read correctly that it didn't matter that much, not least because he would often add, "It's all going well out there so what can I do to help it?"

David also knew from conversations at home that although Roger had not been with the company very long, he was extremely well thought of and that, unless either of them did anything really heinous, any time wasted through their friendship would be overlooked. In any case Henry wanted all his family to be involved in the company, even if he was unsure about how on earth Dianne was likely to fit in. Equally he found David almost as difficult to deal with as there seemed no common ground between their extrovert and introvert personalities.

"Now you're into GCSEs and all that are you going to join us in the business when you leave?" he asked on one occasion.

"I don't know," was David's guarded reply.

"Better come and do a bit during the holidays so you find out what it's like."

"I think I'd like that," he had replied. "But I don't know about full time when I leave school."

"Plenty of time to think about that," said Henry expansively. "You've got A levels to contend with first in any case."

"Yeah," replied David. He had done well enough at school so far but the exam years ahead were beginning to worry him.

So he did start going to the works to work and earn himself some money. To his surprise he not only liked the work, which inevitably could be monotonous, but more especially the camaraderie amongst the working men with whom he rubbed shoulders all day long. He found he could banter with them and have his own leg pulled in return in a way that was impossible at home or even at school. It was to be a portent for the future.

***

With Dianne having gone off to university in London a sort of calm descended on the Wear household that it hadn't known in years. Gerry continued to live at home much to the surprise of all. He seemed to have no desire to set up his own house or indeed to take much interest in the opposite sex, or any sex. Muriel also continued to live 'at home' even if the sexual peccadilloes of the elder members of the family became a bit subdued with age.

To most people it was obvious that Gerry was going to do what he had set out to do which was to take over from his father. In this he had a windfall when he came home from a general sales trip to say that one of their major competitors was in financial difficulties and that they could be bought for a reasonable sum. Thus, Pedro Pumps Ltd came into the Wear fold. Having done this Henry was happy to see Gerry take it on as his responsibility. The only person who seemed unhappy about this development was Muriel but she had no sensible reasons for it.

"Just a gut feeling," she said, "that it's not right."

"Give us a reason," pressed Gerry.

"Can't. Like I say, I just don't like it."

In truth, from Muriel's point of view, the difficulties could be problematical. She had set up her own accounting system that worked very much to Muriel's advantage. The introduction of another company into the mix with the additional interest likely to be taken by the company's auditors was giving Muriel considerable pause for thought. Fortunately for her it was Henry who spotted it first. After at first disbelieving what his intrinsic knowledge of the company told him, he had to tackle her about it.

"We're short of cash and we shouldn't be," he announced to her one day and then watched very closely for her reaction.

There was a pause.

"Is that my problem?" she asked.

"Well, is it?"

"No."

"I beg to differ." Henry could be devastatingly polite.

Another pause.

"I reckon you've got the 'Muriel Bouche Benefit Society' working in your office."

Muriel decided to attack.

"So what if I have? You pay me a pittance for what I do here and nowadays nothing for working my hands off in the house. You spend more bed time with Millie than with me. You don't love me any more!"

Henry drew a deep breath and continued to be very polite.

"My dear Mu, you're muddling things up. What you do here and what goes on at home are not in any way connected. That side of it we'll talk about some other time. I'm talking about the here and now. Especially here and especially now!"

He all but shouted the last sentence. Muriel broke down.

"I'm sorry," she said. "I was just trying to build up a bit of a nest egg for you and me. Maybe one day…"

"Fool! I suspected something like that."

"But Henry…"

He held up his hand to silence her.

"Up to a point I don't mind what you do but you've got careless! If I can spot a problem there are others who will be a lot quicker than I am. I don't want to know what you're doing because it sounds like it might be to our advantage but be very careful. No slip-ups!"

He stared very hard at her and she couldn't take his gaze.

"One final thing. Arrange for some insurance to cover internal theft. If you land up in jail, I don't want to be out of pocket!"

***

"We can't afford it, Dad, she may be flesh and blood but we just can't."

"I know that, you know that, but does she know that?"

"No and she won't want to."

"So who's going to tell her?"

"Who's got the thickest skin?"

"It ought to be you but I guess it has to be me," said Henry.

They were discussing what to do with Dianne when she finally finished at university. She rarely came home for very long during vacations and continued living the dream that T. H. Wear & Co was making a mint of money that she could latch into whenever it suited her. It was on one of those rare occasions when Gerry also happened to be there that Henry made his move.

"So what are you going to do with yourself when you leave uni?" he said.

"Come and work for you, of course."

"Uh, uh. That's not possible."

The temperature in the room rose noticeably.

"What do you mean, not possible?"

"Put simply, we can't afford another member of management staff."

She rounded on Gerry.

"This is you, isn't it? Can't get at me any other way so suddenly find you're hard up!" she yelled.

Gerry tried to maintain his father's quiet politeness.

"Dad's quite right. We can't afford you or anyone else for that matter."

"We're having a rough patch. We might even have to lay off some staff," Henry added in order to drive home the point.

297

"And what about this new company that's all your brainchild?"

"That's part of the problem."

"You're doing this deliberately. I know you are!" She wasn't just yelling now; screeching was more like it.

"Listen! Will you?"

Dianne quieted while Gerry regained his composure and then backed off.

"You tell her, Dad. She might believe you."

"Gerry's right. We can't afford it. Pedro Pumps is OK but it cost us a lot of money, especially by the time we'd moved it here."

"Then why did you buy it?"

Henry ignored the question.

"It's doing OK. It's doing all the right things but it takes time. Give us a year and we should have absorbed it. Added to that the pump market seems to have taken a bit of a downturn and, truthfully, we're short of work. Bottom line – we can't afford you. Give it a year and things should be different."

"So what the bloody hell am I going to do for a year while you don't want me."

"Have a gap year, after instead of before university. Or get a job!"

Gerry said it in jest but Dianne took him seriously.

"Get a job? Don't be daft, I coming to work for you, but a year off? That could be interesting. Got any spare money to get rid of me?"

It was outrageous but it broke the ice.

"Bribery?"

"Yeah!"

She made as though to twist a knife in Gerry's guts.

"We'll see what we can manage as long as you bugger off and don't interfere for at least a year."

Again, Gerry thought he was pulling her leg.

"Too damned right. You won't see me for dust."

And they didn't.

***

In fact, it was nearly eighteen months before Dianne reappeared on the scene and, in her inimitable style, turned up at the factory one Monday morning and announced that she had come to start work. She had not been home and arrived in an old but smart BMW car that she had certainly not had when she left.

Although she had been expected for a full six months everyone had been lulled into expecting a little bit of advance warning. It was Muriel who took the first blast.

"Gerry's away most of the week and your father's not in yet," was her opening gambit.

"What the hell's he doing then? Still in bed?" She leered at Muriel. "He's always been the first here in the morning."

Muriel was stung.

"Not today," she said sullenly.

"Never mind. What am I supposed to be doing? Where's my office? How do I get in touch with Gerry?"

She finally ran out of breath and Muriel continued to play hard to get.

"I really don't know what you're supposed to be doing and I guess you'll be sharing an office with someone, most likely Gerry, but you'll have to wait till Henry gets here. He may have something organised."

"Can't hang around after him. I'll go and find him."

Muriel put her head in her hands when she was gone. If this was the future, it wasn't going to be nice and she would have to be even more careful.

In fact Dianne and Henry missed each other, much to the former's annoyance. She blew through the house like a tornado leaving Millie, like Muriel, to wonder what the future held. She was only slightly contrite when she returned to confront Henry, but at least he had been warned of her arrival and was ready for her.

"Sit," he commanded after she had erupted into his office. She sat in the only chair.

"So what am I doing then?"

"Nothing until you get some of the house rules into your head."

"So."

"First. That door over there that you nearly took off its hinges just now is normally open so that anyone can come in and see me. If it's shut it means that I am not to be disturbed unnecessarily. I may be on the phone or something. Got it?"

She said nothing.

"Second. You may be my daughter but at the moment you are the lowest form of life around here. You're a rookie. You haven't got a clue what makes this place tick. I don't want a strike on my hands or I'd start you on the shop floor as Gerry did and David is about to. Got that too?"

Again, she said nothing but had paled slightly.

"Third. Gerry and I have agreed a purpose for your being here. You'll become buyer and order all the materials we need. It will require tact, which I know you have when it suits you. It will be required all the time. Initially you will work with Muriel because she's been doing a lot of it up to now and knows who's who. Understood?"

"I can't work with Muriel."

"You can and you will."

"And if I don't?"

"You find yourself a job somewhere else."

She chewed her lip.

"OK. I'll give it a whirl."

"And I want to make one other thing very clear to you, Dianne. Just remember it's us doing you the favour, not the other way round. You're here very much on sufferance, so you'd better make it worth our while."

Dianne glared at him. She had never known him so forthright but she had the sense to realise that this was business life, not family life. She got up to go and find Muriel leaving Henry to recover his sense of poise.

***

The return of Dianne more or less coincided with David leaving school and starting full time in the family firm. He achieved an adequacy of A-level grades but nothing spectacular and was more than happy to immerse himself in the sharp end of the company's business. Gerry's ability as a salesman was paying off handsomely and there was more than enough work for all. He kept his relationship with Muriel very much a formal affair, something that, when he thought about it, he had always done. She was his aunt, after all, wasn't she? And you didn't get too close to aunts, did you?

It soon became apparent to all that David was shaping up into a very competent and methodical fitter. His 'holiday job' in the works had evidently taught him a good deal and he was halfway to being good before he even started. When he assembled something, it worked first time. He never had to dismantle a job because a part had been left out. In the relatively short time that Roger Wildsmith had been with the company he had earned reputation for being able to judge his employees to the letter. So it was not long before he called David into his office.

"You assembled that new pump and engine for Jones down at Burnley, didn't you?" he began.

"Yes," said David, panicking that he had done something wrong. "It worked perfectly on test."

"Of course it did. Now I want you to go down there when it's delivered, install it and check that it does what it's supposed to when it gets on site. Can you do that?"

"Yes, but what about Fred who usually does that job?"

"Fred'll be delighted. His missus is getting a bit shaky on her legs and he doesn't like to be away from her too much."

"Are you sure?" The last thing David wanted to do was upset an established practice and one of his mates to boot.

"Yes. Check it with Fred if you want."

David did and Roger was quite correct.

"I'll do the odd one for you just to keep me 'and in," Fred had laughed.

And so, it became a regular feature of his life to be sent out to commission new equipment or to deal with breakdowns and emergency work. His ability to ignore those around him stood him in good stead on these missions; he just got on with the job, was usually successful and always appreciated for his efforts.

"Don't know how you can go off on your own like that, with no idea what you're getting into," was a perpetual refrain from his workmates.

"Gets me away from those two," he would quip in return, jerking a thumb in the direction of the office. They all understood what he meant!

"Yeah. Don't know how you live at home. Must be grim."

"It has its moments. I keep hoping one of them will move out but they don't seem to want to."

"Might miss out on what the other's doing if they did."

"You could be right but I'm working on it."

If he was truthful with himself, he knew that he had thought about this several times but didn't seem to be able get up and get on with it. He supposed he was waiting for something to turn up and as yet it hadn't. And then he heard about a flat in Brampton, some seven or eight miles away from work. Not too far to travel but far enough away for the family not to pester him. He went to Brampton, saw the flat, liked what he found and became its tenant in short order. Conveniently it came with a few sticks of furniture that the previous occupants had decided weren't worth the trouble of getting down the stairs. He never said a word to anyone. The time would come when he needed it.

***

Although Gerry and Dianne continued to row and argue over trivialities, they settled down into a modus operandi that allowed them to work together for the general benefit of T. H. Wear & Co Ltd. They consciously did their best to keep their shouting matches to out of hours times when there weren't others to hear or they carried them on at home. Surprisingly Dianne, like Gerry, was happy to live in the family home despite her long absences. Maybe it gave her volatile nature some sense of security. Henry had set himself up an office in one of the many rooms at Fellside complete with telephone extension from the factory from which he kept in touch, but slightly reduced the number of hours he worked. This allowed Gerry to use his father's office some of the time and leave Dianne on her own in his.

This seemed to motivate her into demanding that the arrangement become permanent.

"Then I can have an office of my own," she said, "and you can have Dad's as you're now the boss and he can work from home. If he comes in he can use yours, or his; whichever you like to call it whilst you're gadding round the country or the world."

"Li'l Sis…" Gerry began.

"And that's the last time you call me Li'l Sis. Got it?" she yelled at him regardless of who was around.

This caused Muriel to appear from her office to tell them to keep their voices down if they insisted in shouting at each other.

"You keep out of this, Mum!" Dianne shouted back at her.

Muriel looked as though she had been slapped across the face, which effectively she had been. She retreated but Gerry was unconcerned. He either knew or had guessed.

"OK, Sis." He was not to be put off insulting her quite so easily. "Forget that idea. Dad would never have it."

"Like I said, you're the boss now, you can do what you like."

"I'm not. Remember it's Dad's business. None of us have a share, any share, in it yet."

"Well it's time we did and whilst we're on the subject it's time I had a pay rise and a big one."

"Why?" Gerry had learnt from his father how to be scathing.

"Just look at the money that I'm saving you on what we buy. I deserve it."

"I grant you that but we need the money to buy new machinery."

"You get by with what you've got if I have to get by on what you pay me."

They carried the argument home which was not unusual but this time Dianne was not listening to any kind of reason.

"And also while we're on the subject I need a new car, like the rest of you."

"Why?" Henry and Gerry said in unison.

"Mine's worn out."

"Rubbish."

"And why shouldn't I have a new car, like the rest of you?" she carried on regardless.

"Perhaps because you don't need one," said Henry.

"And it's up to you to buy your own car unless you do a lot of miles on company business," added Gerry. "And if anyone needs new vehicle on the firm it's David here who needs a new van before the present one dies somewhere down the M6."

"He only works. He doesn't deserve anything!"

It might have been a mistake but David decided to join in the argument.

"I most definitely do. That van's crap and I'm glad to hear that somebody realises it even if that is completely beyond your comprehension."

"You keep out of it. This is nothing to do with you!"

"Oh, yes, it is. You may be clever at what you do but you're pretty unpleasant with it. I wouldn't have you on the premises but then it's not my choice."

He looked pointedly at Henry, who feigned not to notice.

"Shut up, will you?"

"Yes, I will and I'm leaving." And he left the room.

They all presumed that he had simply gone to his room in order to escape and carried on the argument as though uninterrupted. So they were a little surprised when he came down with an overnight bag over his shoulder and a suitcase in his other hand.

"Where are you going?"

"I said I was leaving."

"Where to?"

"You'll find out in due course. I'll see you in the morning, by which time maybe common sense will have prevailed."

"I wouldn't bank on it," said Henry morosely.

And with that David left home for his new flat in Brampton.

Chapter 11

In the cold light of the following morning and after a not very restful night it was patently obvious that David had to go and see his father and broach this latest and much more serious disaster with him. He suspected that Muriel's finale at having her fingers in the till was just the tip of an iceberg and he wanted to get to the bottom of just how much his father knew about it.

"You'll come with me, won't you, Jen?" he almost pleaded with her.

"Of course I will. You can't drive yet, can you?"

"No. I don't mean that. I think I want you around when I'm talking to him. I might get more sense with a female presence. Or at least less pig-headedness."

"OK, we'll see how it works out."

And so it was that by mid-morning they were turning into the bungalow driveway and Mrs Wear was coming down the front steps to welcome them in the floral-pattern housecoat that seemed to be her standard form of dress when at home. No sign of his father, but that was hardly surprising as he seldom moved outside the house. Jennifer came round and helped David up out of the passenger seat, even though he could nearly do it on his own by now.

"I thought you'd be here sometime today so the kettle's hot for some coffee."

"Thanks, Mum. Dad in his chair as usual? I need to see him."

"No. They've gone!"

"They?" questioned David looking sideways at his mother.

"Well, your father and Muriel, of course."

David collapsed back into the car and it was only the pain of banging his plastered arm that prevented him from fainting. Jennifer rushed to his assistance, which he brushed aside as best he could and sheer willpower made him stand again.

"Mum, am I hearing you right? Are you telling me that Dad and Muriel have gone off together?"

"Yup." Mrs Wear seemed delighted by the turn of events.

"But he's not capable of it."

"He is if Muriel's involved." Her eyes sparkled and she hunched her shoulders in her happy way. "There's a letter inside for you."

David nearly collapsed again.

"I'll have that," he said, adding, "And the coffee with plenty of whisky in it."

He looked despairingly at Jennifer and they went indoors.

Propped on the mantelpiece just as in a stage whodunnit was an envelope formally addressed to Mr David Wear and underlined with a flourish. Inside was a single sheet of good-quality writing paper written over in a flowing, almost copperplate hand.

"I have to sit down," said David lowering himself carefully onto a hard chair. Jennifer did not quite know where to put herself. She felt she could not look over his shoulder at the letter but she was desperate for whatever revelations it gave. She was to some extent saved by Mrs Wear coming in with the coffee, together with a half bottle of whisky. She still seemed to be remarkably happy.

David read the letter and it became obvious he was reading it a second time – and then a third. A dazed look came over his face and he emptied a lot of whisky into the coffee mug that had been put beside him. Finally, he handed the letter to Jennifer without saying a word.

Dear David,

This is not a suicide note although writing it makes it feel like that and for you the effect will be very similar. By the time you read this Muriel and I will, I hope, be far, far away, so don't even think about trying to catch up with us. We are lost to you and that is final.

Your mother, Muriel and I have had a very happy life together but somehow you seemed to be blissfully unaware of the situation. Gerry and Dianne coped with it in their own way. Muriel and I had planned on leaving together for a long time but without being quite so sudden about it. You can blame your broken bones and your Jennifer for that. She is much too perceptive for her own good but she will be marvellous for you. Good luck with her. We have your mother's blessing on our going so I beg you not to be too hard on her. It sounds trite but,

Love from your affectionate Dad.

P.S. At least you can now claim the insurance, although I don't think it will cover the big one but I reckon the firm can just about stand that.

Jennifer flopped into a chair and held the letter up in front of her again. Mrs Wear stood smiling benignly at both of them as though her husband going off permanently with the third member of their threesome was the most ordinary thing in the world. Jennifer wanted to hit her if only to wipe the silly smile off her face. In a manner of speaking she did.

"Who are Gerry and Dianne?" she asked in pure innocence and with no idea of the bombshell she was dropping. The happy smile vanished from Mrs Wear's face as she went very pale. David shut his eyes and there was total silence.

"That is not for now," he said slowly, and there was an iron menace in his voice that would brook no further questions.

"The conundrum is, what happens now?" he said in a more reasonable tone.

Mrs Wear came to life.

"There is or there will be a packet for you which I hope will answer all those questions. I can't find it here so I guess it's being sent to you."

"Mother," said David with some of the menace back in his voice. "Just how much do you know about all this?"

She shrugged her shoulders happily but with an unusually serious expression on her face.

"On the one hand quite a lot, in that I knew this was going to happen sometime, although perhaps not quite so abruptly. On the other nothing at all because I have no idea what financial arrangement he has made for any of us, including the company. I have no idea where they've gone. We thought it better that I didn't, you understand?"

"I'm not sure I quite understand this 'we' all the time," said Jennifer. "Do you really mean that you planned all this between the three of you and that David here was oblivious?"

"Yup," she said, with annoying repetition and an expression that inferred that Jennifer was particularly stupid not to comprehend. Before either of them could comment she was prattling on.

"It had to come soon. I know that because that's how I got my new kitchen. It was only a teensy bit of blackmail but I said I wouldn't rock the boat if they left me set up with everything I wanted. A special kitchen has been the one thing I've wanted for years. Snag is, there's only going to be me to cook for in it now. Something's made them move faster than I expected. Got a feeling it's you." She looked hard at Jennifer.

"There I go getting the blame again."

"Yup. I think Muriel thought you would see through her."

"We were getting pretty close to it."

"I thought so. I was hoping to get a new car out of them as well before they left," she added, wistfully. "Hey ho, such is life, but I've got too old for all that sort of thing now!"

She's in a world of her own, thought Jennifer, and then reason took over. If they were to make any sense of this, it was time for her to take control.

"David," she said authoritatively, "we're not going to do any good here. Either we go back to the office or your flat and see if this packet your mother speaks of is anywhere around. Maybe then we shall get some answers or maybe not. No matter, we have some planning and rethinking to do. You've got quite a hole here and getting out of it may not be easy, whatever your father thinks."

David turned his stunned look at her but she must have made sense somewhere in his head because he struggled to his feet and, without a word, blundered towards the car.

"Goodbye, Mrs Wear," she said as she passed her in the hallway. "We'll be in touch when we know a bit more."

That lady merely smiled and, bouncing on the balls of her feet on the front doorstep, still maintained that beatific look on her face. Once again Jennifer wanted to hit her.

"The office, I think," said David as they sped away from this extraordinary ménage.

"Actually, I don't. Let's go to the saltings where you took me last time you saw your father. We need time to think."

What she didn't add was, 'And I wonder if you'll mention marriage again.' She would have to wait and see.

"No, we go to the office first and see if this supposed package has arrived there, and then we go to the saltings."

Jennifer considered this.

"I'll buy that one but you stay in the car. I'll go and see what's what if anything is. You're in no state to see anyone."

"That bad?"

"Yup, as your mother would say."

"Don't you start!"

They drove in silence to the factory. Once there, Jennifer left David in the car and slipped through the front door almost furtively. She wasn't trying to catch anyone out but, by the same token, she didn't want to get involved with anyone other than Miranda if she could avoid it. She was in luck. Miranda was sitting at her desk looking as curiously as she was able at a fat A4-size envelope that Jennifer guessed correctly was what they had come for.

"Has that just come?" she asked.

"Yes, miss," said Miranda and her hand shot to her mouth as she realised what she had said. "Someone I've never seen before called by about ten minutes ago and said that he had instructions to leave it here and that David would be wanting it."

"He does, but you've no idea how it got here?"

"No. This man brought it, short, fair hair, weasel-faced if you know what I mean. Tattoos on the back of his hands. Never seen him here before. Who's it from?"

Jennifer hesitated. It was a reasonable question, after all. There would have to be a conspiratorial little white lie.

"David's not telling but I do think he either knows or has a very good idea. He was certainly expecting it." She had to change the subject. "Otherwise is everything OK, any messages or whatever?"

"No. Nothing that seemed important. Roger's dealt with most of them. A couple of calls for money but Christine has them in hand anyway."

"Fine. In that case we may see you later this afternoon. If not, tomorrow morning."

With that she made a quick exit and just hoped it wasn't too obvious.

Apart from relaying Miranda's comments about the arrival of the envelope, and receiving instructions as to where to turn, they drove in silence to that wild place by the Solway where there were only gulls for company. Once stopped, David started to open the envelope and then stopped and frowned at Jennifer.

"I suspect," he said, "that there may be things in here that I can't show you, much as I would like to, much as I love you, and much as you're involved in all this."

"No problem," she replied. "That possibility had occurred to me, as it had that I owe you an apology anyway."

He looked surprised.

"Back at your mother's I was saying an awful lot of 'we' this and 'we' that when really and truthfully, it's you, not me. I'm only the chauffeur when all's said and done."

He lent across and kissed her. This place really did have an effect on him!

"Silly. You know you're in this almost as deeply as I am. At least I hope you feel you are, but for all that there may be skeletons in this envelope that, for the time being at least, it is better that you do not know about."

"I'll chance it," she said and kissed him across the intervening air.

He drew a deep breath. "Here goes then."

After struggling to open the packet, he finally shook out the papers. They appeared to be all neatly clipped together in sections, filed would be a better word, and at the top was a lengthy covering letter, typed this time. Again, she saw David read it twice before moving on to the other documents. There was another, not quite so lengthy, that appeared to be on official-looking paper, perhaps a solicitor's or accountant's. She attempted to be uninterested and commune with a lonesome seagull that was trying to tell her that it was starving. It grew chilly in the car despite the windows getting fugged up. She drew her coat tighter round her but still David said nothing. In the end he carefully put everything back whence it came and just sat, staring at the scudding clouds.

She dropped her hand gently onto his thigh to remind him of her existence, whereupon he turned a vacant face towards her.

"So?" she said softly.

"Put into the smallest of small nutshells I am now the sole owner of T.H. Wear & Co. Ltd, with only one proviso, and that is that I maintain Mother in the 'manner to which she is accustomed'.

"Aren't I lucky?" he added bitterly before she had time to congratulate him.

"I would have thought so," she said. "Especially when one thinks of the sort of mess you could have had if they had both just gone. We had one of those down at

Halliwell's when a farmer did a bunk. Took us months to sort out."

"I suppose so," he said gloomily.

"Don't you want to own the family company that you run? I would."

"Maybe. If I had someone to share it with."

Her heart leapt but he remained the picture of depression. He continued to stare through the windscreen.

Quite suddenly and apropos of nothing he asked, "Would you marry a mutt like me?"

"Yes," she said.

"Idiot," he said.

"OK. Would you marry a girl like me?"

"Like a shot, but it can't be."

"Why ever not?"

"There's too much you can't know."

"OK. Then start telling me and I'll be the judge of that."

"No!" It was a scream of despair and frustration.

She was quite frightened. What had she let herself in for with this family?

"And I've had another horrible thought. Apart from everything else, have you considered the possibility that Muriel might be my mother?"

It was Jennifer's turn to be thunderstruck and to be at a complete loss for words.

"No, I hadn't," she said in a barely audible voice, adding with slightly more strength, "Does it make any difference?"

"Difference? Of course, it makes a difference!" he shouted angrily.

"What to?"

"Well, us if nothing else. Someone like you is going to run a mile from some sort of bastard like me. A real one I mean."

The silence that followed allowed Jennifer to think and for her conscious mind to agree with what her unconscious self, had already decided upon. It was her turn to get uptight.

"Just listen to me. Hear me out. I don't think that what you're trying to convince yourself of is right. I don't believe they could have lived that lie all these years, however much of a threesome they may have been. Somewhere a hint would have been dropped. Besides all the documentation one needs over the years from a birth certificate onwards would have had to have been forged. You need to be MI6 or seriously the wrong side of the law to do that sort of thing. Forget it. You have to live life as it comes until you really and truly know any different."

"Yes," he said more quietly. "When one looks at it like that you are almost certainly right. Let's go home. I, not we, have to think."

And in total silence they did that. David swore as he banged his arm getting out of the car, but otherwise he just plonked himself in his usual corner of the sofa and continued to stare into space. She got him some tea, and later a meal, and he remained polite but monosyllabic. His only real contribution was to give orders for the next day. She was to be his chauffeur, no more, no less. He had people to see, both at the factory and elsewhere. He would give directions. OK, she had said. What else could she have said? It was not a pleasant evening and it was followed by an uncomfortable night.

He was still moody and grumpy in the morning, especially when he insisted on dressing properly with collar and tie. If she was just his chauffeur or in this case, his valet, then she must take her master's whims in her stride. This she just managed without them actually coming to blows. She dropped him at the office and in almost as many words was told to get lost until just before eleven o'clock. She seethed but bore with it. She then dropped him off at a firm of solicitors in the middle of town and was asked (that was an improvement) to go back to the office and come back when he phoned. Miranda was not impressed with his behaviour either. Jennifer had never heard her so forthright.

"Wha's up wi' David?" was her opening remark. "You two been fighting?"

"No. He's got a lot on his mind suddenly. What's been going on here then?"

"Bit me 'ead off as soon as he come through that door and I'd only just got in meself. Then he's been 'in conference' with Roger for an hour or more. Tried to get hold of Christine but couldn't and now you've taken him off somewhere. When's he coming back?"

Jennifer had never heard such a speech from the usually timid Miranda, although by the end of it she was beginning to subside into her usual downtrodden self.

319

"Sorry," she said. "Really got up my nose, he did. Not like him at all."

"He's going to phone me here when he wants collecting."

"Hoity toity he's got."

"Not really. Anyway, he was simmering down a bit when I left him. Mind if I help you somehow? I can't just sit around."

Miranda looked at her watch. "Is that the time? Go on, you could make us both a cup of coffee, it's been that sort of morning."

"No problem," Jennifer said happily, even if she was taking orders from all and sundry this morning. "How do you like yours?"

"Milk, one sugar, if that's all right." Miranda was beginning to think she had overstepped the mark.

"Coming up," said Jennifer as she departed for the little kitchen along the corridor. There she met Roger, who was on the same sort of mission.

"God, I think I want whisky with it this morning," was his comment.

"I suppose it's no good asking you just what's going on and what all the flap is about?"

"Absolutely no good at all. One, I don't know enough to be helpful, and two, it's more than my job's worth, and I mean that."

"That bad?"

"Aye, but he'll tell you in his own good time. But I'll tell you this much, I reckon he's been wanting to do that ever since you've been here, so just play along and let him

320

get there all by his little self." He tapped the side of his nose conspiratorially to emphasise his point.

She drew a deep breath and deliberately exhaled it noisily.

Roger ignored her and started gathering up mugs and coffee. "How do you like yours?" It was the end of that conversation.

"Oh, don't worry, I'm making for Miranda as well. I'm only the tea girl around here now."

"Balls, if you'll pardon my French," he responded with some asperity. "David couldn't manage without you, even if neither of you two know it yet. There, I've said too much. I'm off before I say more than I should."

And he disappeared into the factory armed with his coffee.

Jennifer found herself standing there with a pot of instant coffee in one hand and a teaspoon in the other, her mouth open and staring at the empty space where Roger had been. Then she blushed furiously and was just grateful that there was no one else around. The phone had just rung so at least Miranda was busy and not going to catch her out. While she cooled down and reality returned, she wondered whether he meant, or even believed, what he had just said. Having found him a wholly down-to-earth individual for whom a spade was simply a spade, she strongly suspected that he did. Also, he appeared to be the most trusted appraiser of people on the premises. There was, therefore, nothing for it but to take his advice and bide her time until David decided to make his own move. Feeling slightly jittery she set off with the coffees to the front office, where she hoped it was just her imagination that saw an odd look on Miranda's face as she walked in. She deflected these thoughts into something she thought might be revealing for Miranda and take the heat away from herself.

"Sounds as though David's been upsetting Roger as well from the tone of his voice in the kitchen just now," she said sitting down in what had been Muriel's chair.

"Not surprised. He don't like meetings about anything that's not directly his business. Muriel used to upset him that way. Try and get him involved in the affairs of the firm or trying to get off with him like. He couldn't stand her but had to put up with 'cos she'd been here since Eve was a lass."

"Really," said Jennifer noncommittally, amazed by these revelations and that Miranda should suddenly become so garrulous.

"Yeah, thought she was God's gift to middle-aged men and old codgers!"

Unfortunately for Jennifer the telephone rang at that instant. It was David with her orders.

Miranda relayed the message: "'Tell Jennifer to pick me up where she left me in about fifteen minutes.' That's all he said. No please, or if she can. He's still got a sore head."

And so have you, thought Jennifer to herself, but out loud she said, "At least I've got time to finish my coffee, just," as she gulped it down.

"Good luck," called Miranda as she went through the door.

***

David did not like Mr Murchison. He never had liked him, but if T. H. Wear needed a solicitor he was as good as they came. Despite that he had not been the firm's solicitor for that long and was presumably one of his father's golfing cronies. Although not that many years older than himself, David found in him a man who could have had 'solicitor' tattooed across his forehead in much the same way as he had a gold watch chain across his waistcoat. He was old-style, pernickety and pompous in everything he did. But there the avuncular solicitor ended. He occupied swish premises in the best part of town equipped with every gizmo of which his profession could avail itself. It all smacked of too high fees for David's peace of mind, but in this instance, he had no choice.

"Well, now David…" he began.

David was not in a good mood: "I think we'll have Mr Wear from now on," he said, adding blandly, "Start as I mean to go on and all that."

Mr Murchison peered over his glasses with a look of some astonishment. He was not used to being told what to do, even if he did realise that he, in turn, was Mr Murchison to perhaps ninety-eight per cent of his clients. He also registered in those few words that David was going to be rather more difficult to deal with than the rest of the Wear clan.

"Now then, Mr Wear, it is my pleasure to inform you that the companies of T.H. Wear & Son Ltd and Pedro Pumps Ltd are now both entirely yours." If he was expecting a reaction from David, he didn't get one. "Except of course that I hold a single share in each in order to maintain the limited liability status. My instructions are to pass that share on to whomsoever you wish at no charge whatsoever." David had the distinct impression that the absence of something to charge for seemed to rankle with him.

"My father and Muriel have set all this up for me, have they?"

"Your father has. I don't think the lady has had any input into it."

"Directly at any rate."

Mr Murchison remained silent.

"Any idea where they've gone?"

"None."

Liar, thought David but refrained from actually saying so.

"Not that I think it would help you any if you did know, and in any case my instructions are not to give any assistance at all in that respect."

David grunted. Mr Murchison coloured just ever so slightly and was aware that David noticed. But in truth all the advice was probably right – it was better if he knew nothing of his father's whereabouts. That way there could be no comeback on whatever he did. He moved on.

"No doubt there are a host of forms to be filled in and signed before all this is wholly legal?"

"There are indeed." The solicitor was visibly relieved. He picked up a manila folder. "They are all in here. You will see that your father has signed and dated them all a couple of weeks ago. You only have to sign where indicated…"

"And read them first," cut in David.

"Well, of course, but I can assure you that they are all in order. Not to mention that it would be extremely difficult to have anything altered."

"Especially as you don't know where my father and Muriel are."

"Exactly so." He didn't colour this time.

"But at the risk of wasting your time and my money I intend to read them. All of them. In present circumstances I don't entirely trust my father and still less, his beloved Muriel."

"I understand."

"I doubt it," said David as he started reading. It took him a good half hour to do so and he rather gloated at keeping Mr Murchison from doing anything else despite the fact that he knew he was paying heavily for it. There were the odd bits of legal explanation required which made his presence the more necessary. In essence he was now reading the originals of the contents of the packet delivered the day before. However, there was also a letter of instruction from his father to the solicitors asking them to set up all the documents he now had in his hand but to hold them in hand 'in case they were needed urgently'. This long pre-dated his having met Jennifer and his father obviously foresaw what was now happening. It was, if anything, a measure of his father's business acumen and David wished that he could anticipate all eventualities with such precision, but the duplicity of the last few years made him very angry indeed, not to mention cynical.

"Thank you, Mr Murchison," he said. "I think I can sign all that lot. Perhaps we could have your secretary to act as witness? I don't want too much to be under the 'Old Pals Act'."

The man behind the desk glowered but was as smooth as silk.

"I will call Mrs Reid," he said.

Whilst waiting for her to come David asked as casually as he was able, "One final question. Is Muriel my mother?"

"No. I can be quite categorical about that." The answer came back without a trace of surprise that it had been asked.

Within ten minutes David was calling his chauffeuse.

***

David was waiting on the curb just where she had left him and, from a distance at least, the expression on his face seemed to have lightened a little. He was still clutching the packet that had come to them the day before.

"Now where to, sir?" Jennifer asked sarcastically before she drew off into the traffic.

"Lunch, I think, or a pie and a pint at least. Go to the Millrace, the pub where we went when you first appeared up here. I don't want to go back to the office just yet."

"Do you normally take your chauffeurs out to lunch, sir?" she enquired in the same tone.

"I'll hit you."

"Oh, good. That means you've simmered down a bit."

"Not much." The desperate mood returned to his face but she had an idea that he was faking it.

Once settled with some sandwiches and glasses of beer and shandy, Jennifer waited for whatever revelation was coming. She did not have too long to wait.

"As you might have guessed I've been with the family solicitors and I did read the papers right. I am now the sole owner of T. H. Wear Ltd."

"Once again, my congratulations."

"Don't be too premature. There's too much you don't know."

She looked imploringly at him, willing him to tell what it was all about. She thought she could see love there but with deep shadow in front of it.

"It can't be that bad. Just tell me about it."

"It can and I can't." There was that ring of steel in his voice again. "Yet," he added in a marginally lighter tone.

"OK. I'll wait. So tell me what you can."

She could almost hear him marshalling his thoughts and working out where to begin.

"I cannot believe," he began, "that I have lived all these years and quite a chunk of them at home, well most of the time anyway, and been so completely bloody oblivious."

"Of what?"

"That my parents and their old friend Muriel have been living together as basically a threesome most of that time without my being aware of it until the other day. In

327

addition, that my mother is basically quite happy for my father to go off with said Muriel, apparently never to return, and my father was equally happy for her to defraud his company. Incidentally he, the solicitor, agrees with you and is very sure about it. It is most unlikely that Muriel is my mother."

"That's a relief anyway."

"I did occasionally wonder," he continued, "why, considering that neither of them is large, they had such an enormous bedroom, with bed to match. Now I know."

This last remark was made with extreme bitterness. It gave Jennifer quite a jolt but she worked hard for it not to show. Her own rather correct upbringing in which such things were hardly thought about, never mind spoken of, was suddenly put into very sharp relief. The idea crossed her mind that David could possibly make his fortune from the *News of the World* but thought better of suggesting it. She felt a bit lost and not quite sure how to help, if indeed he needed help, which was doubtful.

"What can I say," she said tentatively.

"Bugger all!" he exploded, and then apologised for his language, before continuing, "The most galling bit is that he, my father this time, and I suppose she, are so right. The supposedly small amounts that Muriel nicked, that in reality tot up to a very substantial figure, the company hasn't missed. The big one that he gaily says the company can stand – well, it just about can, especially if the insurance company can be persuaded to cough up for the others without there having to be a police investigation."

"I doubt you'll manage that."

"So do I, especially as none of us bloody noticed it until they'd gone."

The bitterness was back in his voice and Jennifer was getting fed up with him wallowing in his own self-pity and at the same time not being willing to include her in it. Perhaps provocation would help.

"Well, it's not my problem. You have to solve it yourself. Perhaps I really should go home this time."

"No!" he shouted and thumped his fist on the table hard enough to bring stares from other patrons. "But on reflection, perhaps you should. And not come back."

His voice had gone from bitter to maudlin. Jennifer was not expecting to be taken at her word but equally was not willing to back down.

"Of course I'm coming back. The plaster's due off your arm on Tuesday, remember? But we did leave in a bit of a rush if your memory goes back that far, and there are things I didn't bring that I need. And you're quite capable of getting yourself to the local shops for food now. Anyway, there's pretty well enough in the flat till I get back."

"Yeah, you may be right. Give me a chance to think without you to distract me." He grinned as he said the last bit and she knew she wasn't lost.

"Then I'd better be on my way if I'm going to get there tonight."

It was a slightly distracted and tense hour or so until Jennifer left with both of them playing hard to get. She stopped at the Lancaster motorway services and rang just to check that David was OK and really meant that she should go. He was still feeling sorry for himself and she rang off, which in its turn upset her. At Hilton Park she phoned again and found him more sensible and worrying if she was all right on her own. More to the point he was concerned about when she was coming back. She promised to be back on Monday latest and for the last bit of the journey she was in happier mood.

"You've had a tiff, again," was almost, but not quite, the first thing her mother said when she arrived.

"Well, yes and no. Is it so obvious?"

"It is to me but others might miss it. What's the problem?"

Just like her mother. Straight to the point and before she was hardly inside the house. And not very sympathetic with it either, it seemed.

"It's Muriel," she started.

"What, she's come back?"

"No, nothing as disastrous as that, but..." And she started to relay all the gory details of what had happened, how David's parents seemed to have lived together with her, and finally how David was now sole owner of the business, even the unlikely possibility of Muriel being his mother. "But there's something there that he won't tell me. He seems to want me to help him make decisions but he won't tell me what the problem is. He gets so belligerent about it. Says it's not for me to know. We got quite uptight over it and I've come away and left him to think about what he wants to do. I hope he's made his mind up by the time I get back."

"I'm glad you're going back. I just think that young man needs you."

"Of course I'm going back, Mum, he's having his plaster off on Tuesday and how is he going to get to the hospital?"

"Well, someone else could take him," suggested her mother tentatively.

"Oh, Mum, don't be silly, I've got to take him. I wouldn't miss this big event for worlds! Anyway, I like him – no, I love him. There, now you know." And she blushed from her shoulders up.

Jennifer found herself enfolded in her mother's arms and doing her best to hold back tears.

"I know you do, my lovely. Even your father has come round to him and Paul's been hearing wedding bells for weeks!"

"Paul?" She stood up straight. "What's it got to do with Paul?"

"Darling, you and David have been the talk of this place ever since you took off 'oop North' in the New Year."

"Really?"

"Yes, really. After all its not every day that one's daughter or sister, as the case may be, goes running round the country after someone they met for half an hour on the other side of the world and…" She held her hand up as Jennifer tried to interject. "And then throws up her job and goes rushing off to help said person when said person happens to break his arm. And doesn't come back." She added the final clincher with some asperity.

Jennifer was a bit downcast.

"I suppose when you put it that way, it does sound a bit daft. Truth stranger than fiction and all that. It's never seemed in the least peculiar to me, but then I guess I'm biased." This last was by way of a rather lame excuse.

Her mother pushed her out to arm's length and looked at her, much as she would with a young teenager who had a problem at school.

"Well what are we going to do about it?"

"Do about it? We?" Jennifer was astounded.

"Yes."

"Why nothing. He'll come round in due course and tell me all about it in his own good time. That's what everybody says anyway. And as for 'we', that would frighten him off completely. He considers you to be awesome. You know that, don't you?"

It was her mother's turn to be surprised.

"Me? Awesome? What are you talking about?"

"David considers you to be very sensible, have us all under control, very loving but awesome nevertheless. I should take it as a compliment if I were you."

They both laughed aloud at this denunciation of her mother's character and reality returned.

"OK. Point taken, so now we're to have a girlie weekend, are we?" and she swept on without waiting for a reply. "Good, we shall enjoy ourselves, shan't we?"

Jennifer smiled and realised that indeed she would.

She made numerous phone calls to David over the weekend and on each occasion, he seemed to be brighter in mood, very much as though he had come to terms with whatever it was that was bugging him. She hoped so. Thus, it was with a light heart and her family's good wishes that she headed north again on the Monday afternoon.

Chapter 12

It was about ten days after the screaming match in the office and its sequel at Fellside, which precipitated David leaving the family home that Gerry came back to the house for reasons that were never clear. Possibly it was because he and Henry seemed to be sharing an office these days, so perhaps it helped to keep the peace. Millie had gone shopping so he made himself a cup of coffee, poured milk over a plate of Frosties and sprawled across the kitchen table to read the day's newspaper. It was pure coincidence that Dianne had forgotten something that she needed at work. She rushed through the house and up to her room to get it.

"Hi, Li'l Sis," called out Gerry as she rushed past him and up the stairs.

He never heard her come back down until she was right next to him. She leant down until her face was level with his and with her right hand positioned the muzzle of a pistol behind his head.

"I did tell you that you would say that once too often," she said quite slowly, and then squeezed the trigger. The pistol was weightless, like an extension of her arm. She hardly heard the noise and did not move with the recoil. She watched attentively as a black/red hole blossomed and swelled.

Gerry pitched forward into the bowl of cereal which started to tinge pink as it collected blood.

She placed the gun by his right hand and left.

***

Millie had had a pleasant morning shopping for a few much needed clothes and had rounded it off with some friends for a light lunch at the Mitre Hotel. She got back to Fellside about half past two feeling that all was right with her world.

Her first anxiety was that the back door, which everyone used, was not only unlocked but slightly ajar. Her second anxiety was that there was an unpleasant smell about the place. Her third anxiety, well, that was on the kitchen table.

"Oh, my God," she breathed. She didn't scream, drop what she was carrying, faint or anything like that. She took in the scene and its implications in an instant and crept out of the room to the phone in the hall.

She called Henry.

She didn't waste time on small talk.

"Gerry's shot himself and he's dead… Of course I'm sure, there's a gun and blood and…" She hesitated, "and bits all over the place… Will you ring the police…? Why me…? Oh, all right."

Millie dialled 999.

"I need Police and Ambulance in that order," she said quite calmly. "My son's shot himself and is dead!" She went on to give the address and other information required. The operator noted her calmness.

Henry did indeed arrive just before the police, took one look and was violently sick into the sink. By the time he had recovered the police had arrived and he had retired to the living room so it was left to Millie to talk to them.

"Madam, you do realise that this is not suicide, don't you?"

"What! It has to be surely?" She was still calm but spoke very softly. "But that means… How do you know?"

"Madam." It was their wonderful politeness that stuck in her mind afterwards. "If you think about it, you physically can't shoot yourself in the back of the head…"

She nodded her head in understanding.

So began the endless round of police questioning. They started with Millie and kept Henry very firmly where he was. The ambulance was sent away until it was wanted again. Millie gave them a succinct rundown as to who lived in the house and how they all fitted together.

Henry told them the same story even if he skated over Muriel's position a bit. He set all the police antennae waving when he told them that David was in Hamburg on business and that he hadn't seen Dianne since mid-morning, although that didn't necessarily mean that she wasn't about somewhere. Police cars sent to fetch her came back empty handed.

The police believed what they had been told even if it didn't make entire sense. Millie was too calm considering that it was her son who had died. Henry was more like a deflated balloon than anything. Muriel was inclined to be belligerent whilst apparently being a mere hanger-on. David was supposedly in Hamburg and they could soon check that out. Dianne had vanished. At least they had a suspect.

***

Jennifer arrived back at the flat to find a cheerful David, principally because he was looking forward to seeing the plaster off his arm the following day.

"You're still not going to be able to do much," she warned. "You'll have exercises to do." He grimaced. "And I'll still be having to drive you around for a bit."

"Well, I like the sound of that at least," was his response. "We shall have to get you properly installed into the establishment when I don't have to have you drive me around."

"Remember Muriel and what I said before," she warned.

"Yes, I am. But she's gone now. I'm the sole owner so I have a free hand!"

"Only one until tomorrow," she laughed. "But remember what I said. I don't think Muriel and her position made anyone very happy, and if you put me in the same position, you're going to jeopardise the fact that she's gone. You do have to be careful."

"I know but I get such good reports on you that I think the entire place will be pleased to see you there!"

"Flattery will get you everywhere! So what do you have in mind? There seem to be some fairly large loose ends to tie up before we do anything."

"One thing at a time," he grinned. "First I have to get this benighted plaster off my arm tomorrow and we have to celebrate that."

Her ears pricked up.

"And for that?" she teased.

"That as well, but nothing elaborate. I can't face a restaurant. At least with a plaster on I could be a visible invalid but without it I'm just an old codger who can't handle his food."

"Not so much of the old codger bit. You make me feel like Muriel."

"Don't remind me. Anyway, I need to talk to you and I can't do that in a restaurant. No. Tomorrow we'll celebrate in the way we did when you first arrived – a trip to the Chinese chippie and a slap-up meal here."

It might not have been her first choice but she was happy to go along with it as it sounded as though he might at last be going to explain a few things and, just perhaps, ask an important question. Subconsciously she knew she had to be patient just a little longer and she might get what she wanted. The following day went as planned but Jennifer found David becoming more and more morose and jumpy as the day went on. Maybe all would be revealed later?

***

Did she but know it, David had worried over his plans for her return most of the time that Jennifer was away. He did not want this to go wrong, although he had a nasty feeling it easily could. Why was it he did not have her aplomb? He could cope with business people and business decisions – well, only just, if he was honest with himself – but personal matters, and especially Jennifer, were another matter entirely. Just look at him. He had failed, quite deliberately he had to admit, to give her his whereabouts in that original note to the Mkonge Hotel. She had found him. He had found out where she lived very easily but what had he done about it? Nothing. He would have thought nothing of calling if he hoped to sell her a pump but to see her for her own sake…? Too embarrassed. What was the matter with him? And now he had a real problem on his hands and he was like the cat on the proverbial hot tin roof about it.

He should have asked her to marry him. He had wanted to ask her. He wanted to marry her but… The revelations about his family had in fact caused him to ask her twice, and twice she had said, 'Yes' in spite of being told she was an idiot, but each time he had ignored her. Why had he done that? Why couldn't he follow through like anyone else would? As always there was that cloud in the background but he would have to get over it, and hopefully get her over it. It was time to finish the arguments with his inner self and get on with it. Now, or at least, very soon. Chin up, act naturally, for later will be either heaven or hell! As his father would have said once upon a time, "Go for it, lad."

***

Their meal, including the going out and getting of it, came up to expectations. Jennifer had the firm conviction that all was right with his world as though he had come to some decision with himself. A good deal of mellow red wine also helped them both to relax.

Tentatively he began, "Jen, you remember you've been asking me questions?"

Whilst she did not move from her comfortable position in his arms, she was suddenly all attention, all alert and hardly daring to breathe. For the last few weeks she had been hoping to get to the bottom of his family and whatever it was that was preventing him from asking her the obvious question. The one that he had indeed asked her twice and from which he had twice shied away. She was tempted to enquire as to what questions but stifled the urge.

Instead she answered with a tentative, "Yes."

She pulled back and looked at him. There was that serious cloud enshrouding his face. She had seen it when she had tried to discuss this before. He was also a bundle of nerves. She could almost hear them jangling. This was patently serious. She had to pull herself together and be serious too.

"Darling, what's the problem? There's obviously something bugging you. Please tell me. I'm all ears." It sounded horribly stilted but it seemed to calm David.

"You've met my parents?" he started.

"Yes."

"Notice anything about them?"

Jennifer cast her mind back to the one significant meeting to which she and David had gone, although she had been excluded from the business part of it. They had hardly spoken. His mother had done her best where the small talk was concerned but, although she had become quite animated in her kitchen and her garden, she couldn't keep it up. Apart from sudden outbursts of bonhomie his father had been almost monosyllabic. The bungalow was immaculate, as was the meal, but the place had the appearance that time had stopped. He had warned her that it would be pretty awful but even so she had been more than glad to get away into some fresh air afterwards.

"They seemed quiet," she replied carefully.

"Be more specific," he almost commanded her.

"Well," she drew the word out as her mind raced on how to be as tactful as possible. "Your mother did her best, but your father was, well…" She paused, searching for a word. "Dead." It was all she could think of but it did best describe him.

"And if I told you that not many years ago, he was the life and soul of every party for miles, captain of his golf club, *raconteur par excellence*, and so on, and so on?"

"I wouldn't believe you," she said. She knew it was the right answer but she did find it close to impossible to visualise. "What went wrong?" She wasn't so sure that this was the right question, just hoping it might help David to get whatever it was off his chest.

341

"No, not you, nor anyone else who hadn't known him before." There was pain in his eyes again. The room seemed to grow dark.

Very quietly she queried, "Before?"

There was another longer pause before he metaphorically shook himself as a dog shakes off water and said, "You have to know. You really do have to know."

"I have been asking you to tell me for a long time now but I've been prepared to wait. What is it I have to know?" she very gently enquired of him.

"It's a long story but you have to know it all. To a large extent I have led you up the garden path. Although I don't think I have actually said so, I have led you to believe that I am an only child groomed to run the family business. Right?"

Jennifer thought. "Yes," she said. "That was certainly my impression."

"Wrong. Totally wrong," said David.

"But you said…"

"No. I hope I didn't say." David ploughed on in a peremptory manner. "I have a sister, I had a brother, and for that matter, another sister. I think you came very close to guessing all that."

He cocked an eye at her.

"Is this the Gerry and Diane, mentioned in your father's letter?"

"As Mum would say, 'Yup'."

Jennifer tried again. "But why have you never spoken of them? Why have I never met them? Have you got some

342

sort of skeleton in the cupboard that you are not telling me about?"

David appeared to relax a little but he laughed a bitter laugh.

"Now there you are much nearer to the truth than you would ever believe. Yes, indeed, much nearer."

"Well, are you going to tell me?"

"Yes. I am. And then, if you want, you can get on the road home and this time I shall not expect you to come back."

"I shall do no such thing," replied Jennifer with some asperity.

"Huh, I wouldn't bank on that," came the tart response.

"Well get on with it then," she answered equally sharply. "Sorry," she added in a small voice as she saw the black cloud again pass across his face. She watched him pause for an instant and then could almost see him decide to jump in with all four feet and to hell with the consequences.

"Yes, I have a sister but she's in prison. For life."

"For life?" Jennifer jumped back out of his arms, wide-eyed and realising how stupid it was to just repeat what he had said, though there seemed no alternative. At least, she didn't have one and realisation was dawning that there was only one obvious thing that you went to prison for life for, and that was murder. Disjointed family they obviously were, but murder? That was something else again.

David carried on relentlessly.

"I had an elder brother too, but she shot him. Dead."

The last word came almost as an afterthought and hung in the air, as the shot itself must have done. He continued. "Daphne, Dianne's twin, died in a stupid but tragic boating accident a good many years ago. Dianne always held Gerry responsible – and I think she is probably right.

Although she was by now expecting something like this Jennifer's hands flew up to her face. She wasn't just wide eyed, her mouth hung open and she was speechless. David's agonised face turned to her and the question as to what she would do now was written all over it. Hesitantly Jennifer put her hands out to his face and he collapsed onto her shoulder and the tears streamed down his face. "Sorry," he mumbled. "My turn to say sorry."

She had not had time to assimilate all this and she did not yet want to cry. That could come later. She had to understand what she was going to cry about first. Unusual it certainly was, but why did it affect him so? She supposed families did not go round shooting each other, even if there were times when they felt like it. She smoothed his hair.

"I think", she said, "that you should tell me all about it. From the beginning. And, don't forget, all of it." There was a formality back in her voice again.

"Yes," he said. "You're a stranger hereabouts, and I'm not being rude, but because of that you are in fact one of the few people who doesn't know about it. There's also an unwritten rule that nobody speaks of what happened. Not to the family anyway. What they do amongst themselves we've given up caring about."

"Ah, that would account for why Roger wouldn't say anything when I asked him what the problems were. Said it was more than his job was worth, literally."

"Yes. He was being a bit dramatic but that's the gist of it. Actually, and I joke not, Dad probably would have sacked him, or tried to, but that's another matter."

"So what actually happened?"

"You see it all goes back a very long way. We're a bit of a spread-about family, I'm the youngest, Diane is five years older than me, Daphne died when she was thirteen and Gerry six years older than them, near enough at any rate. Why such long gaps I don't know, probably just the way it happened. Unless of course Muriel is actually my mother."

"We decided she wasn't."

"Well, yes, but that's as may be. Although I'm beginning to suspect she is mother to the twins, Daphne and Dianne. Anyway, Gerry was always going to be heir to the business and the family prestige. He had a very similar outlook on life to Dad, outward-going, full of *joie de vivre* and all that. I wasn't too bothered. OK, I was interested in what the company did, but it was never going to be the be-all and end-all of my life like it was for Gerry, and for Dad for that matter. Added to that, Gerry could be pretty insensitive and domineering and I wasn't going to be pushed about by my much older brother. I think we all hoped, Dad especially, that there would be niche in the company that I could fit into without my being always subservient to Gerry. It was not to be but that is not really part of this story."

345

He appeared to jerk himself out of what seemed like self-pity and carried on.

"Now Diane, she is something else again. In many ways she is like Gerry, go-getting, always wanting to do things her way, but she is not pleasant with it. He had finesse when he wanted, whereas she has a vicious streak in her and can't contain it. God knows where she gets it from. She and Gerry always fought, even from an early age, both too much alike I suppose. But Gerry never knew when to leave off. I told you he was insensitive. Being six years older he seldom called Diane by her name but always 'L'il Sis'. That was maybe OK when they were children when she really was his little sister, but later on; no. It drove her mad and in the end he did it one time too many."

"I can sympathise with her," said Jennifer. "Brother Paul – you've met him – can be much the same. Not so much domineering as prone to ignoring me. He's always been like that, still is for that matter. Very like Gerry by the sound of it but we do get on pretty well – most of the time. Lots of times I want to hit him where it hurts, or worse – but shoot him? Now that is going a bit too far."

"Well, maybe you understand better than most," said David. "But I need to go back to the beginning. First, you have to remember that I was only about seven, rising eight, when this happened and I've never been told very much about it. Second, although I don't know for sure, I think Muriel is mother to Dianne and Daphne. When she's about to have her hair done it's awfully black about the roots. I'm tall enough to see."

Jennifer smiled. The trouble some people went to; but she supposed it suited Muriel's mentality.

"Third, Dianne and Daphne are – were – twins. Daphne was marginally less belligerent than Dianne.

Jennifer nodded encouragement.

"Dad had a speedboat. He was very flash back then. Gerry was learning to drive and he took it into his head to take the girls, who were then thirteen, out on a boating trip. He hadn't passed his test and was in about the same state where the boat was concerned. He got it wrong and turned the boat over. He and Dianne were thrown into the water, but Daphne, who had been injured in the capsize, was trapped underneath it.

Jennifer sat very still so as not to break the flow.

"With no life jackets, no radio and no flares they had to sit it out until somebody spotted them. I think they came very close to dying of exposure themselves. It certainly did for poor Daphne. It's curious that they appear to have made no attempt to find her. Anyway, the upshot was that Dianne never forgave Gerry for killing her twin sister. Her words not mine."

"Did the passage of time make her more reasonable?"

"No. It was always the last round in their endless friction. If reason, shouting, screaming, sheer frustration could not achieve her goals, it was, 'You should do it for me because you killed my sister!' Mostly it worked. And in order to keep his end up Gerry insisted on calling here 'L'il Sis'. As I believe he had he had done pretty consistently before the accident. As she always said, he would say it once too often.

347

"So there you have the historical bit, now to the more recent past. After a tumultuous adolescence Dianne wanted her share in the action, for which read the company, and if each could have kept themselves to themselves, they would have been an unstoppable pair. She had gone off to university, University College, London and all too plainly about as far away from here as she could get without going abroad. She got her degree, no problem. She's bright with it but what else she did and whom else she met, well that's the enigma. And that's the bit she won't tell me or anybody else."

His voice trailed off again and he continued to stare vacantly into space. Jennifer found she had been sitting on the edge of her seat during this dissertation. Gathering her wits together, she ventured, "And how did you and she get on?"

It seemed to bump David from his lethargy. "Oh, us? Well, pretty well really but for different reasons. I suppose she never saw me as a threat, or if she did then she knew she could keep me on a leash. As a consequence, we weren't automatically at loggerheads with each other and I guess too that I'm all for the quiet life. I don't expect everything to go my way, so I could put up with her tantrums and just switch off and let them roll over me. Gerry couldn't do that: he always rose to the bait."

"Where Paul was concerned, I had to learn the hard way that when he didn't want me – he didn't want me and it was time to make myself scarce. Took a while though."

He cocked an eye at her in acknowledgement.

"That's what she should have done, they both should have done but neither could do it." He paused as though reminiscing but then carried on with the main theme. "She came back from uni and after a year's delay when she took off again, Dad and Gerry made a slot in the company for her. Buyer, and she was good at it too. Very good. Either by stick or by charm she always managed to get hold of everything that little cheaper than we had previously. Dad said she paid her way handsomely. But it was only on the surface. About the only thing she and Gerry didn't do, was to have full-scale rows in the factory with everyone there. They would wait until after hours and then set about each other."

Jennifer smiled. If it hadn't been so serious it could have been funny.

"You may smile and, yes, there is a grain of comedy in it. Truth be told, I think they rather enjoyed their spats, but it was a bit wearing for any of the rest of us who might happen to be around. Certainly on at least one occasion I found myself walking about on tiptoe just in case the noise of normal walking would set one or other of them off. Pathetic really when you think about it, but it could be pretty grim. She just wanted more of everything: responsibility, travel, money, you name it. I honestly don't think she could have handled everything she wanted even if she had got her way. Sorry, I'm daydreaming again, but you must understand that we have all been asking ourselves these questions these last several years." Looking at Jennifer for the first time he said, "But you want to know what actually happened, don't you?"

349

"Yes," she replied quietly.

"In those days we lived in a large red-brick Victorian house of, as the estate agents would say, handsome proportions. After one particularly unpleasant row I left home to live here but Gerry and Dianne continued in the family home. I think it was so that neither one could influence my father without the other knowing. As for parents and Muriel…" He made a face at the thought. "But we all treated it as open house as we each had quite a lot of our belongings left behind there. It was afterwards that it was sold and they moved into the bungalow."

"Afterwards?"

"I'm getting there," he said irritably. "By some quirk of coincidence, fate, call it what you will, both she and Gerry came back to the house separately, independently and for their own supposedly good reasons. There was no premeditation at this stage. Equally by chance Mum and Dad were both out. Dad was in the office and Mum had gone shopping. Me? I had flown to Hamburg for three days and was due back that evening. It seems that Gerry picked up the paper as he came in and spread it, himself and a bowl of cereal out across the kitchen table to read. When Dianne passed through, he called out 'Hi, L'il Sis!' or something similar. As I said, it was once too often. She came downstairs quietly, put a small pistol to the back of his head, made sure he knew it was her and pulled the trigger. And then left the pistol on the table beside him."

There was silence. Total silence. There was nothing Jennifer could say.

"From that she just took off. It was Mum who came back first and found Gerry dead on the kitchen table. Now here's the funny thing, she rose to the occasion, whereas Dad retreated into a shell we none of us knew he had. It was at this point also that Muriel came very much to the fore. She had always been around, all my life anyway, but always a sort of rather shadowy figure in the background even if she had lived in the house all along. Now she became almost the public face of my father. Mum? You can probably imagine her being a mouse playing second fiddle to Dad, but with him having gone almost into a living coma she has become quite animated. Had to, I suppose."

The story was wandering but Jennifer continued to say nothing.

"Guess they all hoped it might look like suicide but the police took one look and said, 'No, it was murder. People don't shoot themselves in the back of the head.' Simple really. We all had to account for our movements but there was no Dianne. And no me either, for that matter, but I was back in Newcastle in the evening as planned to find I had a police reception. The finger of suspicion, as they say, pointed very firmly at Dianne, and the general opinion was that she had headed for London. It was the only place away from here that she knew well and where she could easily get lost. She would have known that the hue and cry could not be long in coming."

"How do you know all this detail?" interrupted Jennifer.

"She told me, but I'll come to that."

351

Jennifer felt put down but held her tongue. David seemed to be on a roll and she hoped talking about it would do him some good. He continued relentlessly.

"About half past eleven that night, long after everyone thought she should have been in London, she walked into a police station in Bedford and gave herself up. I gather she had quite a job convincing them, first, that there had in fact been a murder 300 miles away and, second, that she was owning up to it." He laughed mirthlessly to himself at the thought. "The next day she was brought back north and that was when it got difficult. She just clammed up. Her attitude was, 'I've told you I did it. What. else do you want to know?' Dad had organised solicitors to claim mitigating circumstances, insanity, anything, but she was having none of it. 'I did it. I did it deliberately. I organised myself to do it when I had the opportunity. The opportunity came and I did it. Now just let the law take its course.' And the law did. Put her away for life with minimum fifteen years recommended, and with special reference to psychiatric help. She wouldn't tell anybody anything."

He paused and looked piteously at Jennifer as though to ask whether she really wanted him to go on and tell her the rest of the story, such as it was. She was still in a state of shock and unable to do or say much. He took her silence as a signal to carry on.

"Once she had been sentenced and got into prison proper, not just on remand, she opened up a little. We all went to see her but initially she remained as aloof as before. Indeed, she actually wouldn't talk to anybody at all about anything, even the weather, which made it hard going to say the least. I went regularly, about once a month, and very gradually she told me what happened. Odd bits and pieces with me left to put them together into some sort of coherent whole. She and I didn't fight and I think she felt she could talk to me even if she still said nothing to anybody else. It was, quite simply, the 'L'il Sis' bit that did it on top of the fact that she blamed Gerry fairly and squarely for her sister's death. And quite correctly so but most people would ultimately accept it and get on with their lives. Not her. Gerry would not back off either and, as the pulp novels say, he signed his own death warrant. God knows who she mixed with at college. She said getting the gun was easy if you knew who to talk to and, I think, although she has not yet said so, that somebody also showed her how to use and to care for it. Scary."

"Scary, indeed," echoed Jennifer and shuddered at the thought. Coming from where she did, she was well used to shotguns, their care and safekeeping. She was even a passable shot herself, but a small handgun with the deliberate intention of killing your own brother? No, that was indeed, something else again.

"And your parents, does she talk to them?" she asked.

"No. That's the saddest part of the whole benighted business. Fundamentally she blames them for what she did and I suppose looked at from her end of the telescope she's right. If Mum and Dad had stopped Gerry from making fun of her for all those years, had realised how much it hurt her, how much it brought back the trauma of Daphne's death, then none of this would have happened. Prisons are pretty nasty until you get used to them and Dad never has, especially as she would make a fool of him by not speaking to him at all. He doesn't go now and I don't blame him. Mum gave up even sooner but she seems to have taken it more in her stride than Dad. She's accepted you, but Dad, well I'm not sure that he's even registered your existence. Muriel went once but Diane simply sat with her back to her, making it pretty plain what she thought of that relationship, mother or not!"

They sat staring at the floor, each with their own thoughts. Jennifer trying to make sense of what she had been told, and David knowing that he had to have told Jennifer the whole story but wishing that he hadn't. He was surer by the minute that his greatest wish must have gone up in smoke. Suddenly he was all action. Briskly he stood up and angrily said:

"Time for you to fuck off back to the Cotswold gentry and not bugger about with North Country murderers. It's a long road back to Gloucestershire."

There was a silence such as there must have been after the fatal shot was fired.

"Whatever do you mean?" asked Jennifer in some consternation. "I'm not going anywhere." And added as it dawned on her just what he had said, "And don't think you shock me. I haven't spent most of my life in a farmyard without learning about the birds and the bees, not to mention hearing my fair share of bad language along the way. And from a very tender age too. I'll have you know I can match you word for word if you try me!"

David faltered in his pacing around. "Sorry, I shouldn't have said that, but you can't possibly want to stay here with me after finding all those skeletons in the cupboard, as you so succinctly called it," he said. "I might shoot you," he added somewhat lamely.

She put up her arms to him. "Come here, you great silly," she smiled. "As I said, I'm not going anywhere. I'm just trying to come to terms with the fact that you might shoot me."

This levity between them, which in other circumstances might have been offensive, seemed to break the logjam. With the ghost of an amused smile on her face she carried on. "A couple of times you've asked me a certain question in which I have a very personal interest. You have ignored my very positive answers. Is that question still for answering?"

David stood as though transfixed for what seemed an eternity for both of them, then collapsed beside her and into her arms.

"Yes," he said. "You did say you would but with a family history like mine I didn't think I stood a cat in hell's chance. Jennifer, will you marry me? Really?"

"Yes, David, I will."

Finally, she could cry herself. In joy or sorrow she knew not and cared not. What she wanted more than anything had happened and she was just – well – happy.

"Oh, David," she said as the tears subsided a bit, "I thought we were never going to reach this point. Something always seemed to get in the way."

"I know," was all he said.

She suddenly sat up, all business-like, and pointed a finger at him.

355

"There's one small condition!"

"Condition? What do you mean condition?"

"Honeymoon…?"

"Ah." And David pointed a finger back at her.

"At the Mkonge Hotel," they both said together.

Chapter 13

It was several days later that Jennifer walked into Roger's office and waited quietly. A man in tattered overalls with a welding mask on his head was discussing the assembly of some framework or another. She listened intently and tried to follow the conversation knowing that she would now have to pick up as much knowledge as possible – and fast – if she was not going to both look and feel foolish as David's wife. Her position, if any, in the firm was under discussion – argument might have been a better word – but ultimately would be resolved. Hardly anyone knew about their engagement and today was going to be something of a moment of truth.

With the man gone, Roger relaxed back into his chair.

"And to what do I owe the pleasure of this visit?" he asked.

To which she held out her left hand to display the single stone engagement ring on its correct finger.

"Ah, the young beggar's sorted himself out at last and done what we all know is the best thing he could have done. What's been keeping him?" he said.

Jennifer ignored the question but was pleased with his reaction.

"I thought you should be the first here to see it as you somehow managed to believe in me from the beginning, even if we hadn't actually spoken to each other!"

"Reckon I know a straight person when I meet one," he said.

"So I've been told."

"And I imagine you must know the family history by now. I guess that's what's been holding him back. Not surprising really."

"Yes, and yes. It took him a long time." She hoped she wasn't being derogatory behind David's back but Roger seemed not to notice.

"Phew. That's a relief anyway. Your not being aware of it has been quite a strain."

"With hindsight I now understand your problem when we were making coffee the other day after the balloon went up."

"Yeah, that was tricky."

At that moment John, the design engineer, walked in.

"Sorry to interrupt," he said. "I didn't know you had company, Roger. My, you look well this morning." This last directed at Jennifer.

"Go on, show him. I dare you," smiled Roger.

Jennifer tentatively held out her hand again.

"Eh, lass. That's good to see." The Yorkshire accent seemed broader than ever. "Least I hope it's young David and not some other lucky bugger."

"It is," she said but couldn't manage any more as she was overcome by the rough affection from these colleagues-to-be whose reaction could have been very different.

"I must go and show Christine and Miranda now," she said in an effort to hide her embarrassment and get away.

"Hang on a mo," said Roger and rushed out of his office, apparently only to have a few hurried conversations with the nearest employees. John, who had twigged what he was up to, continued to hold Jennifer in conversation.

"OK, you can go now," he said as he came back with a grin on his face.

"Thanks," she said and walked out innocently heading for the office doorway.

It started with a wolf whistle followed by a bit of banging about but soon grew into a crescendo of noise as every person in the place grabbed something and banged it against something else. Somehow and instinctively she understood what it was all about and held up her hand for all to see which merely served to increase the noise. She looked back to see Roger and John grinning all over their faces over the uproar at her expense. She was glad to escape into the relative calm of the offices.

"Who's a star then?" asked David coming from his office and beaming with pride.

Christine and Miranda were hovering with their very real congratulations only slightly overshadowed by wanting to see her ring. Kisses all round left David looking still proud but embarrassed by the furore that his engagement seemed to have caused. His consolation had to be the affection and respect in which everyone seemed to hold Jennifer. Perhaps his life was going to go right from now on?

***

Back at Valley Court the excitement was equally palpable in the days before Jennifer was expected home shortly after the factory celebrations. There was obvious disappointment that Jennifer had not been at home to announce her engagement but the reality of their being so far apart made for acceptance of the situation. However, her mother had, in her mind at least, virtually made all the arrangements for the wedding and was having extreme difficulty in not actually putting them into practice. Fundamentally it was only the lack of an actual date that stopped her. She also had a suspicion that she wouldn't get carte blanche from her daughter, who might well have her own ideas, even very decided ones, as to what she wanted or, more likely, what she did not want!

As far as Valley Farm itself was concerned both Simon and Paul had, separately and together, walked over the lower ground spying out the land for potential sites for a marquee and car parking. They had also sized up gates and fences needing repair, not to mention what junk should be got rid of or at least hidden away. Appearances had to be maintained even if in the normal way they would not have bothered.

Jennifer herself was blissfully unaware of all this activity and would have been horrified if she had known.

There had been a minor contretemps over whether David was coming south with her.

"I can't go home for the first time after my engagement and not take you with me," she had argued, but David had been adamant.

"I do not want to go through my recent family history in front of strangers, well, not wholly strangers, but that is the first thing they are going to want to know. They might forbid you from marrying me," he had said.

"Don't be silly. They can't do that nowadays."

"I know they can't but they could make their feelings pretty plain and I want their blessing on our marriage, not just their acceptance of a fait accompli."

And so, very reluctantly, Jennifer had headed south on her own with advance warning that the reasons for her doing so would be explained when she got there. To her family's chagrin this she refused to do until they were all settled later that evening and at her insistence were all armed with a strong drink.

"You'll need it," she said enigmatically.

"It can't be that bad," quipped Paul.

"Oh yes it can," she replied.

"Please get on with it. Anyone would think someone had been murdered," pleaded Simon.

"Someone was."

"Aah," he said and took a long swig of his whisky.

As always it was her mother who came to the rescue.

"I think," she said, "you had better tell us the whole story from the beginning."

"That's almost word for word what I asked David to do and he did. So now it's my turn."

To some extent she had edited what she was going to say and thus managed without it all being too garbled. The only serious interruption was a break to refill all their glasses! At the end when they were still digesting the whole sorry tale it was her father who took them all by surprise.

"I know it's going uphill to midnight but if you're talking to that young man before it's tomorrow, tell him from me that the answer's 'Yes'."

The rest of them looked puzzled and Jennifer said, "Sorry?"

He smiled. "A little while back he rang me, damned lucky to get me, and asked if he could marry you, but he wouldn't allow me to give him an answer until 'We had heard the tale' as he put it. As I say, the answer's 'Yes.' He deserves a break."

Jennifer shook her head in disbelief. "That's typical of him," she said.

"But you never said anything about that to me," complained her mother.

"It was my phone call," he grumbled into his drink.

"Bloody old-fashioned if you ask me," said Paul.

The following days were a whirlwind of planning possibilities for what was going to be the wedding of the decade for their small village but would necessarily have to involve a great many friends and relations. First call was to see if the church and its local vicar were available.

As Jennifer's mother said, "As long as she's available we can have the church at any time, it's almost ours anyway!"

Fortunately, she had nothing booked in the late autumn, which was David and Jennifer's preferred time of year for the wedding. From there they moved on to the more mundane aspects, but in due course the bare bones of the event began to fall into place. Decisions were taken as to where the marquee should be, caterers were decided upon and who might be staying in the house so that the farm itself could rise to the occasion and do its bit. A serious start was made on a guest list.

***

Back in Carlisle, or rather Brampton, it was decision time as to where the newly-wed couple would live when all the excitement of the wedding itself was over. Jennifer was adamant that she could not continue to live in a flat even if she had become more accustomed to the idea.

"I must have space," was her mantra on this. Although not quite so concerned, David was happy to go along with her.

"But there is a limit to what we can afford. I may now own T.H. Wear & Co. but Dad didn't leave me any cash for myself!"

Quite unexpectedly through a friend of a friend they lighted upon an old mill across a field from a very minor road. The restoration of this had been started by a couple with little more than good intentions behind them and had faltered and died when their small amount of money ran out. It was habitable after a fashion but they needed for it to be rather better than that. Despite the condition, its situation and rarity value gave it a frighteningly high price tag. A phone call back to Mr H at Halliwells confirmed that, although well outside his orbit, he thought the figure being asked was not unreasonable.

"I've fallen in love with this place. Are you good with bricks and mortar?" she asked David.

"Not that I know of and I'm not sure that this is the opportunity to find out. We've got enough to cope with over the coming months without my learning to be a builder."

"I guess you're right, but I should love it all the same."

It had taken a little time but David had made a sort of peace with his mother, or if nothing else, they had agreed a truce. This had to happen in order to sort out some of the company affairs that had been compounded by his father not having left matters quite as tidy as they seemed at first sight. Business-type discussions had broken down the wall that David, especially, had built between them. Jennifer had deliberately kept a low profile but had maintained contact. Conversation was always a bit difficult and it was when looking for something to talk about on one of her unannounced visits to Mrs Wear that she had mentioned the mill.

"Well, I could help you there," she said quite casually.

For all her apparent vagueness Mrs Wear was quite sharp. Jennifer wondered if it was all a pose. She had instantly seen how the land lay.

"Really?"

"I think so if David will let me."

"That could be a problem."

"I know but bring him round sometime soon and let's see what we can manage between us. Eh?" And she twinkled!

"How on earth can she help us?" was David's immediate reaction.

"I don't know but she was quite certain that she could."

"She's trying to buy me, but I don't see how."

"I don't think so, actually."

"Well, set it up soon and we'll see what you two have been hatching up!"

And so it was that a couple of evenings later, they were in the bungalow with Jennifer all smiles and David trying to look dour.

"What I think you don't realise," Mrs Wear was saying to him, "is that I've always owned the property around here." David sat up very straight as she continued. "You know what your father was like where money was concerned – easy come easy go. Any money about the place was his to spend on enjoying himself. I never complained, we had a good time together."

A wistful look came into her eyes as she only just stopped herself from adding, *The three of us!*

"So you own this place yourself, do you?"

David thought he began to see where this was leading.

"Yes, and I owned the big house in town too. We sold that very well and there was a fair bit of money left over after buying this. I've always been going to do something with it, invest it, buy some more property or something, but I don't seem to have got round to it. So maybe it could help you if you'll let me."

"I'll need to think about it," said David.

"It really is very generous of you to think like this." Jennifer felt she had to say something in the 'thank you line', but David was thinking more practically.

"How would you do it?" he asked.

"I could give you a mortgage on it. I could buy it, do it up and rent it to you, or anything in between."

"You could do that?" David was astounded that she had that much money in her purse, as it were, that she could spend as she wished. As Jennifer had discovered she was plainly much more worldly wise than she gave the impression.

"I shall have to think about it," said David again.

"I'll be in the kitchen then," she said and departed in that direction.

"My, she's wanting a decision here and now!"

"I think only insofar as to whether you will let her."

"Yeah. Well. That's what needs thinking about."

"Do we want the mill or don't we? Seems to me to be the main point. Yes, we may be able to get an ordinary mortgage but that's not going to be easy until it's finished but everyone can see that we aren't in the same predicament as the people we're buying from. With your

366

mother she will be able to see what's going on and finance us accordingly."

"But it means she's got us in her clutches."

"Not if your friend Mr Murchison…"

"He's not my friend!"

"Well, any other competent solicitor. Use the Valley Farm one if you like, but as I was saying you can tie it up as a purely business transaction with the added advantage that it keeps whatever we pay for it in the family."

David said nothing but she knew he was thinking it through.

"Let's at least take her to see the place so that she knows what we are talking about."

Another long pause.

"I'll go that far at the moment." Which left Jennifer to go and fetch Mrs Wear back from the kitchen.

"We'd like to take you to see the place so that you can see that it really exists," said Jennifer.

"Oh, good. I shall enjoy that. It'll give me something else to think about," she said.

David was about to say something but converted it into a cough but he was still looking very dour about the whole prospect.

In the end it was the mill itself that worked its charm on all of them and especially on Mrs Wear. Not being anything of a country person herself she was a bit alarmed by its apparent remoteness but she had the grace to accept that Jennifer, at least, knew what she was taking on in that respect. She also proved to be remarkably astute when it came to property negotiation.

"You should get a job in an estate agents'," commented Jennifer.

"I might just do that, but I want to see you two married first," she said.

With the possibility that there was a method by which they might be able to afford it, David became increasingly enthusiastic. Offers were made, eventually a price was agreed, and then Mr Murchison spent an eternity sorting out the finances to his satisfaction with a suitably sized fee to boot. Jennifer kept clear of those negotiations although she got a whiff from Mrs Wear that David was making life difficult for himself.

They put in many hours themselves tidying the place up but more professional help was needed to make a presentable home of the place. Roger, ever the stalwart for them both, found some part-time building employees who then spent their weekends turning the place into what they wanted. Similarly, plumbers and electricians who served the factory as required were recruited to do the necessary in their respective trades. They would now have somewhere to live once the wedding was over.

***

"We shall have worn out the M6 by the time we're married," grumbled David on one of their many trips south during that long fraught summer running up to their wedding.

"At least I don't have to do all the driving now," answered Jennifer.

"There's some consolation in that."

"Even if there aren't enough hours in the day or days in the week."

Their life had settled down into a routine even if it was one that was erratic and prone to unexpected change. As much by popular consent as by any deliberate policy, Jennifer had taken over Muriel's activities but without the fraudulent ones. Being no longer firmly under anyone's thumb, Miranda had blossomed and was beginning to prove that she had a head on her shoulders and could use it. Jennifer had had a glimpse of this in the unveiling of the fraud and had managed to build upon it. Christine had extended her hours with T.H. Wear and was close to being able to fully quantify their losses with a view to the insurance claim. Roger was a close second to her mother in being able to sum up any situation. "Thank God. It's great to be a happy ship again," he had said.

Jennifer had made many visits home on her own to cover what her mother described as the best bits of the wedding preparations, principally the making of the wedding dress. Somehow, she had found a local lady who made special dresses of all types on an occasional basis. 'I think she waits until she's run out of money and then makes a few dresses to keep her going for a bit longer,' seemed to be the consensus of opinion amongst those who knew of her. Certainly, it was an exciting time for both mother and daughter.

"Wow! I've never known the place look so tidy," commented Jennifer as she and David drove in on this occasion.

"If that's what getting married achieves, you should do it more often!"

"And what's that supposed to mean?"

"Nothing, so long as you only marry me!"

"Well, I hadn't planned on marrying anybody else."

"Good. Then I don't have to take you up to the woods today and apply gentle persuasion?"

"Oh, but you might. Would it be worth it?"

"Yup," he said with finality.

Later he said, "Jen, how do I catch up with Paul?"

"Paul? Saturday morning in the farm office is the best chance but whatever do you want him for?"

David coloured slightly. "It's a bit embarrassing but I wondered if he'd be my best man. You see," he hurried on, "I don't have any real friends. Oh yes, I know lots of people but nobody I would consider a friend good enough to be my best man. I've got to know Paul quite well and he knows the form down here so, you see, it makes some sort of sense," he finished rather lamely.

Jennifer was silent for a moment as she thought furiously. This actually gave her an opportunity for an idea she had in mind.

"You surprise me but I can see where you're coming from. Come to think of it I haven't met any friends of yours I'd class as 'best man' material, but then it's not up to me. I'm not sure how reliable you'll find Paul but then I am his little sister and therefore prejudiced. You also know the problems that can create."

"Very possibly but I'd like to ask him. The more I think about it, the more I think he's the best choice."

370

"OK. Give him a whirl. One thing you're going to have to be careful of is that if you should involve him in any sort of stag night and he gets all his Young Farmers Club friends involved it could take you a week to recover."

"It could be nearly as bad at home, possibly worse. I should have Dad and Gerry's reputation to live up to."

"True. Then I leave that one up to you but please have it well in advance. I don't want you being done for drunken driving on the way to your wedding!"

"No chance," he assured her.

"Good, which brings me on to a very similar subject for very similar reasons. How about Miranda for bridesmaid? She is sort of my protégé after all."

"Well it would be tit for tat but why on earth? I would have thought you had lots of friends down here dying to be your bridesmaid. What about Julie, or whatever her name is, from your old office?"

"That's just my point. My friends are about in the same league as yours and would scratch each other's eyes out to be my bridesmaid. If I have someone from right outside, they all find themselves in the same boat. I think Miranda is capable of carrying it off – if her nerves will stand the pace!"

"That's quite a big if, but if your nerves can cope with her nerves that's fine by me."

"So that's settled then?"

"Yup." And they both laughed.

This was also something of a red letter visit for them as it was when the first of their banns were to be read in church and David had particularly wanted to be there for

371

that even if he couldn't manage all of them. Congratulations were the order of the day afterwards as the whole village seemed to be psyching itself up for the forthcoming event.

"I'm not sure I'm going to be able to cope with the fame of becoming your husband."

"You'll manage and I shall help you, like before." And she kissed him.

***

Inexorably the wedding itself came along. Valley Farm had redecorated a cottage for David and his mother to use in the week leading up to it, although in fact they had not arrived until just beforehand. Mrs Wear had insisted on some celebrations at home and David had had to be part of those. He was surprised and more than pleased that she had not even told his father and Muriel when the wedding was to be. Neither had they been sent an invitation, this last at David's insistence.

"Technically I don't know where they are so I can't tell them what's going on, can I?" she had said, shrugging her shoulders in her inimitable way.

It was a hard week for T.H. Wear & Co.'s customers as the factory was as good as closed, with only Christine and John holding the fort. The latter's comment that he would not be coming to the wedding, 'As somebody has to mind t'shop', was a relief all round. At least there would be somebody who could deal with the telephone, if he did nothing else. Miranda came south by train early in the week in a state of some wonderment and trepidation. Jennifer debated with herself whether the girl had ever been so far from home before. Even Christine left it all to John's tender care at the end of the week and, more spectacularly, so did Roger, who tended to worry about 'his' factory like a mother hen with her chicks.

Most of Jennifer's friends had homes relatively locally even if some of them, she considered, gave themselves airs and graces by living in London. More often than not they were shacked up with some high flyer with loads of money but no time to enjoy it. Their brittle lifestyles had always infuriated her, all the more so now that she was marrying someone who actually made something. She was sure that a good many of them would have taken her father's initial attitude that she was going into 'trade' and therefore somehow letting the side down. If they thought it was all slightly beneath them, at least she was actually marrying David, not just living with him.

The guest list had caused a considerable amount of grief. Numbers were to some extent restricted by the size of the church which Jennifer perceived her father viewing as providential; it kept down the cost! As David had said he was something of a loner not having many friends and, it transpired, even less who were prepared to make the long journey south it was all going to become a rather one-sided affair.

"It's going to be a bit drastic if I have to cut my numbers to match yours," Jennifer complained.

"No need for that, it's just the way it is. If it looks funny, so what. They'll have to put up with it."

373

"I know, but without having your father there? After all he's not dead."

"As good as, and if you'd had him, you'd have to have had Muriel as well."

"No way!" Jennifer was horrified at even the possibility.

"Exactly. So it is how it is."

And it was. Jennifer was fairly drastic in cutting her own list hoping that she did not offend too many of them and included a few unlikely ones, such as Mr Halliwell. To everyone's surprise he actually came, along with his wife who was a stranger to all concerned.

As far as the wedding ceremony itself was concerned, David had made only one specific request and that was that Jennifer should arrive precisely five minutes late, no being clever by being any later or any earlier than that. To her disgust he absolutely refused to be drawn as to why.

By the time the clock had finished striking midday everyone who was going to be in church was there and only the chief usher and the odd gawper, were left outside. At that moment three ladies got out of a car slightly away from the rest and walked in close formation to the church. The middle one was pale of face, around thirty and wearing a tight-fitting black dress that matched her jet-black hair. An odd choice for a wedding. The other two were in more flowery, flowing two-pieces with sensible shoes and looked as though they could be quite formidable personalities. It appeared that they were expected and they were seated in a reserved back pew.

Jennifer arrived as directed but was oblivious as to who was sitting where in a church that was full to overflowing. She only wanted to get to David and get on with it. Relief flooded over her as the wedding ring was placed on what felt like a naked spot where up to now she had worn her engagement ring. Not that she had ever doubted him for one moment but she knew she could enjoy everything that life could throw at them from now on.

However, she was taken aback to find that as they came down the aisle to the strains of the Wedding March there was a woman in black standing not actually in the way but slightly to one side, plainly waiting for her. It also became apparent that David knew who this was because he slowed and brought her over towards the stranger. For a long minute the woman in black stared at her from coal-black eyes that matched her hair and her dress, then moved slightly forward and kissed her.

"You'll do," she said. "Look after him for all our sakes."

"I will," whispered Jennifer, as she realised who this was.

The bridal couple moved on.

The three ladies moved back into their pew and stared straight ahead of them as though they had no part in the proceedings. They sat stiffly to attention with their hands beside them.

That way the handcuffs didn't show.